Mrs. Abby Morton Diaz

The William Henry Letters

Mrs. Abby Morton Diaz

The William Henry Letters

ISBN/EAN: 9783743305656

Manufactured in Europe, USA, Canada, Australia, Japa

Cover: Foto ©Raphael Reischuk / pixelio.de

Manufactured and distributed by brebook publishing software
(www.brebook.com)

Mrs. Abby Morton Diaz

The William Henry Letters

THE

WILLIAM HENRY LETTERS.

BY

MRS. A. M. DIAZ.

WITH ILLUSTRATIONS.

BOSTON:
FIELDS, OSGOOD, & CO.
1870.

UNIVERSITY PRESS : WELCH, BIGELOW, & CO.,
CAMBRIDGE.

EDITOR'S INTRODUCTION.

My dear Young Friends:—

Much to my surprise, I was asked one day if I would be willing to edit the William Henry Letters for publication in a volume.

At first it seemed impossible for me to do anything of the kind; "for," said I, "how can any one edit who is not an editor? Besides, I am not enough used to writing." It was then explained to me that my duties would simply be to collect and arrange the Letters, and furnish any little items concerning William Henry and his home which might interest the reader. It was also hinted, in the mildest manner possible, that I was not chosen for this office on account of my talents, or my learning, or my skill in writing; but wholly because of my intimate acquaintance with the two families at Summer Sweeting place, — for I have at times lived close by them for weeks together, and have taken tea quite often both at Grandmother's and at Aunt Phebe's.

After a brief consideration of the proposal, I agreed to undertake the task; at the same time wishing a more experienced editor could have been found.

1   A

My acquaintance with the families commenced just about the time of William Henry's going to school, and in rather a curious way.

I was then (and am now) much interested in the Freedmen. While serving in the Army of the Potomac, I had seen a good deal of them, and was connected with a hospital in Washington at the time when they were pouring into that city, hungry and sick, and half-naked. I belonged to several Freedmen's Societies, and had just then pledged myself to beg a barrelful of old clothing to send South.

But this I found was, for an unmarried man, having few acquaintances in the town, a very rash promise. I had no idea that one barrel could hold so much. The pile of articles collected seemed to me immense. I wondered what I should do with them all. But when packed away there was room left for certainly a third as many more; and I had searched thoroughly the few garrets in which right of search was allowed me. Even in those, I could only glean after other barrel-fillers. A great many garrets yielded up their treasures during the war; for "Old clo'! old clo'!" was the cry then all over the North.

Now, as I was sitting one afternoon by my barrel, wishing it were full, it happened that I looked down into the street, and saw there my *unknown friend*, waiting patiently in his empty cart. This *unknown friend* was a tall, high-shouldered man, who drove in, occasionally, with vegetables. There were others who came in with vegetables also, and oftener than he; but this one I had particularly noticed, partly because of his bright, good-humored face, and partly because his horse had always a flower, or a sprig of something green, stuck in the harness.

At first I had only glanced at him now and then in the crowd. Then I found myself watching for his blue cart, and next I began to wonder where he came from, and what kind of people his folks were. He joked with the grocery-men, threw apples at the little ragged street children, and coaxed along his old horse in a sort of friendly way that was quite amusing. And though I had never spoken a word to him, nor he to me, I called him my unknown friend, for a sight of him always did me good.

It was a bony old gray horse that he drove, with a long neck poking way ahead; and the man was a farmer-like man, and wore farmer-like clothes; but he had a pleasant, twinkling eye, and the horse, as I said before, was seldom without a flower or bit of green stuck behind his ear or somewhere else about the harness.

And often, when the town was hot and dusty, and business·people were mean, I would say to myself, as my friend drove past on his way home, How I should like to ride out with him, no matter where, if 't is only where they have flowers and green things growing in the garden!

On this particular afternoon, as I have said, I observed my friend sitting quietly in his cart, "bound out," as the fishermen say, — sitting becalmed, waiting for something ahead to get started.

It happened that I was just then feeling very sensibly the heat and confinement of the town, and was more than usually weary of business ways and business people ; actually pining for the balmy air of pine woods and the breath of flowery fields. And perhaps, thought I, my friend may live among warm-hearted country folk, who will be delighted to give to my poor contrabands, and whose garrets no barrelman has yet explored !

So, giving a second look, and seeing that he still sat there, patiently awaiting his turn, I ran down, without stopping to think more about it, and asked if I might ride out with him.

"O yes. Jump in! jump in!" said he, in the pleasantest manner possible ; then he offered me his cushion, and began to double up an empty bag for himself.

"No, no. Give me the bag," said I ; and folding it, I laid it on the board, just to take off the edge of the jolting a little. And my seat seemed a charming one, after having been perched up on an office-stool so long.

That cushion of his took my eye at once. It looked as if it came out of a rocking-chair. The covering was of black cloth, worked in a very old-fashioned way, with pinks and tulips. The colors were faded, but it had a homespun, comfortable, countrified look ; in fact, the first glance at that queer old cushion assured me that I was going to exactly the right place.

Presently we got started, and certainly I never had a better ride, nor one with a pleasanter companion. He asked me all sorts of funny questions about electricity, and oxygen, and flying-machines, and the telegraph, and the moon and stars.

"Now you are a learned man, I suppose," said he ; "and I want you to tell me how that golden-rod gets its yellow out of black ground." I said I was not a learned man at all, and I did n't believe learned men themselves could tell how it got its yellow, and the asters their purple, and the succory its blue, and the everlasting its white, all out of the same black ground. He said he was pretty sure his wife could n't boil up a kettleful and color either of those colors from them.

So we went talking on. He asked me where I 'd been stopping, and what I did for a living. And I told him what I did for a living, and all about soldier life, and the contrabands, and about my barrel. Our road led through woods part of the way, and I drew in long breaths of woody air. He told me a funny woodchuck story, and had a good deal to say about wood-lots, — how some rich men formerly owned great tracts, but becoming poor were forced to sell; and how, when pines were cut off, oaks grew up in their place. And among other things he told me that a hardhack would turn into a huckleberry-bush. I said that seemed like a miracle. He was going on to tell me about one that he had watched, but just then we turned into a pleasant, shady lane.

We had n't gone far down this shady lane before we heard a loud screaming behind us, and looking round saw a small boy caught fast in the bushes by the skirt of his frock.

"Do you see that little boy?" I asked.

"O yes, I see him," he said, laughing. "Hullo, Tommy! what you staying there for?"

The boy kept on crying.

"What you waiting for?" he called out again, just as if he could n't see that the bushes would not let the child stir.

We found out afterwards that little Tommy had hid there to jump out and scare his father, but got caught by the briers. I went to untangle him, — his clothes had several rents, — and was going to put him in the cart; but he would get in "his own self," he said. Then he stopped crying, and wanted to drive. His father said, " No, not till we get through the bars."

Then Tommy began again. And at last he said, half crying and half talking, " When I'm — the — father, and you'm — the — ittle Tommy — you can't — drive — my — horse ! "

His father laughed and said : " Well, when I'm the little Tommy, I'll brush the snarls off my face — so, and throw them under the wheels — so, and let 'em get run over ! "

This made Tommy laugh, and very soon after we came to the bars.

I looked ahead and saw a neat white house, not very large, with green blinds and a piazza, where flowering plants were climbing. There was a garden on one side and an orchard on the other. Just across the garden stood an old, brown, unpainted house. There were tall apple-trees growing near it, that looked about a hundred years old. My friend, Uncle Jacob, — I've heard him called Uncle Jacob so much since that I really don't know how to put a Mister to his name, — said those were Summer Sweeting trees, that had pretty nigh done bearing. He said there used to be Summer Sweeting trees growing all about there ; and that when he took part of the place, and built him a house, he cut down the ones on his land, and set out Baldwins and Tallmans and

Porters ; but his mother kept her's for the good they had done, and for the sake of what few apples they did bear, to give away to the children.

The houses had their backs towards me, and I was glad of that, for I always like back doors better than front ones.

Uncle Jacob whistled, and I saw a blind fly open, and a handkerchief wave from an upper window, where two girls were sitting. Uncle Jacob's wife stepped to the door and waved a sun-bonnet, and then stepped back again.

"Here, Tommy," said Uncle Jacob, "you carry in the magazine to Lucy Maria, and here 's Matilda's gum-arabic. I don't see where Towser is."

I jumped out, and said I guessed I would keep on; for I began to feel bashful about seeing so many women-folks.

"Where you going to keep on to?" Uncle Jacob asked. "This road don't go any farther."

I said I would walk across the fields to the next vil-lage and find a hotel.

"O no," said he, "stay here. Grandmother 'll be glad enough to hear about the contrabands. She 'll knit stockings, and pick up a good deal about the house to send off. And I want to ask much as five hundred questions more about matters and things myself. Come, stay. Yes, we 'll give you a good supper, a first-rate supper. Don't be afraid. My wife 'll — There! I forgot her errand, now! But if you — Whoa! whoa! Georgiana, take this pattern in to your Aunt Phebe, and tell her I forgot to see if I could match it; but I don't believe the man had any like it."

Georgiana was a nice little girl that just then came running across the garden, — William Henry's sister, as I learned afterwards.

Just then Aunt Phebe stepped to the door again.

"Here are two hungry travellers," said Uncle Jacob, "and one of us is bashful."

"Well," said Aunt Phebe, very cheerily, "if anybody is hungry, this is just the right place. How do you do, sir? Come right in. We live so out of the way we 're always glad of company. Father, can't you introduce your friend?"

"Well — no — I can't," said he. "But I guess he 's brother to the President!"

I said my name was Fry.

Aunt Phebe said her father had a cousin that married a *Fry*, and asked what my mother's maiden name was. I told her my mother was a *Young*, and that I was named for my father and mother both, — *Silas Young Fry*.

I heard a tittering overhead, behind a pair of blinds, where I guessed some girls were peeping through. And afterwards, when I was sitting on the piazza, I heard one tell another, not thinking I was within hearing, that a young fry had come to supper.

When we all sat round the table the girls seemed full of tickle, which they tried to hide, — and one of them asked me, — I think it was Hannah Jane, — with a very sober face, —

"Mr. Fry, will you take some fried fish?"

I laughed and said, "No, I never take anything *fried*."

Then we all laughed together, and so got acquainted

very pleasantly; for I have observed that a little ripple of fun sets people nearer together than a whole ocean of calm conversation.

After supper Uncle Jacob read the paper aloud, while the girls washed up the dishes. All were eager to hear; and I found they kept the run of affairs quite as well as townspeople. When there was too much rattling of dishes for Uncle Jacob to be heard, and the girls lost some important item, he was always willing to read it over. Little Tommy was rolled up in a shawl and set down in the rocking-chair (that cushion did come out of it) while his mother mended his clothes. This was the way he usually got punished for tearing them. He was done up in a shawl, arms and all, and kept in the rocking-chair while the clothes were being mended, and he was obliged to remain pretty quiet, or the chair would tip. Aunt Phebe said Tommy was so careless, something must be done, and keeping him still was the worst punishment he could have.

When the girls finished their dishes and took out their sewing, and were going to light the large lamp, their mother said that we mustn't think of settling ourselves for the evening. She said we must all go in to grandmother's, for she'd be dreadful lonely, missing Billy so.

Then Aunt Phebe told me how her nephew, Billy, a ten-year old boy, had gone away to school only the day before, and how they all missed him.

"Isn't he pretty young to go away to school?" I asked.

"That's what I told his father," said she.

"His father sent him away to keep him," said Uncle Jacob. "Grandmother was spoiling him."

1 *

" Ruining the boy with kindness ? " said Lucy Maria.

" Well," said Aunt Phebe, " I suppose 't was so.   I know 't was so.   But we did hate to have Billy go! "

Uncle Jacob then took me across the garden, and introduced me to Mr. Carver, the father of William Henry, and to Grandmother, — old Mrs. Carver, as the neighbors called her.

She was a smiling, blue-eyed old lady, though with a little bit of an anxious look just between the eyes.   I thought there was no doubt about her being a grandmother that would spoil boys.

" Why, there 's Towser, now ? " said Uncle Jacob. " He did n't come to meet me to-night."

" He 's been there, off and on, pretty much all day," said grandmother.   " You see what he 's got his head on, don't you ? "

" Billy's old boots ! " said Uncle Jacob.

" Yes.   He set a good deal by Billy.   I have n't put the boots away yet," she said, with a sigh.

" Here, Towser ! come here, sir ! " cried Uncle Jacob.

Towser was a big, shaggy, clever-looking dog.   He got up slowly, sniffed at my trousers, then walked to Uncle Jacob, then round the room, then to the door, then up stairs and down again, and then back· he went and lay down by the boots.

" He misses my grandson," said grandmother to me, trying to smile about it.

The little girl, Georgiana, sat on a cricket, holding a kitten, tying and untying its ribbon.   A square of patchwork had fallen on the floor.   She stooped to pick it up and dropped her spool.   That rolled away towards the door, and kitty jumped for it and soon got the thread in a tangle. The door opened so suddenly that she hopped up about two feet into the air and tumbled head over heels.

It was Lucy Maria who opened the door. The other girls came soon after ; and when Tommy was asleep Aunt Phebe came too. We had a very sociable time. I don't call myself a talker, but I did n't mind talking there, they seemed so easy, just like one's own folks. I told grandmother many things about the contrabands, and about Southern life, and Southern people, and about soldier life and battles and rations and making raids, and the Washington hospitals, and how needy the contrabands were, and about my barrel. "Poor creatures ! " said she. "I must look up some things for them to-morrow." Aunt Phebe thought there might be a good many things lying about that would be of use to folks who had n't anything.

"Billy's boots ! " cried Hannah Jane.

"Why, yes," said her mother, "no use keeping boots for a growing boy."

This and other remarks brought us back to William Henry again, and grandmother seemed glad of it. She liked to keep talking about her boy.

"I shall feel very anxious," she said. "I hope he will write soon as he gets there. I told him he 'd better write every day, so I could be sure just how he was. For if well one day, he might n't be the next.

"O grandmother, that 's too bad ! " said Lucy Maria. " 'T is cruel to ask a boy to write every day ! "

"I would n't worry, mother," said Aunt Phebe. " Billy 's always been a well child. "

" These strong constitutions," said grandmother, " when they do take anything, 't is apt to go hard with 'em."

" He's taken pretty much everything that can be given to him already," said Aunt Phebe.

" I suppose they'll put clothes enough on his bed," said grandmother. " I can't bear to think of his sleeping cold nights."

" Perhaps they have blankets in that part of the country," said Uncle Jacob.

" But people are not always thoughtful about it," said grandmother. " I really hope he'll take care of himself, and not be climbing up everywhere. Houses and trees were bad enough; but now they have gymnastic poles and everything else, to tempt boys off the ground. O dear! when we think of everything that might happen to boys, 't is a wonder one of them ever lives to grow up. Is n't there a pond near by ? "

" O yes," said Lucy Maria, " Crooked Pond. That's what gives the name to the school, — Crooked Pond School."

" I hope he won't be whipped," said his little sister.

" Whipped ! " cried Aunt Phebe, " I should like to see anybody whipping our Billy ! "

" O mother, I should n't," said Matilda.

" 'T is n't an impossible thing," said grandmother. " He's quick. Billy's good-hearted, but he's quick. He might speak up. I gave him a ·charge how to behave. But then, what's a boy's memory ? I don't suppose he'll remember one half the things I told him. I meant to have charged him over again, the last thing, not to stay out in the rain and get wet, where there's nobody to see to his clothes being dried."

" Well," said Uncle Jacob, " if a boy does n't know enough to go into the house when it rains, he better come home ? "

" What I hope is," said Aunt Phebe, " that he 'll keep himself looking decent."

" If he does," said Lucy Maria, " then 't will be the first time. The poor child never seemed to have much luck about keeping spruced up. If anybody here ever saw William Henry with no buttons off and both shoes tied, and no rip anywhere, let 'em raise their hands ! "

Everybody laughed. I thought grandmother's eye wandered round the circle, as if half taking it all in earnest, and half hoping some hand would go up. But no hand went up.

" Billy always was hard on his clothes," she said, with a sigh. " If he only keeps well I won't say a word ; but there 's always danger of boys eating unwholesome things, where there 's nobody to deny them."

" Billy's stomach 's his own, and he must learn to have the care of it," said Mr. Carver.

Mr. Carver seemed a very quiet, thoughtful man, and of quite a different turn from his brother.

I suggested that boarding-house diet was apt to be plain ; and then told grandmother about a nephew of mine, a nice boy, who was rather older than her grandson, who was named after me, and of whom I thought everything. I told her he had been away at school a year, and that he enjoyed himself, and went ahead in his studies, and never had a sick day, and came home with better manners than he had when he went away. As this pleased her, I said everything I could think of about my nephew, including some anecdotes of little Silas, when he was quite small; and she told a few about William Henry, the others helping her out, now and then, with some missing items.

Uncle Jacob said he should n't dare to say how many times she 'd been frightened almost to death about Billy. Many and many a time she was sure he was lost, or drowned, or run over, or carried off, and would never come back alive; but he always managed to come out straight at last. Uncle Jacob said that if all the worry that was worried in this world were piled up together, 't would make a mountain; but if all of it that need n't be worried were knocked off, what was left would n't be bigger than a huckleberry hill.

Mr. Carver said there was one thing which made him entirely willing to trust William Henry away, and that was, he had always been a boy of principle. "I have watched him pretty closely," said Mr. Carver, "and have noticed that he has a kind of pride about him that will not permit him to lie, or equivocate in any way.

"That 's true!" cried Aunt Phebe. "True enough! Billy don't always look fit to be seen, but he is n't deceitful. I 'll say that for him!"

"When he went to our school," said Matilda, "and was in the class below me, and there was a fuss among the boys, and all of 'em told it a different way, the teacher used to say she would ask William Henry, and then she could tell just how it happened."

"He could n't have a better name than that," said Mr. Carver.

Grandmother wiped her eyes, she seemed so gratified that her boy's good qualities were remembered at last.

I am almost certain that an editor should not be so long in telling his story. But I should like to say a little more about that first night, — just a very little more.

Grandmother would n't hear of my going to a hotel. Anybody that had been a soldier, and was doing good, should never go from her house to find a night's lodging. And she might as well have said, particularly anybody that had a little Silas away at school, for I saw she felt it.

It required very little urging to make me stay; for in all my travels I had never met with a pleasanter set of people. My choice was offered me, whether to lodge in the front chamber, or in the little back chamber where Billy slept. Of course I chose the last; for people's best, front, spare chambers never suit me very well.

Billy's room was a snug little room, low in the walls, and papered with flowery paper. There were two windows, the curtains to which were made of paper like that on the walls. You had to roll them up with your hands, and tie them with a string that went over the top. The room was over the sink-room, and in going into it we stepped one step down. There was no carpet on the floor, excepting a strip by the bedside and a mat before the table. Grandmother said the table Billy and she made together, so the legs did n't stand quite true. It was covered with calico, and more calico was puckered on round the edge and came down to the floor. That was done, she said, to make a place for his boots and shoes. She thought 't was well for a boy to have a place for his things, even if he did always leave them somewhere else. There was nothing under the table but one rubber boot, with the rubber mostly cut off, and some pieces of new pine, easy to whittle, that Billy had picked up and stowed away there. A narrow looking-glass hung over the table. It had a queer picture at the top, of two Japanese figures. The glass had a little

crack in one corner, — cracked by his ball bouncing up when he was trying it. Some green tissue-paper hung around this fracture with a very innocent, orna-mental air. Not far from the glass I observed a rusty jack-knife stuck in the wall, close to the window-frame; and on its handle was hanging a string of birds'-eggs.

In stepping up to examine these I stumbled against an old hair-covered trunk, quite a large one. The cover seemed a little askew, and not inclined to shut. This trunk was the color of a red cow, and for aught I know was covered with the skin of a red cow. In the middle of the cover the letters W. C. were printed in brass nails, which led me to guess that the trunk had belonged to William Henry's father. Grandmother raised the cover, to see what kept it from shutting, and found 't was a great scraggly piece of sassafras (saxifax) root, which lay on top.

There was everything in that trunk, — everything. Of course I don't mean meeting-houses, or steamboats, or anacondas; but everything a boy would be likely to have. I saw picture papers, leather straps, old pocket-books, a pair of dividers, the hull of a boat, a pair of boot-pullers, a chrysalis, several penholders, a large clam-shell, a few pocket combs, — comb parts gone, — fishing-lines, reels, bobs, sinkers, a bullet-mould, arrows, a bag of marbles, a china egg, a rule, hammers, a red comforter, two odd mittens, "that had lost the mates of 'em," a bird-call, a mask, an empty cologne-bottle, a dime novel, odd cards, — all these, and more, were visible by merely stirring the top layer a little. Also several tangles of twine, twining and intertwining among the mass. Grandmother shook up the things some, — by means of a handle which probably belonged to a hatchet, but the hatchet part was buried, — and I saw that the bottom was covered with marbles, dominos, nails, bottles, slate-pencils, bits of brass clock machinery, and all the innumerable nameless, shapeless things-which would be likely to settle down to the bottom of a boy's trunk. Grandmother said she should set it to rights if it were n't for fish-hooks ; but anybody's hands going in there would be likely to get fish-hooks stuck into them.

In one end of the trunk was quite a fanciful box. It was nothing but a common pine box, painted black, with "cut out" pictures pasted on it. There were ladies' faces, generals' heads, bugs, horses, butterflies, chairs, ships, birds, and in the centre of the cover, outside, there was a large red rose on its stalk. At the centre, inside, was a laughing, or rather a grinning face, cut from some comic magazine. In this box was kept some of his more precious treasures, — a little brass anchor, a silver pencil-case, a whole set of dominos, and a ball, very prettily worked, orange-peel pattern, in many colors. This was a present from his teacher. There was also a curious pearl-handled knife, with the blades broken short off. She said he never felt so badly about breaking any knife as when that got broken, for it was one his cousin brought him home from sea. He was keeping it to have new blades put in.

"How much this trunk reminds me of little Silas's bureau-drawer!" I said, taking up an old writing-book. As I spoke several bits of paper fell out and among them were some very funny pictures, done with a lead-pencil and then inked over.

"What are these?" I asked. "Does he draw?"

"Well — not exactly," she answered, — "nothing that can be called drawing. He tries sometimes to copy what he sees."

"I suppose I may look at them," I said, picking up one of the bits of paper. "Pray what is this?"

Grandmother put on her spectacles, and turned the paper round, as if trying to find the up and down of it.

"O, this is Uncle Jacob chasing the calf," said she; "those things that look like elbows are meant for his legs kicking up. And on this piece he's tried to make the old gobbler flying at Georgiana. You see the turkey is as big as she is. But maybe you don't know which the turkey is! That one is the fat man, and that one is the cat and kittens. And that one is a dandy, making a bow. He saw one over at the hotel that he took it from."

She was sitting by the bed, and as she named them, spread them out upon it, one by one, along with some others I have not mentioned, all very comical. When I had finished laughing over them I said, —

"I should like to send these pictures in my barrel. 'T would give the little sick contrabands something to laugh at."

"Well, I'll tell Billy when he comes," she answered, then gathered them up and smoothed the quilt again.

The bedstead was a low one, without any posts, except
that each leg ended at the top with a little round, flat head
or knob.   The quilt was made of light and dark patchwork.   Grandmother told me, lowering her voice, that
Billy's mother made that patchwork when she was a little
girl just learning to sew; but 't was kept laid away, and
about the last work she ever did was to set it together.
And 't was her request that Billy should have it•on his
bed.   She said Billy was a very *feeling* boy, though he
did n't say much.   One time, a couple years ago, she
hung that quilt out to blow, and forgot to take it in till
after the dew began to fall, so, being a little damp, she
put on another one.   But next morning she looked in,
and there 't was, over him, spread on all skewy !

"Sometimes I think," she added, "that boys have
more feeling than we think for ! "

"I know they have ! " I answered.

A picture of William Henry's mother hung opposite
the bed.   It was not a very handsome face, nor a pretty
face.   But it had such an earnest, loving, wistful expression, that I could not help exclaiming, " Beautiful ! "

"Yes, she was a beautiful woman.   We all loved her.
She was just like a daughter to me.   Billy does n't know
what he 's lost, and 't is well he don't.   I try to be a
mother to him; but they say," said the tender-hearted old
lady, — "they say a grandmother is n't fit to have the
bringing up of a child !   Billy has his faults."

"Now if I were a child," I exclaimed, "I should
rather you would have the bringing up of me than anybody I know of !   And 't is my opinion, from what I
hear, that you 've done well by Billy.   Of course boys

are boys, and don't always do as they ought to. Now there's little Silas. He's been a world of trouble first and last. But then boys soon get big enough to be ashamed of all their little bad ways. The biggest part of 'em like good men best, and mean to be good men. And I think Billy's going to grow up a capital fellow! A capital fellow! If a boy's true-hearted he'll come out all right. And your boy is, is n't he?

"O very!" she said. "Very!"

I was so glad to think, after the old lady had gone down, that I'd said something which, if she kept awake, thinking about the boy, would be a comfort to her.

Next morning grandmother brought out quite an armful of old clothes. A poor old couple, living near, she said, took most of hers and Mr. Carver's; but what few there were of Billy's that were decent to send I might have. A couple of linen jackets, a Scotch cap, two pairs of thin trousers, not much worn, but outgrown, a small overcoat, several pairs of stockings, and some shoes. And the boots also, and some underclothing, that William Henry might have worn longer, she said, if he were only living at home, where she could put a stitch in 'em now and then.

Grandmother sighed as she emptied the pockets of crumbles, green apples, reins, bullets, and knotted, gray, balled-up pocket-handkerchiefs. Among the clothes she brought out a funny little uniform, which I had seen hanging up in his room, — one that he had when a soldier, or trainer, as she called it, in a military company, formed

near the beginning of the war. It consisted of a blue
flannel sack, edged with red braid, red flannel Zouave
trousers, and a blue flannel cap, bound with red, and having a square visor. That uniform would fit some little .
contraband, she said.

"Had n't you better keep those?" I asked. "Won't
he want them?"

"O no," she said. "He's outgrown them. And 't is
no use keeping them for moths to get into."

She gave me some picture-books, and two primers, a
roll of linen, and quite a good blanket, all of which I
received thankfully.

In rolling up the different articles, I saw her eye resting so lovingly on the little uniform, that I said, " Here,
grandmother, had n't you better take back these?"

"O, I guess not," she answered. "I guess you better
send them. But," she added a moment after, "perhaps
they might as well stay till you send another barrel."

"Just exactly as well," I said. And the old lady
seemed as if she had recovered a lost treasure.

Aunt Phebe added a good many valuable articles, so
that by the time Uncle Jacob was ready to start I had
collected two immense bundles, and felt almost brave
enough to face another barrel. For they all said they
would beg from their friends, and save things, and that I
must certainly come again.

"For you know," said Aunt Phebe, "'t is a great deal
better to hear you tell things than to read about them in
the newspapers."

They stood about the door to see us off, and Matilda
stroked the old horse, and talked to him as if he under-

stood. She broke off two heads of phlox, red and white, and fastened them in behind his ear. Uncle Jacob told me, as we rode along, that the old horse really expected to be patted and talked to before starting. And indeed I noticed myself that after being dressed up he stepped off with an exceedingly satisfied air, just as I have seen some little girls, — and boys too, for that matter, and occasionally grown people.

But it is quite time to give you the Letters. There should be more of them, for the correspondence covers a period of about two years. 'T is true that, after the first, William Henry did not write nearly as often. But still there are many missing. Little Tommy cut up some into strings of boys and girls, and at' one time when grandmother was n't very well, and had to hire help, the girl took some to kindle fire with. The old lady said she was sitting up in her arm-chair, by the fireplace one day, when she saw, in the corner, a piece of paper with writing on it, half burnt up. She poked it out with a yardstick, and 'twas one of Billy's letters! Quite a number which were perfect have been omitted. This is because that some coming between were missing; and so, as the children say, there would n't be any sense to them. Others contained mostly private matters. Very few were dated. This is, however, of small importance, as the Letters probably will never be brought forward to decide a law case.

THE WILLIAM HENRY LETTERS.

THE first letter from William Henry which has been preserved seems to have been written a few weeks after entering his school, and when he had begun to get acquainted with the boys. Could the letter itself be made to appear here, with its *very* peculiar handwriting, and with all the other distinctive marks of a boy's first exploit on paper, it would be found even more entertaining than when given in the printed form.

MY DEAR GRANDMOTHER, —

I think the school that I have come to is a very good school. We have dumplings. I 've tied up the pills that you gave me in case of feeling bad, in the toe of my cotton stocking that 's lost the mate of it. The mince pies they have here are baked without any plums being put into them. So, please, need I say, No, I thank you, ma'am, to 'em when they come round? If they don't agree, shall I take the pills or the drops? Or was it the hot flannels, — and how many?

I 've forgot about being shivery. Was it to eat roast onions? No, I guess not. I guess it was a wet band tied round my head. Please write it down, because you

2

told me so many things I can't remember. How can anybody tell when anybody is sick enough to take things? You can't think what a great, tall man the schoolmaster is. He has got something very long to flog us with, that bends easy, and hurts, — Q. S. So Dorry says. Q. S. is in the abbreviations, and stands for a sufficient quantity. Dorry says the master keeps a paint-pot in his room, and has his whiskers painted black every morning, and his hair too, to make himself look scareful. Dorry is one of the great boys. But Tom Cush is bigger. I don't like Tom Cush.

I have a good many to play with; but I miss you and Towser and all of them very much. How does my sister do? Don't let the cow eat my peach-tree. Dorry Baker he says that peaches don't grow here; but he says the cherries have peach-stones in them. In a month my birthday will be here. ' How funny 't will seem to be eleven, when I 've been ten so long! I don't skip over any button-holes in the morning now; so my jacket comes out even.

Why did n't you tell me I had a red head? But I can run faster than any of them that are no bigger than I am, and some that are. One of the spokes of my umbrella broke itself in two yesterday, because the wind blew so when it rained.

We learn to sing. He says I 've a good deal of voice; but I 've forgot what the matter is with it. We go up and down the scale, and beat time. The last is the best fun. The other is hard to do. But if I could only get up, I guess 't would be easy to come down. He thinks something ails my ear. I thought he said I had n't got any at all. What have a feller's ears to do with singing, or with scaling up and down?

Your affectionate grandchild,

WILLIAM HENRY.

P. S. Here's a conundrum Dorry Baker made: In a race, why would the singing-master win? Because "Time flies," and he *beats time*.

I want to see Aunt Phebe, and Aunt Phebe's little Tommy, dreadfully.

W. H.

This second letter must have been pleasing to Aunt Phebe, as it shows that William Henry was beginning to have some faint regard for his personal appearance.

MY DEAR GRANDMOTHER, —

I've got thirty-two cents left of my spending-money. When shall I begin to wear my new shoes every day? The soap they have here is pink. Has father sold the bossy calf yet? There's a boy here they call Bossy Calf, because he cried for his mother. He has been here three days. He sleeps with me. And every night, after he has laid his head down on the pillow, and the lights are blown out, I begin to sing, and to scale up and down, so the boys can't hear him cry. Dorry Baker and three more boys sleep in the same room that we two sleep in. When they begin to throw bootjacks at me, to make me stop my noise, it scares him, and he leaves off crying. I want a pair of new boots dreadfully, with red on the tops of them, that I can tuck my trousers into and keep the mud off.

One thing more the boys plague me for besides my

head. Freckles. Dorry held up an orange yesterday. "Can you see it?" says he. "To be sure," says I.

"Did n't know as you could see through 'em," says he, meaning freckles. Dear grandmother, I have cried once, but not in bed. For fear of their laughing, and of the bootjacks. But away in a good place under the trees. A shaggy dog came along and licked my face. But oh! he did make me remember Towser, and cry all over again. But don't tell, for I should be ashamed. I wish the boys would like me. Freckles come thicker in summer than they do in winter.

Your affectionate grandchild,

WILLIAM HENRY.

If William Henry's recipe for the prevention of spunkiness were generally adopted, I fancy that many a boy would be seen practising the circus performance here mentioned. It must have been "sure cure!" I well remember the "plaguing" of my school days, and know from experience how hard it is for a boy (or a man) always to keep his temper. The fellows used to make fun of my name. In our quarrels, when there was nothing else left to say, they would call out, — leaving off the Silas, — "Y Fry? why not bake?" or "boil," or "stew." Of course to such remarks there was no answer.

It is to be regretted that so few of Grandmother's letters were preserved. As Billy here makes known the state of his pocket-book, we may infer that she had been inquiring into his accounts, and perhaps cautioning him against spending too freely.

MY DEAR GRANDMOTHER, —

I do what you told me. You told me to bite my lips and count ten, before I spoke, when the boys plague me, because I'm a spunky boy. But doing it so much makes my lips sore. So now I go head over heels sometimes, till I'm out of breath. Then I can't say anything.

This is the account you asked me for, of all I've bought this week : —

Slippery elm	1 cent.
Corn-ball	1 cent.
Gum	1 cent.

And I swapped a whip-lash that I found for an orange that only had one suck sucked out of it. The "Two

Betseys," they keep very good things to sell.   They are two old women that live in a little hut with two rooms to

it, and a ladder to go up stairs by, through a hole in the wall.   One Betsey, she is lame and keeps still, and sells the things to us sitting down.   The other Betsey, she can run, and keeps a yard-stick to drive away boys with.   For they have apple-trees in their garden.   But she never touches a boy, if she does catch him.   They have hens and sell eggs.

The boys that sleep in the same room that we do wanted Benjie and me to join together with them to buy a great confectioner's frosted cake, and other things. And when the lamps had been blown out, to keep awake and light them up again, and so have a supper late at night, with the curtains all down and the blinds shut up, when people were in bed, and not let anybody know.

But Benjie had n't any money.   Because his father works hard for his living, — but his uncle pays for his schooling, — and he would n't if he had.   And I said I would n't do anything so deceitful. And the more they said you must and you shall, the more I said I would n't and I should n't, and the money should blow up first.

So they called me "Old Stingy" and "Pepper-corn" and "Speckled Potatoes." Said they'd pull my hair if't were n't for burning their fingers. Dorry was the maddest one. Said he guessed my hair was tired of standing up, and wanted to lie down to rest.

I wish you would please send me a new comb, for the large end of mine has got all but five of the teeth broken out, and the small end can't get through. I can't get it cut because the barber has raised his price. Send quite a stout one.

I have lost two of my pocket-handkerchiefs, and another one went up on Dorry's kite, and blew away.

Your affectionate grandchild,

WILLIAM HENRY.

MY DEAR GRANDMOTHER, —

I did what you told me, when I got wet. I hung my clothes round the kitchen stove on three chairs, but the cooking girl she flung them under the table. So now I go wrinkled, and the boys chase me to smooth out the wrinkles. I 've got a good many hard rubs. But I laugh too. That 's the best way. Some of the boys play with me now, and ask me to go round with them. Dorry has n't yet. Tom Cush plagues the most.

Sometimes the schoolmaster comes out to see us when we are playing ball, or jumping. To-day, when we all clapped Dorry, the schoolmaster clapped too. Somebody told me that he likes boys. Do you believe it?

A cat ran up the spout this morning, and jumped in the window. Dorry was going to choke her, or drown her, for the working-girl said she licked out the inside of a custard-pie. I asked Dorry what he would take to let her go, and he said five cents. So I paid. For she was just like my sister's cat. And just as likely as not some-

body's little sister would have cried about it. For she had a ribbon tied round her neck.

The woman that I go to have my buttons sewed on to, is a very good woman. She gave me a cookie with a hole in the middle, and told me to mind and not eat the hole.

Coming back, I met Benjie, and he looked so sober, I offered it to him as quick as I could. But it almost made him cry; because, he said, his mother made her cookies with a hole in the middle. But when he gets acquainted, he won't be so bashful, and he 'll feel better then.

We walked away to a good place under the trees, and he talked about his folks, and his grandmother, and his

Aunt Polly, and the two little twins.　They 've got two cradles just like each other, and they are just as big as each other, and just as old.　They creep round on the floor, and when one picks up anything, the other pulls it away.　I wish we had some twins.　I told him things too.

Kiss yourself for me.

Your affectionate grandchild,

WILLIAM HENRY.

P. S.　If you send a cake, send quite a large one.　I like the kind that Uncle Jacob does.　Aunt Phebe knows.

MY DEAR GRANDMOTHER, —

I was going to tell you about " Gapper Skyblue." " Gapper " means grandpa.　He wears all the time blue overalls, faded out, and a jacket like them. . That 's why they call him " Gapper Skyblue."　He 's a very poor old man.　He saws wood.　We found him leaning up against a tree.　Benjie and I were together.　His hair is all turned white, and his back is bent.　He had great patches on his knees.　His hat was an old hat that he had given him, and his shoes let in the mud.　I wish you would please to be so good as to send me both your old-fashioned india-rubbers, to make balls of, as quick as holes come.　Most all the boys have lost their balls.　And please to send some shoe-strings next time, for I have to tie mine up all the time now with some white cord that I found, and it gets into hard knots, and I have to stoop my head way down and untie 'em with my teeth, because I cut my thumb whittling, and jammed my fingers in the gate.

2*

C

Old Gapper Skyblue's nose is pretty long, and he looked so funny leaning up against a tree, that I was just going to laugh. But then I remembered what you said a real gentleman would do. That he would be polite to all people, no matter what clothes they had on, or whether they were rich people or poor people. He had a big basket with two covers to it, and we offered to carry it for him.

He said, "Yes, little boys, if you won't lift up the covers."

We found 't was pretty heavy. And I wondered what was in it, and so did Benjie. The basket was going to "The Two Betseys."

When we had got half-way there, Dorry and Tom Cush came along, and called out: "Hallo! there, you two. What are you lugging off so fast?"

We said we did n't know. They said, "Let's see." We said, "No, you can't see." Then they pushed us.

Gapper was a good way behind. I sat down on one cover, and Benjie on the other, to keep them shut up.

Then they pulled us. I swung my arms round, and made the sand fly with my feet, for I was just as mad as anything. Then Tom Cush hit me. So I ran to tell Gapper to make haste. But first picked up a stone to send at Tom Cush. But remembered about the boy that threw a stone and hit a boy, and he died. I mean the boy that was hit. And so dropped the stone down again and ran like lightning.

"Go it, you pesky little red-headed firebug!" cried Tom Cush.

"Go it, Spunkum! I'll hold your breath," Dorry hollered out.

The dog, the shaggy dog that licked my face when I was lying under the trees, he came along and growled and snapped at them, because they were hurting Benjie. You see Benjie treats him well, and gives him bones. And the master came in sight too. So they were glad to let us alone.

The basket had rabbits in it. Gapper Skyblue wanted to pay us two cents apiece. But we wouldn't take pay. We wouldn't be so mean.

When we were going along to school, Bubby Short came and whispered to me that Tom and Dorry were hiding my bird's eggs in a post-hole. But I got them again. Two broke.

Bubby Short is a nice little fellow. He's about as old as I am, but over a head shorter and quite fat. His cheeks reach way up into his eyes. He's got little black eyes, and little cunning teeth, just as white as the meat of a punkin-seed.

I had to pay twenty cents of that quarter you sent, for

breaking a square of glass. But did n't mean to, so please excuse. I have n't much left.

Your affectionate grandchild,

WILLIAM HENRY.

P. S. When punkins come, save the seeds — to roast. If you please.

MY DEAR GRANDMOTHER, —

One of my elbows came through, but the woman sewed it up again. I 've used up both balls of my twine. And my white-handled knife, — I guess it went through a hole in my pocket, that I did n't know of till after the knife was lost. My trousers grow pretty short. But she says 't is partly my legs getting long. I 'm glad of that. And partly getting 'em wet.

I stubbed my toe against a stump, and tumbled down and scraped a hole through the knee of my oldest pair. For it was very rotten cloth. I guess the hole is too crooked to have her sew it up again. She thinks a mouse ran up the leg, and gnawed that hole my knife went through, to get the crumbles in the pocket. I don't mean when they were on me, but hanging up.

My boat is almost rigged. She says she will hem the sails if I won't leave any more caterpillars in my pockets. I 'm getting all kinds of caterpillars to see what kind of butterflies they make.

Yesterday, Dorry and I started from the pond to run and see who would get home first. He went one way, and I went another.

I cut across the Two Betseys' garden. But I don't see how I did so much hurt in just once cutting across.

I knew something cracked, — that was the sink-spout I jumped down on, off the fence. There was a board I hit, that had huckleberries spread out on it to dry. They went into the rain-water hogshead. I did n't know any huckleberries were spread out on that board.

I meant to go between the rows, but guess I stepped on a few beans. My wrist got hurt dreadfully by my getting myself tripped up in a squash-vine. And while I was down there, a bumble-bee stung me on my chin. I stepped on a little chicken, for she ran the way I thought she was n't going to. I don't remember whether I shut the gate or not. But guess not, for the pig got in, and went to rooting before Lame Betsey saw him, and the other Betsey had gone somewhere.

I got home first, but my wrist ached, and my sting smarted. You forgot to write down what was good for bumble-bee stings. Benjie said his Aunt Polly put damp sand on to stings. So he put a good deal of it on my chin, and it got better, though my wrist kept aching in the night. And I went to school with it aching. But did n't tell anybody but Benjie. Just before school was done, the master said we might put away our books. Then he talked about the Two Betseys, and told how Lame Betsey got lame by saving a little boy's life when the house was on fire. She jumped out of the window with him. And he made us all feel ashamed that we great strong boys should torment two poor women.

Then he told about the damage done the day before by some boy running through their garden, and said five dollars would hardly be enough to pay it. " I don't know what boy it was, but if he is present," says he, " I call upon him to rise."

Then I stood up. I was ashamed, but I stood up. For you told me once this saying: "Even if truth be a loaded cannon walk straight up to it."

The master ordered me not to go on to the play-ground for a week, nor be out of the house in play-hours.

From your affectionate grandchild,

WILLIAM HENRY.

I was very sorry that while in the neighborhood of the Crooked Pond school, a short time since, lack of time prevented my finding out the Two Betseys' shop. These worthy women, as will be seen further on, became William Henry's firm friends.

MY DEAR GRANDMOTHER, —

Lame Betsey gave me something to put on my wrist that cured it. I went there to ask how much money must be paid. I had sold my football, and my brass sword, and my pocket-book. They told me they should not take any money, but if I would saw some wood for them, and do an errand now and then, they should be very glad. When I told Dorry, he threw up his hat, and called out, "Three cheers for the 'Two Betseys.'" And when his hat came down, he picked it up and passed it round; "for," says he, "we all owe them something." One great boy dropped fifty cents in. And it all came to about four dollars. And Bubby Short carried it to them. But I shall saw some wood for them all the same.

Last evening it was rainy. A good many boys came into our room, and we sat in a row, and every one said some verses, or told a riddle. These two verses I send for Aunt Phebe's little Tommy to learn. I guess he's done saying "Fishy, fishy in the brook" by this time. Dorry said he got them out of the German.

"When you are rich,	"Better honest and poor,
You can ride with a span;	And go as you can,
But when you are poor,	Than rich and a rogue,
You must go as you can.	And ride with a span."

This riddle was too hard for me to guess. But Aunt Phebe's girls like to guess riddles, and I will send it to them. Mr. Augustus says that a soldier made it in a Rebel prison. Mr. Augustus is a tall boy, that knows a good deal, and wears spectacles, and that's why we call him Mr. Augustus.

RIDDLE.

I'm one half a Bible command,
That aye and forever shall stand;
And, throughout our beautiful land,
'T is needed now to foil the traitorous band.

I'm always around, — yet they say
Too often I'm out of the way,
Thereby leading astray;
I'm decked in jewels fine and rich array.

Although from my heart I am stirred,
I can utter but one little word,
And that very seldom is heard;
My elder sister sometimes kept a bird.

Reads the riddle clear to you?
I am very near to you:
Both very near and dear — to you,
Yet kept in chains. Does that seem queer to you?

That about being "stirred from the heart" is all true. So is that about being "around." The "Bible command," spoken of at the beginning, is only in three words, or two words joined by "and." This word is the first half. But I must n't tell you too much.

They are all *dear*. But some kinds are dearer than others.

I wish my father would send me one.

That about the bird is first-rate, though I never saw one of that kind of — I won't say what I mean (Dorry says you must n't say what you mean when you tell riddles). But maybe you 've seen one. They used to have them in old times.

I 've launched my boat. She 's the biggest one in school. Dorry broke a bottle upon her, and christened her the " General Grant." The boys gave three cheers when she touched water, and Benjie sent up his new kite. It 's a ripper of a kite with a great gilt star on it that 's got eight prongs.

My hat blew off, and I had to go in swimming after it. It is quite stiff. The master was walking by, and stopped to see the launching. When he smiles, he looks just as pleasant as anything.

He patted me on my cheek, and says he, "You ought to have called her the ' Flying Billy.'" And then he walked on.

"What does 'Flying Billy' mean?" says I.

"It means you," said Dorry. "And it means that you run fast, and that he likes you. If a boy can run fast, and knows his multiplication-table, and won't lie, he likes him."

But how can such a great man like a small boy?

From your affectionate grandchild,
WILLIAM HENRY.

P. S. When the boys laugh at me, I laugh too. That's a good way.

P. S. There's a man here that's got nine puppies. If I had some money I could buy one. The boys don't plague me quite so much. I'm sorry you dropped off your spectacles down the well. I suppose they sunk. I've got a sneezing cold.

W. H.

About the spectacles, I may as well confess that I was the means of their being lost.

One day Uncle Jacob came into the office hastily, and, with a look of distress, said to me very solemnly, —

"Mr. Fry, if you can, I want you to leave everything, and ride out with me!"

"Oh! what is the matter?" I exclaimed.

"Why," said he, "ever since we sent out word about old clothes, they've been coming in so fast the rooms are all filled up, and we don't know where to go!"

He then went on to tell that the notice had spread into all the neighborhoods round about, and that bundles of every description were constantly pouring in. They were left at the back door, front door, side door, dropped on the piazza, and in at the windows. Men riding by tossed them into the yard, and little boys came tugging bundles, bigger than they could lift, or dragged them in roller-carts, or wheeled them in wheelbarrows. He said he found bundles waiting for him at the store, at the post-office, and he could hardly ride along the street without some woman knocking at the window, and holding up one, and beckoning with her forefinger for him to come in after it! Even in the meeting-house somebody took a roll of something from under a shawl and handed him! He would have brought the parcels, or a part

of them, but there was every kind of a thing sent in, — white
vests and flounced lace or muslin gowns, and open-work
stockings; and some things were too poor, and some were
too nice, and his folks thought Mr. Fry should come out.

So what could I do but go? And, as it happened, I could
"leave everything" just as well as not, and was glad to.

Grandmother received me in the kindest manner, gave me
a pair of black yarn stockings, asked about the contrabands,
talked about Billy, read me his letters, and, on the whole,
seemed much easier in her mind concerning him than when
I saw her before.

She was skimming pans of milk. With her permission I
watched the skimming, for pans of milk to a city man were
a rare sight to see! I was also given some of the cream,
and a baked Summer Sweeting to eat with it.

The cream was put into a large yellow bowl, and the bowl
set in a six-quart tin pail. It was then ready to be lowered
into the well; for, as country people seldom have ice, they
use the well as a refrigerator, and it is there they keep their
butter, cream, fresh meat, or anything that is likely to spoil.

"Do let me lower it down the well for you," I said; seeing that her hand trembled a little; and besides, I hardly
thought it prudent for her to go out, as the grass was damp,
there having been quite a sprinkle of rain.

"Well, if you 've a mind to take the trouble," she said,
as she handed me the pail, at the same time telling me to be
particular about putting stones around the bowl, in the bottom, to steady it. She then handed me the line, and cautioned
me about hitting another pail, which was already down the
well.

Just as I went out Uncle Jacob passed through the gate
into the garden, to pick his mother some beans.

"Sha' n't I do that?" he asked.

"O no," said I; "I am very glad to make myself useful."

Little Tommy stood by the well watching me, and I was talking to him and playing with Towser, and by not attending to my business, I must have tied a granny-knot, though I meant to tie a square one; and about half-way down the pail slipped off, and went plump to the bottom.

Little Tommy ran into the house calling out, "Grandmother! Grandmother! that man lost your pail! Mr. Fwy let go of your pail!"

Grandmother came running out and looked down. Her spectacles were tipped up on top of her head; and when she bent over the well-curb they slipped off, just touched the tip of her nose, and were out of sight in a moment.

Uncle Jacob came up laughing and said, "Of course the specs must go down to see where the cream went to!" But Grandmother thought it was no laughing matter.

Mr. Carver and Uncle Jacob had a good many spells of fishing in the well. At last Uncle Jacob was lucky enough to catch the handle of the pail with his hook, and then he drew the pail up. It was found to be in quite a damaged condition. The water looked creamy for some time. The glasses never came to light. It seemed, therefore, no more than my duty to send Grandmother another pair, which I did soon after in a bright new six-quart pail, wishing with all my heart they were gold-bowed ones. But I could not afford to do more than replace the lost ones.

I will add that the six-quart pail was filled with the best of peaches.

The next three letters seem to have been sent at one time. Before they reached Grandmother she had worked herself into a perfect fever of anxiety.

Owing to the rabbit affair, of which they contain the whole story, William Henry had not felt like writing, so that, even before his letter was begun, they at the farm were already looking for it to arrive. Then it took a longer time than he expected to finish up his account of the matter; and when at last the letter was sealed and directed, the boy who carried it to the post-office forgot his errand, and it hung in an over-coat pocket several days. No wonder, then, the old lady grew anxious.

I was at the farm at the time they were looking for the letters, and I really tried very hard to be entertaining; but not the funniest story I could tell about the funniest little rollypoly contraband in the hospital could excite more than a passing smile.

Aunt Phebe gave me my charge before I went in.

"You must be lively," said she. "Be lively! Turn her thoughts off of Billy! That's the way! Though I do feel worried," she added. "'T is a puzzle why we don't have letters. I'm afraid something *is* the matter, or else it seems to me we should. He's been very good about writing. If anything has happened to Billy, I don't know what we should do. 'T would come pretty hard to Grandmother. And I do have my fears! But 't won't do to let her know I worry about him. And you better be very lively! We all have to be!"

I observed that Mr. Carver, although he talked very calmly with his mother, and urged her to rest easy, was after all not so very much at ease himself. He sat by the window apparently reading a newspaper. But it was plain that he only wished Grandmother to think he was reading; for he paid but little attention to the paper, and was constantly looking across the garden to see when Uncle Jacob should get back from the post-office; and the moment Towser barked he folded his paper and went out. Grandmother put on her "out-door" spectacles, and stood at the window. When Mr. Carver returned she glanced rapidly over him with an earnest, beseeching look, which seemed to say that it was not possible but that somewhere about him, in some pocket, or in his hat, or shut up in his hand, there must be a letter.

"The mail was late," Mr. Carver said; "Uncle Jacob could n't wait, and had left the boy to fetch it."

Grandmother was setting the table. In her travels to and from the buttery she stopped often to glance up the road, and during meal-time her eyes were constantly turning to the windows.

Presently Aunt Phebe came in.

"The boy did n't bring any letters," said she; "but I 've been thinking it over, and for my part I don't think 't is worth while to worry. No news is good news. Bad news travels fast. A thousand things might happen to keep a boy from writing. He might be out of paper, or out of stamps, or out of anything to write about, or might have lessons to learn, or be too full of play, or be kept after school, or might a good many things!"

"You don't suppose," said Grandmother, "that — you don't think — it could n't be possible, could it, that Billy 's been punished and feels ashamed to tell of it?"

"Nonsense!" said Aunt Phebe. "Now don't, Grandmother, I beg of you get started off on that notion! Yesterday 't was the measles. And day before 't was being drowned, and now 't is being punished!"

"'T would n't be like William not to tell of it," said Mr. Carver.

"Not a bit like him," said Aunt Phebe.

"No," said Grandmother, "I don't think it would. But you know when anybody gets to thinking, they are apt to think of everything."

I told them there was a possibility of the letter being mis-sent. And that idea reminded me of just such an anxious time we had once about little Silas. His letter went to a town of the same name in Ohio, and was a long time reaching us. I made haste to tell this to Grandmother, and thought it comforted her a little.

When I left the next morning, Mr. Carver followed me out and asked me to make inquiries in regard to the telegraphic communication with the Crooked Pond School, and to be in readiness to telegraph; for, in case no letter came that day, he should send me word to do so.

But no word arrived, as the next mail brought the following letters, with their amusing illustrations.

MY DEAR GRANDMOTHER, —

I suppose if I should tell you I had had a whipping you would feel sorry. Well, don't feel sorry. I will begin at the beginning.

We can't go out evenings. But last Monday evening one of the teachers said I might go after my overjacket that I took off to play ball, and left hanging over a fence. It was a very light night. I had to go down a long lane to get where it was; and when I got there, it was n't there. The moon was shining bright as day. Old Gapper Skyblue lives down that lane. He raises rabbits. He keeps them in a hen-house.

Now I will tell you what some of the great boys do sometimes. They steal eggs and roast them. There is a fireplace in Tom Cush's room. Once they roasted a pullet. The owners have complained so that the master said he would flog the next boy that robbed a hen-house or an orchard, before the whole school.

Now I will go on about my overjacket. While I was looking for it I heard a queer noise in the rabbit-house. So I jumped over. Then a boy popped out of the rabbit-

house and ran. I knew him in a minute, for all he ran
so fast, — Tom Cush.

Now when he started to run, something dropped out
of his hand. I went up to it, and 't was a rabbit, a dead

one, just killed; for when I stooped down and felt of it,
it was warm. And while I was stooping down, there
came a great heavy hand down on my shoulder. It was
a man's great heavy hand.

Gapper had set a man there to watch. He hollered
into my ears, " Now I 've got you ! "   I hollered, too, for
he came sudden, without my hearing.

" You little thief ! " says he.

" I did n't kill it," says I.

" You little liar ! " says he.

" I 'm not a liar," says I.

" I 'll take you to the master," says he.

" Take me where you want to," says I.

Then he pulled me along, and kept saying, " Who did,
if you did n't? If you did n't, who did ? "

And he walked me straight up into the master's room, without so much as giving a knock at the door.

"I've brought you a thief and a liar," says he.   Then he told where he found me, and what a bad boy I was. Then he went away, because the master wanted to talk with me all by myself.

Now I did n't want to tell tales of Tom, for it 's mean to tell tales.   So all I could say was that I did n't do it.

The master looked sorry.   Said he was afraid I had begun to go with bad boys.   "Did n't I see you walking in the lane with Tom Cush yesterday?" says he.   I said I was helping him find his ball.   And so I was.

"If you were with the boys who did this," said he, "or helped about it in any way, that 's just as bad."

I said I did n't help them, or go with them.

"How came you there so late?" says he. ·

"I went after my overjacket," says I. ·

"And where is your overjacket?" says he.

I said I did n't know.   It was n't there.

Then he said I might go to bed, and he would talk with me again in the morning.

When I got to our room, the boys were sound asleep. I crept into bed as still as a mouse.   The moon shone in on me.   I thought my eyes would never go to sleep again.   I tried to think how much a flogging would hurt. Course, I knew 't would n't be like one of your little whippings.   I was n't so very much afraid of the hurt, though.   But the name of being whipped, I was afraid of that, and the shame of it.   Now I will tell you about the next morning, and how I was waked up.

Your affectionate grandchild,

MY DEAR GRANDMOTHER, —

I had to leave off and jump up and run to school without stopping to sign my name, for the bell rang. But, now school is done, I will write another letter to send with that, because you will want to know the end at the same time you do the beginning.

It was little pebbles that waked me up the next morning, — little pebbles dropping down on my face. I looked up to find where they came from, and saw Tom Cush standing in the door. He was throwing them. He made signs that he wanted to tell me something. So I got up. And while I was getting up, I saw my overjacket on the back of a chair. I found out afterwards that Benjie brought it in, and forgot to tell me.

Tom made signs for me to go down stairs with him. He would n't let me put my shoes on. He had his in his hand, and I carried mine so. So we went through the long entries in our stocking-feet, and sat down on the doorstep to put our shoes on. Nobody else had got up. The sky was growing red. I never got up so early before, except one Fourth of July, when I did n't go to bed, but only slept some with my head leaned down on a window-seat, and jumped up when I heard a gun go off. Tom carried me to a place a good ways from the house. Our shoes got soaking wet with dew.

Now I will tell you what he said to me.

He asked me if I saw him anywhere the night before. I said I did.

He asked me where I saw him.

I said I saw him coming out of the hen-house, where

3   D

Gapper Skyblue kept his rabbits. He asked me if I was sure, and I said I was sure.

" And did you tell the master ? " says he.

I said, " No."

" Nor the boys ?

" No."

Then he told me he had been turned away from one school on account of his bad actions, and he would n't have his father hear of this for anything; and said that, if I would n't tell, he would give me a four-bladed knife, and quite a large balloon, and show me how to send her up, and if I was flogged he would give me a good deal more, would give money, — would give two dollars.

" I don't believe he 'll whip you," says he, " for he likes you. And if he does, he would n't whip a small boy so hard as he would a big one."

I said a little whipping would hurt a little boy just as much as a great whipping would hurt a great boy. But I said I would n't be mean enough to tell or to take pay for not telling.

He did n't say much more. And we went towards home then. But before we came to the house, he turned off into another path.

A little while after, I heard somebody walking behind me. I looked round, and there was the master. He 'd been watching with a sick man all night.

He asked me where I had been so early. I said I had been taking a walk. He asked who the boy was that had just left me. I said 't was Tom Cush. He asked if I was willing to tell what we had been talking about. I said I would rather not tell.

Says he, " It has a bad look, your being out with that boy so early, after what happened last night."

Then he asked me where I had found my overjacket. I said, " In my chamber, sir, on a chair-back."

" And how came it there ? " says he.

" I don't know, sir," says I.

And, Grandmother, I almost cried ; for everything seemed going against me, to make me out a bad boy. I will tell the rest after supper.

Your affectionate grandchild,

WILLIAM HENRY.

MY DEAR GRANDMOTHER, —

Now I will tell you what happened that afternoon.

The school was about half done.

The master gave three loud raps with his ruler.

This made the room very still.

He asked the other teachers to come up to the platform. And they did.

Next, he waved his ruler, and said, " Fold."

And we all folded our arms.

It was so still that we could hear the clock tick.

He told Tom Cush to close the windows and shut the blinds.

Then he talked to us about stealing and telling lies. Said he did n't like to punish, but it must be done. He said he had reason to believe that the boy whose name he should call out was not honest, that he took other people's things and told lies.

Then he told the story, all that he knew about it, and said he hoped that all concerned in it would have honor enough to speak out and own it.

Nobody said anything.

Then the master said, " William Henry, you may come to the platform."

I went up.

Somebody way in the back part shouted out, " Don't believe it ! "

" Silence ! " said the master. And he thumped his ruler on the desk.

Then he told me to take off my jacket, and fold it up. And I did.

He told me to hand my collar and ribbon to a teacher. And I did.

Then he laid down his ruler, and took his rod and bent it to see if it was limber. It was n't exactly a rod. It was the thing I told you about when I first came to this school.

He tried it twice on the desk first.

Then he took hold of my shoulder and turned my

back round towards him. He said I had better bend down my head a little, and took hold of the neck of my shirt to keep me steady. I shut my teeth together tight.

At that very minute Bubby Short cried out, " Master! Master! Stop! Don't! He did n't do it! He did n't kill it! I know, who! I 'll tell! I will! I will! I don't care what Tom Cush does! 'T was Tom Cush killed it!"

The master did n't say one word. But he handed me my jacket.

The boys all clapped and gave three cheers, and he let them.

Then he said to me, whispering, " Is this so, William?" And I said, low, " Yes, sir."

Then he took hold of my hand and led me to my seat. And when I sat down he put his hand on my shoulder just as softly, — it made me remember the way my mother used to before she died, and, says he, " My dear boy," then stopped and began again, " My dear boy," and stopped again. If he 'd been a boy I should have thought he was going to cry himself. But of course a man would n't. And what should he cry for? It was n't he that almost had a whipping. At last he told me to come to his room after supper. Then Bubby Short was called up to the platform.

Now I will tell you how Bubby Short found out about it.

He sleeps in a little bed in a little bit of a room that lets out of Tom's. 'T is n't much bigger than a closet. But it is just right for him. That morning when Tom got up so early and threw pebbles at me, Bubby Short had been keeping awake with the toothache. And he heard Tom telling another boy about the rabbit.

He made believe sleep. But once, while Tom was dressing himself, he peeped out from under the bedquilt, with one eye, to see a black-and-blue spot, that Tom said he hit his head against a post and made, when he was running.

But they caught him peeping out, and were dreadful mad because he heard, and said if he told one single word they would flog him. But he says he would have told before, if he had known it had been laid to me.

Was n't he a nice little fellow to tell?

O, I was so glad when the boys all clapped! And when we were let out, they came and shook hands with Bubby Short and me. Great boys and all. Mr. Augustus, and Dorry, and all. And the master told me how glad he was that he could keep on thinking me to be an honest boy.

Now are n't you glad you did n't feel sorry?

Your affectionate grandchild,

WILLIAM HENRY.

The next time I went down to the farm I was told, of course, all about the foregoing letters, — how they were received, and what effect they produced in the family when they were read. Grandmother, however, gives a happy account of the reception and reading of them in the following reply, which she wrote soon after they were received.

Grandmother's Letter to William Henry, in reply.

MY DEAR LITTLE BOY, —

Your poor old grandmother was so glad to get those letters, after such long waiting! My dear child, we were anxious; but now we are pleased. I was afraid you were down with the measles, for they 're about. Your aunt Phebe thinks you had 'em when you were a month old; but I know better.

Your father was anxious himself at not hearing; though he did n't show it any. But I could see it plain enough. As soon as he brought the letters in, I set a light in the window to let your aunt Phebe know she was wanted. She came running across the yard, all of a breeze. You know how your aunt Phebe always comes running in.

"What is it?" says she. "Letters from Billy? I mistrusted 't was letters from Billy. In his own hand-writing? Must have had 'em pretty light. Measles commonly leave the eyes very bad."

But you know how your aunt Phebe goes running on. Your father came in, and sat down in his rocking-chair, — your mother's chair, dear. Your sister was sewing on her doll's cloak by the little table. She sews remarkably well for a little girl.

"Now, Phebe," says I, "read loud, and do speak every word plain." I put on my glasses, and drew close up, for she does speak her words so fast. I have to look her right in the face.

At the beginning, where you speak about being whipped, your father's rocking-chair stopped stock still. You might have heard a pin drop. Georgianna said, "O dear!" and down dropped the doll's cloak. "Pshaw!" said Aunt Phebe, "'t is n't very likely our Billy 's been whipped."

Then she read on and on, and not one of us spoke. Your father kept his arms folded up, and never raised his eyes. I had to look away, towards the last, for I could n't see through my glasses. Georgianna cried. And, when the end came, we all wiped our eyes.

"Now what's the use," said Aunt Phebe, "for folks to cry before they 're hurt ? "

"But you almost cried yourself," said Georgianna. "Your voice was different, and your nose is red now." And that was true.

After your sister was in bed, and Aunt Phebe gone, your father says to me : " Grandma, the boy's like his mother." And he took a walk around the place, and then went off to his bedroom without even opening his night's paper. If ever a man set store by his boy, that man is your father. And, O Billy, if you had done anything mean, or disgraced yourself in any way, what a dreadful blow 't would have been to us all !

The measles come with a cough. The first thing is to drive 'em out. Get a nurse. That is, if you catch them. They 're a natural sickness, and one sensible old woman is better than half a dozen doctors. Saffron's good to drive 'em out.

Aunt Phebe is knitting you a comforter. As if she had n't family enough of her own to do for !

From your loving

GRANDMOTHER.

I think this the proper place to insert the following letter from Dorry Baker to his sister. I am sorry we have so few of Dorry's letters. Two very entertaining ones will be given presently, describing a visit Dorry made to William Henry's home. The two boys, as we shall see, soon after their acquaintance, grew to be remarkably good friends. Mr. Baker, Dorry's father, hearing his son's glowing accounts of William Henry's family, took a little trip to Summer Sweeting place on purpose to see them, and was so well pleased with Grandmother, Mr. Carver, Uncle Jacob, and the rest, as to suggest to his wife that they should buy some land in the vicinity, and turn farmers. He and Grandmother had a very pleasant talk about their boys; and not long after, knowing, I suppose, that it would gratify the old lady, he sent her some of Dorry's letters, that she might have the pleasure of reading for herself what Dorry had written about her Billy, and about Billy's people and Billy's home. Perhaps, too, Mr. Baker was a little bit proud of the smart letters his son could write.

Dorry's Letter to his Sister.

DEAR SIS, —

If mother's real clever, I want you to ask her something right away. But if it's baking-day, or washing-day, or company's coming off, or preserves going on, or anything's upset down below; or if she's got a headache or a dress-maker, or anything else that's bad, — then wait.

I want you to ask her if I may bring home a boy to spend Saturday. Not a very big boy, — do very well to " Philopene" with you : won't put her out a bit.

If you don't like him at first, you will afterwards. When he first came we used to plague him on account of his looks. He's got a furious head of hair, and freckles. But we don't think at all about his looks now. If anything, we like his looks.

He's just as pleasant and gen'rous, and not a mean

3 *

thing about him. I don't believe he would tell a lie to save his life. I know he would n't. He 's always willing to help everybody. And had just as lief give anything away as not. And when he plays, he plays fair. Some boys cheat to make their side beat. You don't catch William Henry at any such mean business. All the boys believe every word he says. Teachers too.

I will tell you how he made me ashamed of myself. Me and some other boys.

One day he had a box come from home. 'T was his birthday. It was full of good things. Says I to the boys, " Now, maybe, if we had n't plagued him so, he would give us some of his goodies."

That very afternoon, when we had done playing, and ran up to brush the mud off our trousers, we found a table all spread out with a table-cloth that he had borrowed, and in the middle was a frosted cake with " W. H." on top done in red sugar. And close to that were some oranges, and a dish full of nuts, and as much as a pound of candy, and more figs than that, and four great cakes of maple-sugar, made on his father's land, as big as small johnny-cakes, and another kind of cake. And doughnuts.

" Come, boys," says he, " help yourselves."

But not a boy stirred.

I felt my face a-blushing like everything. O, we were all of us just as ashamed as we could be ! We did n't dare go near the table. But he kept inviting us, and at last began to pass them round.

And I tell you the things were tip-top and more too. Such cake ! And doughnuts, that his cousin made !

And tarts! You must learn how. But I don't believe you ever could. Of course we had manners enough not to take as much as we wanted. I want to tell you some more things about him. But wait till I come. He's most as old as you are, and is always a laughing, the same as you are.

Ask mother what I told you. Take her at her cleverest, and don't eat up all the sweet apples.

From your brother,
DORRY.

P. S. Put some away in meal to mellow. Don't mellow 'em with your knuckles.

Mrs. Baker, I imagine, was not particularly fond of boys. She gave her permission, however, for Dorry to bring a "muddy-shoed" companion home with him, as we see by the following letter from William Henry to his grandmother.

A Letter from William Henry.

MY DEAR GRANDMOTHER, —

Dorry asked his sister to ask his mother if he might ask me to go home with him. And she said yes; but to wait a week first, because the house was just got ready to have a great party, and she could n't stand two muddy-shoed boys. May I go?

Tom Cush was sent home; but he did n't go. His father lives in the same town that Dorry does. He has been here to look for him.

I never went to make anybody a visit. I hope you will say yes. I should like to have some money. Ev-

erybody tells boys not to spend money; but if they knew
how many things boys want, and everything tasted so
good, I believe they would spend money themselves.
Please write soon.

> From your affectionate grandchild,
> WILLIAM HENRY.

To this short letter Grandmother sent at once the following reply; and in the succeeding letters from William Henry
we get a pretty good idea of what sort of people Dorry's folks
were, and also hear something about Tom Cush.

Grandmother's Second Letter.

MY DEAR BOY, —

Do you have clothes enough on your bed? Ask for
an extra blanket. I do hope you will take care of yourself. When the rain beats against the windows, I think,
"Now who will see that he stands at the fire and dries
himself? And you 're very apt to hoarse up nights.
We are willing you should go to see Dorry. Your uncle
J. has been past his father's place, and he says there 's
been a pretty sum of money laid out there. Behave well.
Wear your best clothes. Your aunt Phebe has bought
a book for her girls that tells them how to behave. It is
for boys too, or for anybody. I shall give you a little
advice, and mix some of the book in with it.

Never interrupt. Some children are always putting
themselves forward when grown people are talking. Put
" sir " or " ma'am " to everything you say. Make a bow
when introduced. If you don't know how, try it at a
looking-glass. Black your shoes, and toe out if you pos-

sibly can. I hope you know enough to say "Thank you," and when to say it. Take your hat off, without fail, and step softly, and wipe your feet.

Be sure and have some woman look at you before you start, to see that you are all right. Behave properly at table. The best way will be to watch and see how others do. But don't stare. There is a way of looking without seeming to look. A sideways way.

Anybody with common sense will soon learn how to conduct properly; and even if you should make a mistake, when trying to do your best, it is n't worth while to feel very much ashamed. *Wrong* actions are the ones to be ashamed of. And let me say now, once for all, never be ashamed because your father is a farmer and works with his hands. Your father's a man to be proud of; he is kind to the poor; he is pleasant in his family; he is honest in his business; he reads high kind of books; he's a kind, noble Christian man; and Dorry's father can't be more than all this, let him own as much property as he may.

I mention this because young folks are apt to think a great deal more of a man that has money.

Your aunt Phebe wants to know if you won't write home from Dorry's, because her Matilda wants a stamp from that post-office. If the colt brings a very good price, you may get a very good answer to your riddle.

From your loving
GRANDMOTHER.

P. S. Take your overcoat on your arm. When you come away, bid good by, and say that you have had a good time. If you have had, — not without.

William Henry's Reply.

DEAR GRANDMOTHER, —

I am here. The master let us off yesterday noon, and we got here before supper, and this is Saturday night, and I have minded all the things that you said. I got all ready and went down to the Two Betseys to let some woman look at me, as you wrote. They put on both their spectacles and looked me all over, and picked off some dirt-specks, and made me gallus up one leg of my trousers shorter, and make some bows, and then walk across the room slow.

They thought I looked beautiful, only my hair was too long. Lame Betsey said she, used to be the beater for cutting hair, and she tied her apron round my throat, and brought a great pair of shears out, that she used to go a-tailoring with. The Other Betsey, she kept watch to see when both sides looked even.

Lame Betsey tried very hard. First she stood off to look, and then she stood on again. She said her mother used to keep a quart-bowl on purpose to cut her boys' hairs with; she clapped it over their heads, and then clipped all round by it even. The shears were jolly shears, only they could n't stop themselves easy, and the apron had been where snuff was, and made mè sneeze in the wrong place. Says I, "If you 'll only take off this apron, I 'll jump up and shake myself out even." I 'm so glad I 'm a boy. Aprons are horrid. So are apron-strings, Dorry says.

They gave me a few peppermints, and said to be sure not to run my head out and get it knocked off in the

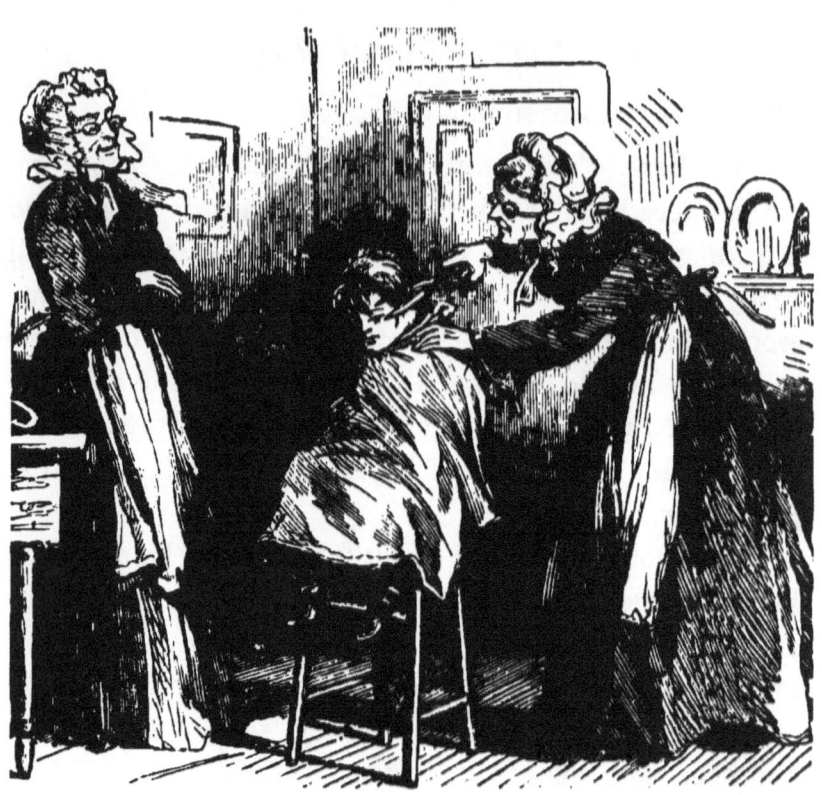

cars, and not to get out till we stopped going, and to beware of pickpockets.

O, we did have a jolly ride in the cars! Do you think
my father would let me be the boy that sells papers in
the cars? I wish he would. I did n't see any pickpockets. We got out two miles before we got there. I
mean to the right station. For Dorry wanted to make
his sister Maggie think we had n't come.

We took a short cut through the fields. Not very short.
And went through everything. My best clothes too. But
I guess 't will all rub off. There were some boggy places.

When we came out at Dorry's house, it was in the

back yard. I said to Dorry, "There's your mother on the doorstep. She looks clever."

Dorry said, "She? She's the cook. I'll tell mother of that. No, I won't neither."

I suppose he saw I'd rather he would n't. The cook said everybody had gone out. Then Dorry took me into a jolly great room and left me. Three kinds of curtains to every window! What's the use of that? Gilt spots on the paper, and gilt things hanging down from up above. A good many kinds of chairs. I was going to sit down, but they kept sinking in. Everything sinks in here. I tried three, and this made me laugh, for I seemed to myself like the little boy that went to the bears' house and tried their chairs, and their beds, and their bowls of milk. Then I came to a looking-glass big enough for the very biggest bear. I thought I would make some bows before it, as you said. I was afraid I could n't make a bow and toe out at the same time. Because it is hard to think up and down both at once. While I was trying to, I heard a little noise, I looked round, and — what do you think? Bears? O no. Not bears. A queen and a princess, I thought. All over bright colors and feathers and shiny silks. The queen — that's Dorry's mother you know, — could n't think who I was, because they had been to the depot, and thought we had n't come. So she looked at me hard, and I suppose I was very muddy. And she said, "Were you sent of an errand here?" Before I could make up any answer, Dorry came in. He had some cake, and he passed it round with a very sober face. Then he introduced me, and I made quite a good bow, and said, "Very well, I thank you, ma'am."

I tried to pull my feet behind me, and wished I was sitting down, for she kept looking towards them; and I wanted to sit down on the lounge, but I was afraid 't would n't bear. She was quite glad to see Dorry. But did n't hug him very hard. I know why. Because she had those good things on. Dorry's grandmother lives here. She can't bear to hear a door slam. She wears her black silk dress every day. And her best cap too. 'T is a stunner of a cap. White as anything. And a good deal of white strings to it. Everything makes her head ache. I 'd a good deal rather have you. When boys come nigh, she puts her hand out to keep them off. This is because she has nerves. Dorry says his mother has 'em sometimes. I like his father. Because he talks to me some. But he 's very tired. His office tires him. He is n't a very big man. He does n't laugh any. If Maggie was a boy she 'd be jolly. She 'll fly kites, or anything, if her mother is n't looking. Her mother don't seem a bit like Aunt Phebe. I don't believe she could lift a tea-kettle. Not a real one. When she catches hold of her fork, she sticks her little finger right up in the air. She makes very pretty bows to the company. Sinks way down, almost out of sight. She gave us a dollar to spend; was n't she clever? Dorry says she likes him tip-top. If he 'll only keep out of the way.

I guess I 'd rather live at our house. About every room in this house is too good for a boy. But I tell you they have tip-top things here. Great pictures and silver dishes! Now, I 'll tell you what I mean to do when I 'm a man. I shall have a great nice house like this, and nice things in it. But the folks shall be like our folks. I

E

shall have horses, and a good many silver dishes. And great pictures, and gilt books for children that come a-visiting. And you shall have a blue easy-chair, and sit down to rest.

Now, maybe you 'll say, " But, Billy, Billy, where are you going to get all these fine things?" O you silly grandmother! Don't you remember your own saying that you wrote down? — " What a man wants he can get, if he tries hard enough." Or a boy either, you said. I shall try hard enough. There 's more to write about. . But I 'm sleepy. I would tell you about Tom Cush's father coming here, only my eyes can't keep open. Is n't it funny that when you are sleepy your eyes keep shutting up and your mouth keeps coming open? Please excuse the lines that go crooked. There 's another gape! I guess Aunt Phebe will be tired reading all this. I 'm on her side. I mean about measles. I 'd rather have 'em when I was a month old. I suppose I was a month old once. Don't seem as if 't was the same one I am now. But if I do have 'em, — there I go gaping again, — if I catch 'em, and all the doctors do come, I 'll — O dear! There I go again. I do believe I 'm asleep — I 'll — I 'll get some natural-born old woman to drive 'em out, as you said, and good night.

WILLIAM HENRY.

MY DEAR GRANDMOTHER, —

I am back again, and had a good time ; but came back hungry. I 'll tell you why. The first time I sat down to table I felt bashful, and Dorry's mother said a great deal about my having a small appetite, and afterwards I did n't like to make her think it was a large one.

I guess I behaved quite well at the table. But I could n't look the way you said. It made me feel squint-eyed. Once I almost laughed at table. The day they had roast duck, it smelt nice. I thought it would n't go round, for they had company besides me ; and I said, " No, I thank you, ma'am." Dorry whispered to me, " You must be a goose not to love duck " ; and that was when I almost laughed at table. His grandmother shook her head at him.

Now I 'll tell about Tom Cush's father. That Saturday, when we were eating dinner, somebody came to the front door, and inquired for us two, — Dorry and me. It was Tom Cush's father. He wanted to ask us about Tom, and whether we knew anything about him. But we knew no more than he did. He talked some with us. The next evening, — Sunday evening, — Tom Cush's mother sent for Dorry and me to come and see her. His father came after us. She said they wanted to know more about what I wrote to you in those letters.

O, I don't want ever again to go where the folks are so sober. The room was just as still as anything, not much light burning, and great curtains hanging way down, and she looked like a sick woman. Just as pale ! Only sometimes she stood up and walked, and then sat down again, and leaned way forward, and asked a question, and looked into our faces so. We did n't know what to do. Dorry talked more than I could. Tom's father kept just as sober ! He said to Dorry : " It is true, then, that my boy would n't own up to his own actions ? " or something like that.

Dorry said, " Yes, sir."

Tom's father said, "And he was willing to sit still and see another boy whipped in his place?"

"Yes, sir," Dorry said. But he did n't say it very loud.

Then they stopped asking questions, and not one of us spoke for ever so long. O, 't was so still! At last Dorry said, just as softly, "Can't you find him anywhere?" And then I said that I did n't believe he was lost.

Then Tom's father got up from his chair and said, "Lost? That's not it. That's not it. 'T is his not being honorable! 'T is his not being true! Lost? Why, he was lost before he left the school." Says he: "When he did a mean thing, then he lost himself. For he lost his truth. He lost his honor. There's nothing left worth having when they are gone."

O, I never saw Dorry so sober as he was that night going home. And when we went to bed, he hardly spoke a word, and did n't throw pillows, or anything. I shut my eyes up tight and thought about you all at home, and Aunt Phebe, and Aunt Phebe's little Tommy, and about school, and about Bubby Short, and all the time Tom's mother's eyes kept looking at me just as they did; and when I was asleep I seemed back again in that lonesome room, and they two sitting there.

From your affectionate grandchild,
WILLIAM HENRY.

P. S. I want to tell that when I was at Dorry's I let a little vase fall down and break. I did n't think it was so rotten. I felt sorry; but did n't say so; I did n't know how to say it very well. I wish grown-up folks would know that boys feel sorry very often when they don't say so, and sometimes they think about doing right, too. And mean to, but don't tell of it. Next time I shall tell about Bubby Short and me going to ride in Gapper's donkey-cart. He 's going to lend it to us. I should like to buy them a new vase.

W. H.

P. S. Benjie 's had a letter, and one twin fell down stairs.

There is one sentence in the first paragraph of the following letter which reminds me of a very windy day, when I was staying at Summer Sweeting place.

In returning from a walk, by a short cut across the field, I met a boy who was running just about as fast as he could.

Soon after I came to another and much smaller boy, who was not running at all, but was sitting flat upon the ground, under a tree, and crying with might and main. This smaller boy proved to be Tommy. On a branch of the tree, just out of his reach, hung a broom, towards which his weeping eyes were turned in despair. A paper of peanuts which I happened to have soon quieted him, because, in order to crack them, he had to shut his mouth. At the first of it, however, he went on with his crying while picking out the meats, which so amused me that I was obliged to turn aside and laugh.

It appeared that Tommy had been riding horseback on his mother's broom " to see Billy," and when he had made believe get there, he wanted to hitch his horse. A larger boy, out of mischief, or rather in mischief, bent down a branch of the tree, telling Tommy there was a tiptop thing to tie up to. He helped Tommy to tie the horse to the branch, and then ran off across the field. It is very plain what happened when the branch sprang back to its place.

I unhitched the *animal*, and then Tommy and I mounted it, he behind me, and away we cantered to the house, my amazing gallops causing the little chap to laugh as loudly as he had cried.

MY DEAR GRANDMOTHER, —

Please to tell my sister I am much obliged to her for picking up that old iron for me.   But that old rusty fire-shovel handle, I guess that will not do to put in again.   For my father said, the last time, that he had bought that old fire-shovel handle half a dozen times. But Aunt Phebe's Tommy, he pulls it out again to ride horseback on.

I know a little girl just about as big as my sister, named Rosy.   Maybe that is not her name.   Maybe it is, because her face is so rosy.   She had a lamb.   And she's lost it.   It ate out of her hand, and it followed her. It was a pet lamb.   But it's lost.   Gapper came up to inquire about it.   Mr. Augustus wrote a notice and nailed it on to the Liberty Pole, and then Dorry chalked out a white lamb on black pasteboard, and painted a blue ribbon around its neck, and hung that up there too.

Gapper let Bubby Short and me have his donkey-cart to go to ride in.   He kicked up when we licked him, and broke something.   But a man came by and mended it. So we did n't get back till after dark.   But the master did n't say anything after we told the reason why.   Did you ever see a ghost?   Do you believe they can whistle? I'll tell you what I ask such a question for.

There is an old house, and part of it is torn down, and nobody lives in it.   It is built close to where the woods begin. The boys say there is a ghost in it. I'll tell you why. They say that if anybody goes by there whistling, something inside of that house whistles the same tune. Dorry says it's a jolly old ghost. Mr. Augustus thinks 't is all very silly. Now I'll tell you something.

The night Bubby Short and I were coming back from taking a ride in Gapper's donkey-cart, we tried it. We did n't dare to lick him again, for fear he would kick up, so we rode just as slow! — and it was a lonesome road, but the moon was shining bright.

Says Bubby Short, " Do you believe that's the honey-moon?"

" No," says I. " That's what shines when a man is married to his wife."

" Are you scared of ghosts?" said Bubby Short.

" Can't tell till I see one," says I.

" How far off do you suppose they can see a fellow?" says he.

Says I, "I don't know. They can see best in the dark."

" Do you think they'd hurt a fellow?" says he.

" Maybe," says I. " There's the old house."

" I know it," says he; " I've been looking at it."

Says I, " Are you scared to whistle?"

" Scared! No," says he. " Let's whistle, I say."

" Well," says I, " you whistle first."

" No," says he, " you whistle first."

" Let *him* whistle first," says I.

" He won't do it. Ghosts never whistle first," says he.

I asked him who said that, and he said 't was Dorry.

Then I said, " Let's whistle together."

So we waited till we almost got past, and then whistled " Yankee Doodle." And, grandmother, it did, — it whistled it.

Bubby Short whispered, " Lick him a little."

Then I whispered back, " 'T won't do to. If I do, he won't go any."

But in a minute he began to go faster of his own accord. He heard somebody ahead calling. It was Gapper, coming to see what the matter was that kept us so late. Now what do you think about it ?

From your affectionate

WILLIAM HENRY.

P. S. My boots leak. Shall I get them tapped, or get a new pair, or throw them away, or else keep the legs to make new boots of ?

W. H.

Here we have William Henry trying his hand at story-telling.

MY DEAR GRANDMOTHER, —

Sometimes Dorry writes stories in his letters for his sister, just as he tells them to her, talking, at home. Now I 'll write one for my sister, and I 'll call it by a name. I 'll call it

THE STORY OF THE GREAT STORM.

Once there was a little boy named Billy, and Gapper lent him his donkey to go ride. That 's me, you know. Next day Gapper came and said, " You boys lost my whip." Now I remembered having the whip when we crept in among the bushes, — for we got sight of a wood-chuck, and came near finding his hole. So when school was done at noon, I asked leave to put some bread and meat in my pocket, instead of eating any dinner, and go to look for Gapper's whip. And he said I might. 'T was two miles off. But I found it. And I dug for a good deal of saxifax-root. And picked lots of boxberry-plums.

And I never noticed how the sky looked, till I heard a noise something like thunder. It was very much like thunder. Almost just like it. I thought it was thunder. Only it sounded a great ways off. I was walking along slow, snapping my whip and eating my dinner, for I thought I would n't hurry for thunder, when something hard dropped down close to me. Then another dropped, — and then another. And they kept dropping. I picked one up and found they were hail-stones, and they were bigger than bullets.

It kept growing dark, and the hailstones came thicker, and hit me in the face. Then they began to pour right down, and I ran. They beat upon me just like a driving storm all of sharp stones. The horses and cows cut across the fields like mad. The horses flung up their heads. I was almost to that old house and ran for that, and kicked the door through to get in, for I thought I should be killed with the hail. The shingles off the roof were flying about; and when I got inside, 't was awful. I thought to be sure the roof would be beat in. Such a noise! It sounded just exactly as if a hundred cartloads of stones were being tipped up on to the roof. And then the window-glass! It was worse than being out doors, for

4

the window-glass was flying criss-cross about the room,
like fury, all mixed up with the hail. I crouched down
all in a bunch and put my arms over my head, and so
tried to save myself. But then I spied a closet door a
crack open, and I jumped in there. And there I sat all
bent over with my hands up to my ears, and thought, O,
what would become of me if the old house should go?
And now the strangest part is coming. You see 't was a
pretty deep closet — School-bell ! I did n't think 't was
half time for that to ding. I 'll tell the rest next time.
Should you care if I brought home Dorry to make a
visit ? He wants to bad. 'T would be jolly if Bubby
Short went too.

From your affectionate grandchild,
WILLIAM HENRY.

MY DEAR GRANDMOTHER, —

Everybody 's been setting glass. Counting the house
and the schoolhouse, and the panes set over the barn
door, and four squares in the hen-house, we had to set
four hundred and twenty-three squares. The expressman has brought loads and loads. All the great boys
helped set. We slept one night with bedquilts and rugs
hung up to the windows. The master tried to shut his
blind in the storm, but the hail drove him in, and he
could n't even shut down his window again. A rich man
has given to the Two Betseys better windows than they
had before. Now I will tell about my being in that
closet.

When it began to grow stiller, I took my hands down
from my ears, and one hand when it came down touched

something soft. Quite soft and warm. I jumped off from it in a hurry. Then I heard a kind of bleating noise, and a little faint " ba'a ba'a." But now comes the very strangest part. Farther back in the closet I heard somebody move, somebody step. I was scared, and gave the door a push, to let the light in. Now who do you think was there? Aunt Phebe must stop reading and let you guess. But maybe you're reading yourself. Then stop and guess. 'T was n't a ghost. 'T was n't a man. 'T was n't a woman. 'T was Tom Cush! and Rosy's lamb!

Says he, " William Henry!" Says I, " Tom!" Then we walked out into the room, and O, what a sight! Says I, " I thought 't was going to be the end of the old house."

Says Tom, " I thought 't was going to be the end of the world."

In the corners the hailstones were heaped up in great banks. You might have shovelled up barrels full. Most of them were the size of bird's eggs. But some were bigger. Then we looked out doors. The ground was all white, and drifts in every cornering place, and the leaves stripped off the trees. Then we looked at one another, and he was just as pale as anything. He leaned against the wall, and I guessed he was crying. To see such a great boy crying seemed most as bad as the hailstorm. Maybe he did n't cry. When he turned his head round again, says he: " Billy, I 'm sick, and what shall I do?"

" Go home," says I.

" No," says he, " I won't go home. And if you let

'em know, I 'll — " And then he picked up Gapper's whip, — " I 'll flog you."

" Flog away," says I ; " maybe I shall, and maybe I sha' n't."

He dropped the whip down, and says he, " Billy, I sha' n't ever touch you. But they must n't know till I 'm gone to sea."

I asked him when he was going. And he told me all about it.

When he was sent away from school, he went into town and inquired about the wharves for a chance to go, and got one, and came back to get some things he left hid in the old house, and to wait till 't was time to go. He sold his watch, and bought a great bag full of hard bread and cheese and cakes.

He was mad at Gapper for setting a man to watch, and so he took Rosy's lamb. · He was going to kill it. And then skin it. But he could n't do it. It licked his hand, and looked up so sorryful, he could n't do it. And when he cut his foot — he cut it chopping something. That 's why he stayed there so long. And he was the ghost that whistled. He knew the fellows would n't go in to see what it was that whistled. And he ate up most all his things, and tied a string to the lamb, and let it out nights to eat grass, and then pulled it in again."

I would n't have stayed there so for anything. He went into town three times, nights, to get victuals to eat. I don't see what he wants to be such a kind of a boy for. He says he means to go to sea, and if ever he 's good he 's going home. I told him about his father and mother, and he walked while I was talking, and kept his back towards me. I asked him what ailed him, and he said 't was partly cutting him, and partly sleeping cold nights, and partly the crackers and cheese. I gave him the rest of my meat, and he was glad enough.

He said he was ashamed to go home.

Now I have got to the end of another sheet of paper. I wish I had n't begun to tell my sister this story. It takes so long. And I want every minute of the time to play in. For 't is getting a little cooler, and a fellow can stand it to run some. The master says it 's good weather for studying. Dorry says he never saw any weather yet good enough for studying. I shall write a very short letter next time, to tell the rest of it.

From your affectionate grandchild,

WILLIAM HENRY.

P. S. I forgot to put this letter in the office. I guess I will not write any more letters till I go home. I was going to tell more, but I can do it better talking. I went to see Tom Cush the next day, and he had gone. Rosy's got her lamb back again. But her flower-garden was killed by the hail. Not one leaf left. She found her lamb on the doorstep, waiting to get in.

We have next a letter from Aunt Phebe, a dear, good-hearted woman, who took almost a mother's interest in William Henry. Indeed, I have heard her remark, that she hardly knew any difference between her feelings for him and for her own children.

Some of her letters will be found to contain good advice, given in a very amusing way.

Letter from Aunt Phebe.

DEAR BILLY, —

You rogue, you! I meant to have written before.
You've frightened us all to pieces with your ghost that
was n't a ghost, and your whipping that was n't a whipping, and your measles that you did n't have. Grandmother may talk, but she's losing her memory. You
were red as a beet with 'em. As if I did n't carry you
about all night and go to sleep walking!

Grandmother says, " Yes, indeed! bring Dorry, and let
him stay a week if he wants to." Bless her soul! She'll
always keep her welcome warm, so never mind her memory. And Bubby Short, too. Pray bring Bubby Short.
I want to see his black eyes shine. Don't Benjie want
to come? I've got beds enough, and girls enough to
work, and a great batch of poor mince-pies that I want
eaten up. Don't see how I came to make such a miss in
my pies this baking. Your uncle J. thinks I skinched on
plums. There never was such a man for plums. I do
believe if they were put into his biscuits he'd think he'd
got no more than his rights.

Your uncle J. says: " Tell the boys to come on. I've
got apples to gather, and husking to do." They'd better
bring some old clothes to wear. This is such a tearing
place. I've put my Tommy into jacket and trousers.
He used to hitch his clothes upon every rail. Such a
climber! I don't know what that boy 'll be when he
grows up.

I send you a good warm comforter, knit in stripes; and
all the family are knit into it, especially Tommy. The

pink stripes are his good-boy days, and the black ones are his naughty actions. I showed him where I knit 'em in. That clouded gray and black stripe is for my two great girls quarrelling together about whose work 't was to do some little trifle. I told 'em they should be knit in, big as they are, if they could n't behave and be accommodating. That bright red stripe is for Hannah Jane's school report, all perfect. That blue stripe is for your sister Georgianna when she made a sheet. It matches her eyes as near as I could get the yarn. My blue dye is weak this fall. Indigo is high. Your uncle J. says it 's on account of the Rebs feeling so blue. That gray stripe, dotted with yellow, means a funny crying spell Tommy had at table. I came home, and there he sat in his high chair, with his two hands on the arms of it, his mouth wide open, eyes shut, and the tears streaming down, making the dolefullest noise, — "O-oh, a-ah; o-oh, a-ah." Lucy Maria said he 'd been going on in that strain almost half an hour, because we did n't have mince-meat for supper. That green stripe is for the day we all took the hay-cart and went to ride in the woods. The orange-colored one is for the box of oranges your uncle J. fetched home. "A waste of money," says I. "Please the children," says he; "and the peel will save spice." Makes me laugh when your uncle J. sets out to save. My girls and Tommy have got the very best of fathers, only they don't realize it. But young folks can't realize. The pale rose-colored stripe is for the travelling doctor's curing your grandmother's rheumatics, and promising she never should have another touch of 'em if she was careful. The dark red stripe is for the red cow's getting choked to death with a turnip.

She was a prime butter cow. Any man but your uncle J. would look sober for a month about it. But he says, "O, there's butter enough in the world, Phebe. And the calf will soon be a cow on its own hook." That's your uncle J.

The plain dark purple stripe is for my Matilda's speaking disrespectfully to grandmother. She was sorry enough afterwards, but I told her it should go in. That bright yellow stripe is for the day your father went to market and got such a great price for his colt. The bright fringe, mixed colors, is for us all in both houses, when we got news of your coming home, and felt so glad. There's a stitch dropped in one place. That may go for a tear-drop, — a tear of mine, dear, if you please. Do you think we grown-up women, we jolly, busy women, never shed tears? O, but we do sometimes, in an out-of-the-way corner, or when the children are all gone to school, or everybody is in bed. Bitterer tears they are, Billy, than boys' tears. One more stripe, that plain white one in the centre, is for the little Tommy that died. I couldn't bear to leave him out, Billy. He had such little loving ways. You don't remember him.

There's your uncle J.'s whistle. He always whistles when he gets to the bars, to let me know it's time to begin to take up dinner.

From your loving

AUNT PHEBE.

I will insert here two of Dorry Baker's letters to his sister. When they were written Dorry and Bubby Short were making William Henry a visit.

Dorry to his Sister.

DEAR SIS, —

Who's been giving you an inch, that you take so many "l's"? Or is father putting an "L" to his house, or some great "LL. D." been dining there, or what is the matter, that about every "l" in your letter comes double? I wouldn't spell "painful" with two "l's" if the pain was ever so bad. But I know. You are thinking about Billy and the good times we are having. Aunt Phebe says you might have come too, just as well as not; for her family is so big, three or four more don't make a mite of difference.

We got here last night. Billy's grandmother's a brick. She took Billy right in her arms, and I do believe she cried for being glad, behind her spectacles. His sister is full as pretty as you. Billy brought her a round comb. Aunt Phebe's little Tommy's as fat as butter. He sat and sucked his thumb and stared, till Billy held out a whistle to him, and then he walked up and took it, as sober as a judge.

" And I've brought you something, Grandmother," says Billy.

He went out and brought in a bandbox tied up. I wondered, coming in the cars, what he had got tied up in that bandbox. He out with his jackknife, and cut the strings, and took out — have you guessed yet? Of course you have n't, — took out a new cap like grandma's. He stuck his fist in it, and turned it round and round, to let her see it.

" Now sit down," says he, " and we'll try it on."

She would n't, but he made her.

"Come here, Dorry," says he, "and see which is the front side of this."

When her old cap was pulled off, there was her gray hair all soft and crinkly.   He got the cap part way on.

"You tip it down too much," says I.

"We 'll turn it round," says he.

"'T is upside down," said Billy's father.

"Now 't is one-sided," says Uncle J., "like the colt's blinders."

"'T was never meant for my head," says Grandmother.

"Send for Phebe," says Uncle J.

But "Phebe" was coming. There was a great chattering outside, and the door opened, and in came Aunt Phebe, laughing, and her three great girls laughing too, with their red cheeks, and their great braids of hair tied up in red bow-knots of ribbon. And they all went to kissing Billy.

And then says Aunt Phebe, "What in the world are you doing to your grandmother? A regular milliner's cap, if I breathe! Well done, Grandmother! Here, let me give it a twist. It's hind side before. What do boys know? or men either? What are all these kinds of strings for?"

"The great ones to hang down, and the little ones to tie up," says Billy.

The girls stood by to pick the bows apart, and fuzz up the ruffles where they were smashed in; and Billy's father and Uncle Jacob, they sat and laughed.

Grandmother could n't help herself, but she kept saying, "Now, Phebe! now, girls! now, Billy!"

"And now, grandmother!" says Aunt Phebe. "There! fold your hands together. Don't lean back hard, 't will jam easy. Now see, girls! Is n't she a beauty?" And, Maggie, I do believe she's the prettiest grandmother there is going. Her face is just as round and smiling!

"Now sit still, Grandmother," said Aunt Phebe. And she winked to the girls, and they whisked two tables up together, spread on the cloth, set on the dishes; then out into the entry, and brought in great loaves of plum-cake, and pies and doughnuts, and set out the table, — all done while you 'd be tying your shoe. Then they set a row of lights along the middle, and we all sat round, — Grandmother at the head, and Aunt Phebe's little Tommy in his high chair; and I 'll tell you what, if these are poor mince-pies, I hope I shall never see any good ones.

"Why did n't you have some fried eggs?" said Uncle Jacob.

"Now did anybody ever hear the like?" said Aunt Phebe. "Fried eggs! when they 're shedding their feathers, and it takes seventy-six fowls to lay a dozen, and every egg is worth its weight in currency! Better ask why we don't have cranberry sauce!"

"There!" says Uncle J. "I declare, if I did n't forget that errand, after all!"

"When I told you to keep saying over 'Cranberries, cranberries,' all the way going along!" says Aunt Phebe.

"They would 'a' set my teeth on edge before I got to Ne'miah's corner," said Uncle J. "The very thoughts of 'em is enough. Lucy Maria, please to pass that frosted cake. I declare, I 'm sorry I forgot that errand."

For all we were so hungry, there was a great deal left, and I was glad to see it going into Billy's buttery. Billy says it 's just like his aunt Phebe to come to supper, and make that an excuse to bring enough to last a week, to save Grandmother steps.

I do like to stay where folks are jolly. They keep me a-laughing; and as for Bubby Short, his little black eyes have settled themselves into a twinkle, and there they stay. I never had such a good time in my life.

From your same old brother,

DORRY.

P. S. We have got good times enough planned out
to last a month. Uncle J. says we may have his old
horse, and Young Gray, and Dobbin, and the cow too, if
we want, to ride horseback on, or tackle up into anything
we can find, from a hay-cart to a wheelbarrow. I shall
want to write, but sha' n't. There 'll be no time. When
I get home, I 'll talk a week.

Love to all inquiring friends.

Maggie could have formed but little idea of the nature of
the offer mentioned in Dorry's postscript, because she had
never, at that time, stood on the spot and seen with her own
eyes all the "wheel-ed things" that were to be seen in
Uncle Jacob's back-yard.

How gladly would I, if space permitted, go into a minute
description of that roomy enclosure, with its farming imple-
ments, garden tools, cattle, pump, fowls, watering-trough,
grindstone, woodpile, haystack, etc., and carryalls, carts,
wagons, wheelbarrows, roller-carts, and tip-carts, some in
good repair, others very far out of it! "Entertainment for
man and beast" might truly have been written over the
entrance!

Mother Delight (an old nurse-woman) once remarked of
Uncle Jacob, that he was a very *buying man*. This was a
true remark, and yet he never bought without a reason.
For instance, if Quorm (a Corry Pond Indian) brought bushel-
baskets along to sell, Uncle Jacob took one, not because
he had not bushel-baskets enough, but to encourage Quorm.
And if Old Pete Brale wanted to let Uncle Jacob have an
infirm, rickety wagon, and take his pay in potatoes, Uncle
Jacob traded, that Pete Brale might be kept from starvation.
And so of other things.

It may be imagined, therefore, that as time went on all
manner of vehicles were there gathered together. Some of

these were in good running order, while others had been bought partly with a view to their being repaired and sold at a profit. The expression on Aunt Phebe's face when Uncle Jacob brought home an addition to his interesting collection was very striking. I remember particularly observing this at the coming into harbor of a rattling, shackly, green-bottomed carryall, which had a door at the back, and seats running lengthwise. It formerly belonged to some person who, having then a large family of small children to get to meeting, contrived a conveyance which would take in and discharge again the greatest number with the least trouble.

In this odd vehicle, which had been run under an overhanging apple-tree, I often sat through the summer afternoon, now reading my book, now watching the animal life about me, gaining useful knowledge from both. Sometimes, when feeling like a boy again, — as I often did and do feel, — I would amuse myself with playing *go to ride* in a comical old chaise. It was set high, and pitched forward, the lining was ragged, the back "light" gone, the stuffing running out of the cushions; yet there I liked to sit, and "ride," and joggle up and down, as in the happy days of boyhood. But not, as in those happy days, "hard as I could," for reasons easy to guess.

I trust no one will imagine that spacious yard to have been merely a sort of safe anchorage, where all manner of disabled craft might run in for shelter! Lest any words of mine should imply this, or seem to cast blame on Uncle Jacob, let me hasten to say that he really required a variety of "wheel-ed things" to carry on his business.

Neither of the Mr. Carvers got their living wholly, or even chiefly, by farming. They drew wood from lots owned by themselves, or by others, and used their teams in any way, according as employment was offered them. Thus heavy carts were wanted for heavy work, and light carts for light work, besides carryalls for dry and for rainy weather, and riding wagons, because they were handy.

For all the Summer Sweeting folks were hard workers, they knew how to get up a good time, and enjoyed it too, as we shall see by the account of one which Dorry gives in the following letter : —

Dorry to his Sister.

DEAR SIS, —

O, we 've hurrahed and hurrahed and hurrahed ourselves hoarse ! Such a bully time ! You 'd better believe the old horses went some ! And that hay-cart went rattle and bump, rattle and thump, — seemed as if we should jolt to pieces ! But I 've counted myself all over, and believe I 'm all here ! Bubby Short's throat is so sore that all he can do is to lie flat on the floor and wink his eyes. You see we cheered at every house, and they came running to their windows, and some cheered back again, and some waved and some laughed, and all of them stared. But part of the way was through the woods.

This morning Billy and Bubby Short and I went over to Aunt Phebe's of an errand, to borrow a cup of dough. I wish mother could see how her stove shines ! And while we were sitting down there, having some fun with Aunt Phebe's little Tommy, Uncle Jacob came in and said, " Mother, let 's go somewhere."

She said, " Thank you ! thank you ! we shall be very happy to accept your invitation. Girls, your father has given us an invitation ! Boys, he means you too ! "

" But you can't go, — can you ? " Uncle Jacob cried out, and made believe he did n't know what to make of it. O, he's such a droll man! "I thought you could n't leave the ironing," says he.

"O yes, we can!" Hannah Jane said; and "O yes, we can!" they all cried out.

Aunt Phebe said it would be entirely convenient, and told her girls to shake out the sprinkled clothes to dry.

"O, now," said Uncle Jacob, "who'd have thought of your saying 'yes.' I expected you could n't leave."

"Then they kept on talking and laughing. O, they are all so funny here! Uncle Jacob tried to get off without going; but at last he said, "Well, boys, we must catch Old Major."

"That's the old gray horse, you know. And we were long enough about it. For, just as we got him into a corner, he 'd up heels, and away he 'd go. And once he slapped his tail right in my face. But after a while we got him into the barn.

Then pretty soon Uncle Jacob put on a long face, and looked very sober, and put his head in at the back kitchen door, and said he guessed we should have to give up going, after all, for the mate to Old Major had got to be shod, and the blacksmith had gone away.

"Harness in the colt, then," Aunt Phebe said. "No matter about their matching, if we only get there!"

That colt is about twenty years old. He 's black, and short, and takes little stubby steps; and he 's got a shaggy mane, that goes flop, flop, flop every step he takes. But Old Major is bony, and has a long neck, like the nose of a tunnel. Such a span as they made! What would my mother say to see that span!

They were harnessed in to the hay-cart. A hay-cart is a long cart that has stakes stuck in all round it. We put boards across for benches. Aunt Phebe brought out a whole armful of quite small flags, that they had Independent Day, and we tied one to the end of every stake.

Such a jolly time as we did have getting aboard! First all the baskets and pails full of cake and pies were stowed away under the benches, and jugs of water, and bottles of milk, and a hatchet, and some boiled eggs, and apples and pears. Then uncle called out, "Come! where is everybody? Tumble in! tumble in! Where's little Tommy?"

Then we began to look about and to call "Tommy!" "Tommy!" "Tommy!" At last Bubby Short said, "There he is, up there!" We all looked up, and saw Tommy's face part way through a broken square of glass — I mean where the glass was broken out. He said he could n't "tum down, betause the *roosted* was on his feets." You see, he 'd got his feet tangled up in Lucy Maria's worsteds.

"O dear!" Lucy Maria said; "all that shaded pink!"

When they brought him down, Uncle Jacob looked very sober, and said, "Why, Tommy! Did you get into all that shaded pink?"

"Did n't get in *all* of it," said Tommy. Then he told us he was taking down the "gimmerlut to blower a hole with." Next he began to cry for his new hat; and when he got his new hat, he began to cry for a posy to be stuck in it. That little fellow never will go anywhere without a flower stuck in his hat. Aunt Phebe says his grandmother began that notion when her damask rose-bush was in bloom.

After we were all aboard, Uncle Jacob brought out the teakettle, and slung it on behind with a rope. He said maybe mother would want a cup of tea. Then they laughed at him, for he is the tea-drinker himself. Next he brought out a long pan.

"Now that's my cookie-pan!" Aunt Phebe said. "You don't cook clams in my cookie-pan!"

He made believe he was terribly afraid of Aunt Phebe, and trotted back with it just like a little boy, and then came bringing out an old sheet-iron fireboard.

"Is this anybody's cookie-pan?" said he, then stowed it away in the bottom of the cart. Bubby Short wanted to know what that was for.

"That's for the clams," Uncle Jacob said.

But we could n't tell whether he meant so. We never can tell whether Uncle Jacob is funning or not. I have n't told you yet where we were bound. We were bound to the shore. That's about six miles off. The last thing that Uncle Jacob brought out was a stick that had strips of paper tied to the end of it.

"That's my flyflapper!" Aunt Phebe said. "What are you going to do with my flyflapper?"

He said that was to brush the snarls off little Tommy's face. Tommy is a tip-top little chap; but he's apt to make a fuss. Sometimes he teased to drive, and then he teased for a drink, and then for a sugar-cracker, and then to sit with Matilda, and then with Hannah Jane. And, every time he fretted, Uncle Jacob would take out the flyflapper, and play brush the snarls off his face, and

say, "There they go! Pick 'em up! pick 'em up!"
And that would set Tommy a-laughing. Tommy tumbled out once, the back end of the cart. Billy was driving, and he whipped up quick, and they started ahead,
and sent Tommy out the back end, all in a heap. But
first he stood on his head, for 't was quite a sandy place.
I drove part of the way, and so did Bubby Short. We
did n't hurrah any going. Some men that we met would
laugh and call out, "What 'll you take for your span?"
And sometimes boys would turn round, and laugh, and
holler out, "How are *you*, tea-kettle?" I think a hay-
cart is the best thing to ride in that ever was. Just as
we got through the woods, we looked round and saw
Billy's father coming, bringing Billy's grandmother in a
horse and chaise. Then we all clapped. For they said
they guessed they could n't come.

When we got to the shore the horses had to be hitched
to the cart, for there was n't a tree there, nor so much as
a stump. Uncle Jacob called to us to come help him dig
the clams. Billy carried the clam-digger, and I carried
the bucket. Is n't it funny that clams live in the mud?
How do you suppose they move round? Do you suppose
they know anything? Uncle Jacob struck his clam-digger
in everywhere where he saw holes in the mud; and as
fast as he uncovered the clams we picked them up, and
soon got the bucket full.

Then he told us to run like lamplighters along the
shore, and pick up sticks and bits of boards. "Bring
them where you see a smoke rising," says he.

O, such loads as we got, and split up the big pieces
with the hatchet! Uncle Jacob had fixed some stones in

a good way, and put his iron fireboard on top, and made a fire underneath. Then he spread his clams on the fireboard to roast. O, I tell you, sis, you never tasted of anything so good in your life as clams roasted on a fireboard!

And he put some stones together in another place, and set on the tea-kettle, and made a fire under it, — to make a cup of tea for mother, he said. Tommy kept helping making the fire, and once he joggled the teakettle over. Aunt Phebe and the girls sat on the rocks, the side where the wind would n't blow the smoke in their eyes. But Billy's grandmother had a soft seat made of seaweed and the chaise cushions, and shawls all over her, and Billy's father read things out of the newspaper to her. He said they two were the invited guests, and must n't work.

It took the girls ever so long to cut up the cakes and pies, and butter the biscuits. I know I never was so hungry before! The clams were passed round, piping hot, in box covers, and tin-pail covers, and some had to have shingles. You 'd better believe those clams tasted good! Then all the other things were passed round. O, I don 't believe any other woman can make things as good as Aunt Phebe's! Georgianna had a frosted plum-cake baked in a saucer; and, every time she moved her seat, Uncle Jacob would go too, and sit close up to her, and say how much he liked Georgie, she was the best little girl that ever was, — a great deal better than Aunt Phebe's girls. Then Georgianna would say, " O, I know you! you want my frosted cake!" Then Uncle Jacob would pucker his lips together, and shut up his eyes, and shake his head so solemn! He keeps everybody a-laughing, even Billy's grandmother. He was just as clever to her! picked out the best mug there was to put her tea in, — Aunt Phebe don't carry her good dishes, they get broken so, — and shocked out the clams for her in a saucer. When you get this letter, I guess you'll get a good long one. After dinner we scattered about the shore. 'T was fun to see the crabs and frys and things the tide had left in the little pools of water. And I found lots of *blanc-mange* moss. We boys ran ever so far along shore, and went in swimming. The water·wás n't very cold.

When it was time to go home, Uncle Jacob drummed loud on the six-quart pail, and waved his handkerchief. And the wind took it out of his hand, and blew it off on the water. Billy said, " Now the fishes can have a pocket-handkerchief." And that made little Tommy laugh. Tommy had been in wading without his trousers being rolled up, and got 'em sopping wet. Just as we were going to leave, a sail-boat went past, quite near the shore, with a party on board. We gave them three cheers, and they gave us three cheers and a tiger ; then they waved, and then we waved. Uncle Jacob had n't any pocket-handkerchief, so he caught Georgianna up in his arms, with her white sunbonnet on, and waved her ; then the people in the boat clapped.

O, we had a jolly time coming home! In the woods we all got out and rested the horses, and I came pretty near catching a little striped squirrel. I should give it to you if I had. Did you ever see any live fences ? Fences that branch out, and have leaves grow on them ? Now I suppose you don't believe that! But it 's true,

for I 've seen them.   In the woods, if they want to fence
off a piece, they don't go to work and build a fence, but
they bend down young trees, or the branches of trees, and
fasten them to the next, and so on as far as they want the
fence to go.   And these trees and branches keep growing, and look so funny, something like giants with their
legs and arms all twisted about.   And every spring they
leaf out the same as other trees, and that makes a real
live fence.   My squirrel was on that kind of fence.   I
wish it was my squirrel.   He had a striped back.   I got
close up to him, that is, I got quite close up, — near
enough to see his eyes.   What things they are to run !

Coming home we sang songs, and laughed; and every
time we came to a house we cheered all together, and
waved our flags.   Everybody came to their windows to
look, for there is n't much travelling on that road.   O,
I 'm so out of breath, and so hoarse !   But I 'm sorry
we 've got home, I wish it had been ten miles.   Now I
hear them laughing and clapping over at Aunt Phebe's.
What can they be doing?   Now Uncle Jacob is calling
us to come over.   Bubby Short 's jumped up.   He says
his throat feels better now.   I wonder what Uncle Jacob
wants of us.   We must go and see.   Good by, sis.   This
letter is from your

BROTHER DORRY.

I remember what they were clapping about.   It happened
that I came out from the city that day.   The weather was so
fine, I felt as if I must take one more look at the country, before winter came and spoiled every bright leaf and flower.   I
think the flowers and leaves seem very precious in the fall,
when we know frost is waiting to kill them.

It was quite a disappointment to find the people all gone, and I was glad enough when at last the old hay-cart came rattling down the lane. Such a jolly set as they were! I jumped them out at the back of the cart.

That little Tommy was always such a funny chap. Just like his father for all the world. When the girls took their things off, he got himself into an old sack, and then tied on one of his mother's checked aprons, and began to parade round. When Lucy Maria saw him she took him up stairs and put more things on him, and dressed him up for Mother Goose. I don't know when I 've seen anything so droll. They put skirts on him, till they made him look like a little fat old woman. He had a black silk handkerchief pinned over his shoulders, and a ruffle round his neck, and an old-fashioned, high-crowned nightcap on. Then spectacles. They put a peaked piece of dough on the end of his nose, to make it look like a hooked nose, and then set him down in the arm-chair. He kept sober as a judge. Bubby Short laughed till he tumbled down and rolled himself across the floor. Lucy Maria sent us out of the room to see something in the yard, and when we came back, there was a little old man with his hat on, and a cane, sitting opposite Mother Goose. He was made of a stuffed-out overcoat, trousers with sticks of wood in them, and boots. "That is Father Goose," Lucy Maria said. Then Bubby Short had to tumble down again; and this time he rolled way through the entry, out on the doorstep!

Then came such a pleasant evening! Aunt Phebe said 't was a pity for Grandmother to go to getting supper, they might as well all come over. Where anybody had to boil the teakettle and set the table, half a dozen more or less did n't matter much.

So we all ate supper together, and it seemed to me 'I never did get into such a jolly set! Uncle Jacob and Aunt Phebe were so funny that we could hardly eat. And in the evening — But 't is no use. If I begin to tell, and tell all I want to, there won't be any room left for the letters.

Now comes quite a gap in the correspondence. There must have been many letters written about this time, which were, unfortunately, not preserved. The next in order I find to be a short epistle from Bubby Short, written, it would seem, soon after the winter holidays.

A Letter from Bubby Short.

DEAR BILLY, —

My mother is all the one that I ever wrote a letter to before. So excuse poor writing, and this pen is n't a very good pen to write with I bet. I am very sorry that you can't come back quite yet. I hope that it won't be a fever that you are going to have. Does your grandma think that 't is going to be a fever? Do you take bitter medicine? I never had a fever. I take little pills every time I have anything. My mother likes little pills best now. But she used to make me take bitter stuff. Once she put it in my mouth and I would n't swallow it down. Then she pinched my nose together and it made me swallow it down. Once I ate up all the little pills out of the bottle, and she was very scared about it. It was n't very full. But the doctor said that it would n't hurt me any if I did eat them. How many presents did you have? I had five. Dorry he says he hopes that it won't be a slow fever that you are going to have if you do have any fever, for he wants you to hurry and come back. Some new fellows have come. One is a tip-top one. And one good "pitcher." I hope you will come back very soon, 'cause I like you very much.

Do you know who 't is writing? I am that one all you fellers call

BUBBY SHORT.

As may be gathered from the foregoing letter, William Henry did not go back to school with the rest. He was taken ill just at the close of vacation, and remained at home until spring. Grandmother said it was such a comfort that it did n't happen away. And it seemed to me that this thought really made her enjoy his being sick at home.

Indeed, the people at Summer Sweeting place seemed ready to get enjoyment from everything, even from gruel, which is usually considered flat. I passed a day there at a time when William Henry was subsisting on this very simple but wholesome food. Aunt Phebe and Uncle Jacob came in to take tea at grandmother's. The old lady was bringing out her nice things to set on the table, when Aunt Phebe said suddenly, I suppose seeing a hungry look in Billy's eyes. She said, —

" Now, Grandmother, I would n't bring those out. Let 's have a gruel supper, and all fare alike ! We 'll make it in different ways, — milk porridge, oatmeal, corn-starch, — and I think 't will be a pleasant change."

" Gruel is very nourishing, well made," said Grandmother ; " but what will Mr. Fry say ? "

" Mr. Fry will say," I answered, " that milk porridge, with Boston crackers, is a dish fit for a king."

" I 'm afraid Jacob won't think he 's been to supper," said Grandmother.

" O yes," said Uncle Jacob, " I 'll think I have at any rate. But I like mine the way the man in the moon did his, or part of the way."

" Yes," said Aunt Phebe, " I understand ! The last part. — the ' plum ' part ! "

" O, don't all eat gruel for me," said Billy. " Course I sha' n't be a baby, and cry for things ! "

5

But Aunt Phebe seemed resolved to develop the gruel idea to its utmost. She made all kinds, — Indian meal, oatmeal, corn-starch, flour, mixed meals, wheat; made it sweetened, and spiced with plums, and plain. One kind, that she called "thickened milk," was delicious. "Course" we had one cup · of tea, and bread and butter, and I can truly say that I have eaten many a worse supper than a "gruel supper."

Here is a letter from William Henry to Dorry, written when he began to get well: —

William Henry's Letter to Dorry.

DEAR DORRY, —

I'm just as hungry as anything, now, about all the time. My grandmother says she's so glad to see me eat again; and so am I glad to eat myself. Things taste better than they did before. Maybe I shall come back to school again pretty soon, my father says; but my grandmother guesses not very, because she thinks I should have a relapse if I did. A relapse is to get sick when you're getting well; and, if I should get sick again, O what should I do! for I want to go out-doors. If they'd only let me go out, I'd saw wood all day, or anything. There is n't much fun in being sick, I tell you, Dorry; but getting well, O, that's the thing! I tell you getting well's jolly! I have very good things sent to me about every day, and when I want to make molasses candy my grandmother says yes every time, if she is n't frying anything in the spider herself; and then I wait and whistle to my sister's canary-bird, or else look out the window. But she tells me to stand a yard back, because she says cold comes in the window-cracks: and my uncle Jacob he took the yardstick one day, and measured a yard, and put a

chalk mark there, where my toes must come to, he said.
If I hold the yardstick a foot and a half up from the floor,
my sister's kitty can jump over it tip-top.   My sister has

made a Red-Riding-Hood cloak for her kitty, and a muff
to put her fore paws in, and takes her out.

Yesterday Uncle Jacob came into the house and said
he had brought a carriage to carry me over to Aunt
Phebe's; and when I looked out it was n't anything
but a wheelbarrow.   My grandmother said I must
wrap up, for 't was the first time; so she put two over-

coats on me, and my father's long stockings over my shoes and stockings, and a good many comforters, and then a great shawl over my head so I need n't breathe the air; and 't was about as bad as to stay in. Uncle Jacob asked her if there was a Billy in that bundle, when he saw it. "Hallo, in there!" says he. "Hallo, out there!" says I. Then he took me up in his arms, and carried me out, and doubled me up, and put me down in the wheelbarrow, and threw the buffalo over me; but one leg got undoubled, and fell out, so I had to drag my foot most all the way. Aunt Phebe undid me, and set me close to the fire; and Lucy Maria and the rest of them brought me story-books and picture-papers; and Tommy, he kept round me all the time, making me whittle him out little boats out of a shingle, and we had some fun sailing 'em in a milk-pan. Aunt Phebe had chicken broth for dinner, and I had a very good appetite. She let me look into all her closets and boxes, and let me open all her drawers. But I had to have a little white blanket pinned on when I went round, because she was afraid her room was n't kept so warm as my grandmother's. Soon as Uncle Jacob came in and saw that little white blanket he began to laugh. "So Aunt Phebe has got out the *signal of distress*," says he. He calls that blanket the "signal of distress," because when any of them don't feel well, or have the toothache or anything, she puts it on them. She says he shall have to wear it some time, and I guess he 'll look funny, he 's so tall, with it on. The fellers played base-ball close to Aunt Phebe's garden. I tell you I shall be glad enough to get out-doors. I tell you it is n't much fun to look out the window and see 'em play ball. But Uncle Jacob says if the ball hit me 't would knock me over now. Aunt Phebe was just as clever, and let me whittle right on the floor, and did n't care a mite. And we made corn-balls. But the best fun was finding things, when I was rummaging. I found some pictures in an old trunk that she said I might have, and I want you to give them to Bubby Short to put in the Panorama he said he was going to make. He said the price to see it would be two cents. They are true ones, for they are about Aunt Phebe's little Tommy. One day, when he was a good deal smaller feller than he is now, he went out when it had done raining one day, and the wind blew hard, and he found an old umbrella, and did just what is in the pictures. The school-teacher that boarded there, O, she could draw cows and pigs and anything ; and she drew these pictures, and wrote about them underneath.

I wish you would write me a letter, and tell Benjie to and Bubby Short.

From your affectionate friend,

WILLIAM HENRY.

P. S.   What are you fellers playing now ?

Thinking the school-teacher's pictures might please other little Tommys, I have taken some pains to procure them for insertion here. Little "fellers" usually are fond of carrying umbrellas, — large size preferred. Nothing suited Tommy better than marching off to school of a rainy day with one up full spread, provided he could hold it. His cousin Myra once took an old umbrella and cut it down into a small one, by chopping off the ends of the sticks, supposing he would be delighted with it. But no, he wanted a "*man's one.*"

TOMMY ON HIS TRAVELS.

TOMMY sets forth upon his travels around the house, taking with him his whip.

At the first corner he picks up an umbrella. A larger boy opens the umbrella, and shows him the way to hold

it. Being an old umbrella, it shuts down again. But Tommy still keeps on in his way.

At the second corner a gust of wind takes down the

umbrella, and blows his capes over his head. He pushes on, however, whip in hand, dragging the umbrella behind him.

On turning the third corner a hen runs between his legs, and throws him down in the mud.

He is taken inside, stripped and washed, and left sitting upon the floor in his knit shirt, waiting for clean clothes. He can reach the handle of the molasses-jug. He does reach the handle, and tips over the jug. His mother finds him eating molasses off the floor with his forefinger. Tommy looks up with a sweet smile.

Here we have William Henry back at school again.

William Henry to his Grandmother.

MY DEAR GRANDMOTHER, —

I've been here three days now. I came safe all the way, but that glass vial you put that medicine into, down in the corner of the trunk, broke, and some white stockings down there, they soaked it all up; but I sha' n't have to take it now, and no matter, I guess, for I feel well, all but my legs feeling weak so I can't run hardly any. When I got here, the boys were playing ball; but they all ran to shake hands, and slapped my shoulders so they almost slapped me down, and hollered out, " How are you, Billy ? ' " How fares ye ? " " Welcome back ! " " Got well ? " " Good for you, Billy ! " Gus Beals — he 's the great tall one we call " Mr. Augustus " — he called out, " How

are you, red-top ? " And then Dorry called out to him, " How are you, hay-pole ? " Dorry and Bubby Short want me to tell you to thank Aunt Phebe for their dough-

5 *

nuts, and you, too, for that molasses candy.   The candy
got soft, and the paper jammed itself all into the candy,
but Bubby Short says he loves paper when it has molasses candy all over it.   I gave some of the things to Benjie.
Something hurt me all the way coming, in the toe of my
boot; and when I got here I looked, and 't was a five-
cent piece right in the toe!   I know who 't was!   'T was

Uncle Jacob when he made believe look to see if that
boot-top was n't made of mighty poor leather.   I went
to spend it yesterday, down to the Two Betseys' shop.
Lame Betsey called me a poor little dear, and was just
going to kiss me, but I twisted my face round.   I'm too
big for all that now, I guess.   She looked for something
to give me, and was just going to give me a stick of
candy; but the other Betsey said 't was no use to give
little boys candy, for they 'd only swallow it right down;
so she gave me a row of pins, for she said pins were
proper handy things when your buttons ripped off.   Just
when I was coming back from the Two Betseys' shop I
met Gapper Skyblue.   He goes about selling cakes now.
A good many boys were round him, in a hurry to buy
first, and all you could hear was, " Here, Gapper! "

" This way, Gapper ! " " You know me, Gapper ! " " Me,
me, me ! " One boy — he's a new boy — spoke up loud
and said, " Mr. Skyblue, please attend to me, if you please,
for I have five pennies to spend ! " He came from Jersey. The fellers call him " Old Wonder Boy," because
he brags and tells such big stories. But now, just as
soon as he begins to tell, Dorry begins too, and always
tells the biggest, — makes them up, you know. O, I tell
you, Dorry gives it to him good ! You'd die a laughing
to hear Dorry, and so do all the fellers. W. B., — that's
what we call Old Wonder Boy sometimes, — W stands
for Wonder, and B stands for Boy, — he says cents are
not cents; says they are pennies, for the Jersey folks
call them pennies, and he guesses they know. He says
he gets his double handful of pennies to spend every day
down in Jersey. But Bubby Short says he knows that's
a whopper, for he knows there would n't anybody's mother
give them their double handful of pennies to spend every
day, nor cents either, nor their father either. And then
Dorry told Old Wonder Boy that he supposed it took his
double handful of pennies to buy a roll of lozenges down
in Jersey. Then W. B. said that our lozenges were all
flour and water, but down in Jersey they were clear
sugar, and just as plenty as huckleberries. Dorry said
he did n't believe any huckleberries grew out there, or if
they did, they'd be nothing but red ones, for the ground
was red out in Jersey. But W. B. said no matter if the
ground was red, the huckleberries were just as black as
Yankee huckleberries, and blacker too, and three times
bigger, and ten times thicker. Said he picked twenty
quarts one day.

Dorry said, " Poh, that was n't much of a pick!"
Says he, " Now I'll tell you a huckleberry story that's
worth something." Then all the boys began to hit
elbows, for they knew Dorry would make up some funny
thing. Says he: "I went a huckleberrying once to
Wakonok Swamp, and I carried a fourteen-quart tin pail,
and a great covered basket, besides a good many quart
and pint things. You'd better believe they hung thick
in that swamp! I found a thick spot, and I slung my
fourteen-quart tin pail round my waist, and picked with
both hands, and ate off the bushes with my mouth all the
while. I got all my things full without stirring two yards
from the spot, and then I did n't know what to do. But
I'll tell you what I did. I took off my jacket, and cut
my fishing-line, and tied up the bottom ends of my jacket
sleeves and picked them both full. And then I did n't
know what to do next. But I'll tell you what I did. I
took off my overalls, and tied up the bottoms of their legs,
and picked them so full you would n't know but there
was a boy standing up ' in 'em!" Then the boys all
clapped.

" Well," Old Wonder Boy said, " how did you get them
home?"

" O, got them home easy enough," Dorry said. " First
I put the overalls over my shoulders, like a boy going
pussy-back. I slung all the quart and pint things round
my waist, and hung the covered basket on one arm, and
took the fourteen-quart tin pail in that same hand. Then
I tied my jacket to the end of my fishing-pole, and held
it up straight in my other hand like — like a flag in a
dead calm!"

O, you ought to 've seen the boys, — how they winked at one another and puffed out their cheeks; and some of 'em rolled over and over down hill to keep from laughing! Bubby Short got behind the fence, and put his face between two bars, and called out, " S — e — double l ! " But Dorry says they don't know what a " s — e — double l " is down in Jersey. But I don't believe that W. B. believes Dorry's stories; for I looked him in the face, and he had a mighty sly look when he asked Dorry how it was he got his huckleberries home.

To-day they got a talking about potatoes. Old Wonder Boy said that down in Jersey they grow so big you have to pry 'em up out of the hill, and it don't take much more than two to make a peck. Dorry told him that down in Maine you could stand on top the potato-hills and look all round the country, they were so high; and he asked W. B. how they planted 'em in Jersey, with their eyes up or down? He said he did n't know which way they did turn their eyes. Then Dorry told him the Yankees always planted potatoes eyes up, so they could see which way to grow. Said he planted a hill of potatoes in his father's garden, last summer, with their eyes all down, and waited and waited, but they did n't come up. And when he had waited a spell longer, he raked off the top of that hill of potatoes, and all he saw was some roots sticking up. And he began to dig down. And he kept digging. Followed their stems. But he never got to the potato-tops; and says he, " I never did get to those potato-tops ! " O, you ought to 've heard the boys !

Old Wonder Boy wanted to know where Dorry

thought they 'd gone to. Dorry thought to himself a minute, and looked just as sober, and then says he, just like a school-teacher, "The earth, in the middle, is afire. I think when they got deep enough to feel the warm, they guessed 't was the sun, and so kept heading that way."

Is the world afire in the middle? Dorry told me that part of his story was really true. How Uncle Jacob would laugh to sit down and hear Dorry and Old Wonder Boy tell about whales. W. B. calls 'em wales. His uncle is a ship-captain, he says, and once he saw a wale, and the wale was making for his ship, and it chased 'em. And, no matter how they steered, that wale would chase. And by and by, in a calm day, he got under the vessel and boosted her up out of water, when all the crew gave a yell, — such a horrid yell that the wale let 'em down so sudden that the waves splashed up to the tops of the masts, and they thought they were all drowned.

"O, poh!" Dorry cried out. "My uncle was a regular whaler, and went a whaling for his living. And once he was cruising about the whaling-grounds and 't was in a place where the days were so short that the nights lasted almost all day. And they got chased by a whale. And he kept chasing them. Night and day. And there came up a gale of wind that lasted three days and nights; and the ship went like lightning, night and day, the whale after them. And, when the wind went down, the whale was so tuckered that he could n't swim a stroke. So he floated. Then the cap'n sang out to 'em to lower a boat. And they did. And the cap'n got in and took a couple of his men to row him. The whale was rather longer than a liberty-pole. About as long as a liberty-pole and a half. He was asleep, and they steered for the tail end. A whale's head is about as big as the Two Betseys' shop, and 't is filled with clear oil, without any trying out. The cap'n landed on the whale's tail, and went along up on tiptoe, and the men rowed the boat alongside, and kept even with him ; and, when he got towards her ears, he took off his shoes, and threw 'em to the men to catch. After a while he got to the tip-top of her head. Now I 'll tell you what he had in his hand. He had a great junk of cable as big round as the trunk of a tree, and not quite a yard long. In one end of it there was a point of a harpoon stuck in, and the other end of it was lighted. He told the men to stand ready. Then he took hold of the cable with both hands, and with one mighty blow he stuck that pointed end deep in the whale's head, and then gave one jump into the boat, and he cried out to the men, ' Row ! row for your lives ! To the tail end ! If you want to live, row !' And before that whale could turn round they were safe aboard the ship ! But now I 'll tell you the best part of the whole story. They did n't have any more long dark nights after that. They kept throwing over bait to keep her chasing, and the great lamp blazed, and as fast as the oil got hot it tried out more blubber, and that whale burned as long as there was a bit of the inside of him left. Flared up, and lighted up the sea, and drew the fishes, and they drew more whales ; and they got deep loaded, and might have loaded twenty more ships. And when they left they took a couple in tow, — of whales, — and knocked out their teeth for ivory, and then sold their carcasses to an empty whaler."

Dorry says some parts of this story are true.   But he did n't say which parts.   Said I must look in the whale-book and find out.

Your affectionate grandchild,

WILLIAM HENRY.

P. S.   I wish you would please to send me a silver three-cent piece or five-cent.   Two squaws have got a tent a little ways off, and the boys are going to have their fortunes taken.   But you have to cross the squaws' hands with silver.   W. H.

Georgianna's Letter to William Henry.

MY DEAR BROTHER BILLY, —

O Billy, my pretty, darling little bird is dead!   My kitty did it, and O, I don't know what I shall do, for I love my kitty if she did kill my birdie ; but I don't forget about it, and I keep thinking of my birdie every time my kitty comes in the room.   I was putting some seeds in the glass, and my birdie looked so cunning ; and I held

a lump of white sugar in my lips, and let him peck it.
And while I was thinking what a dear little bird he was,
I forgot he could fly out; but he could, for the door was
open, and he flew to the window.   I did n't think anything about kitty.   It flew up to that bracket you made,
and then it went away up in the corner just as high as it
could, on a wooden peg that was there.   I did n't know
what made it flutter its wings and tremble so, but grandmother pointed her finger down to the corner, on the
floor, and there was my kitty stretching out and looking
up at my bird.   And that was what made poor birdie
tremble so.   And it dropped right down.   Before we
could run across to catch kitty, he dropped right down
into her mouth.   I never thought she could get him.   I
did n't know what made grandmother hurry.   I did n't
know that kitties could charm birds, but they do.   She
did n't have him a minute in her teeth, and I thought it
could n't be dead.   But, O Billy, my dear birdie never
breathed again!   I warmed him in my hands, and tried
to make him stir his wings, but he never breathed again.
Now the tears are coming again.   I thought I was n't
going to cry any more.   But they come themselves;
when I don't know it, they come; and O, it was such a
good birdie!   When I came home from school I used to
run to the cage, and he would sing to meet me.   And I
put chickweed over his cage.

Grandmother has put away that empty cage now.
She 's sorry, too.   Did you think a grandmother would be
sorry about a little bird as that?   But she 'd rather give
a good deal.   When she put the plates on the table, and
rattled spoons, he used to sing louder and louder.   And

H

in the morning he used to wake me up, singing away so loud! Now, when I first wake up, I listen. But O, it is so still now! Then in a minute I remember all about it. Sometimes kitty jumps up on the bed, and puts her nose close down, and purrs. But I say, "No, kitty. Get down. You killed little birdie. I don't want to see you." But she don't know what I mean. She rubs her head on my face, and purrs loud, and wants me to stroke her back, and don't seem as if she had been bad. She used to be such a dear little kitty. And so she is. She's pretty as a pigeon. Aunt Phebe says she never saw such a pretty little gray and white kitty as she is. I was going to have her drowned. But then I should cry for kitty too. Then I should think how she looked all drowned, down at the bottom, just the same way I do now how my birdie looked when it could n't stir its little wings, and its eyes could n't move. My father says that kitty did n't know any better. I hope so. I took off that pretty chain she had round her neck. But grandmother thinks I had better put it on again. Aunt Phebe's little Tommy says, "Don't kye, Dordie, I'll *bung* dat tat. I'll take a tick and *bung* dat tat!" He calls me Dordie, I guess I rather have kitty alive than let her be drowned, don't you? Grandmother wants you not to catch cold and be sick.

From your affectionate sister,

GEORGIANNA.

P. S. Grandmother showed me how to write this letter.

A caged bird is never a very interesting object to me. But this little canary of Georgie's was really a beautiful creature, and very intelligent. They used to think that he listened for her step at noon and night; for no sooner was it heard in the entry than he peeped out with his little bright eyes, and tuned up, and sang away, as if to say, " Glad! glad! glad you 've come! glad you 've come!"

Then she would go to the cage and talk to him, and let him take sugar from her mouth, and would hang fresh chickweed about its cage. Mornings she used to sing, from her bed, and the bird would answer. Indeed, he really seemed quite a companion for her.

At the time the accident happened I had been staying for a few weeks at the hotel, a mile or two off, and called at the farm that very day. · Lucy Maria told me, as I stopped at their door, what the kitten had done, and how Georgianna had cried and mourned and could not be comforted.

I found her sitting on the door-step. She had· placed the bird in a small round basket, lined with cotton-wool, and was bending over, and stroking it. I had always noticed the bird a great deal, used to play with it, and whistle to make it sing louder and louder. The sight of me brought all this back to her mind, and she burst into tears again, sobbing out, " O, he never — will sing — any more! Dear little birdie! He had to fall down! IIe could n't — help it!"

I talked with her awhile, in a cheerful way, and when she had become quite calm I held out my hand and said, " Come, Georgie, don't you want to go with me and find a pretty place where we can put birdie away, under the soft grass? And we will plant a flower there."

The idea of the soft grass and the flower seemed to please her. She took my hand, and we went to look about.

We thought the garden not a very good place, because it was dug up every year, and the field would be mowed and trampled upon. But just over the fence, back of the garden, we came upon some uneven ground, where the old summer-sweeting trees grew. In one place there was a sudden pitch downwards, into a little hollow, which grass and plantain leaves made almost forever green. For here was what they called the Boiling Spring. The water bubbled out of the ground on the slope of the bank, and in former times, before the well was dug, had been used in the family. Several trees grew about there, — wild cherry, damson, and poplar, — and a profusion of yellow flowers, wild ones. Some of these grandmother called " Ladies' Slipper "; the others, " Sullendine." The spring had once been stoned up and boxed over. But the boards were now rotting away, the stones falling in, and our little hollow had quite a deserted look. The water trickled out and ran away around the curve of the bank.

Grandmother came with us, and Georgie's teacher, and Matilda and Tommy. We hollowed out a little place under the wild-cherry tree, wrapped the birdie in cotton-wool, lay him in, and covered him over with the green sod. I then went down by the stone wall, where sweetbriers were growing, dug up a very pretty little one, and set it out close by, so that it might lean against the cherry-tree. Tommy kept very sober, and scarcely spoke a word, till it was all over. He then said to me, in a very earnest tone, " Mr. Fwy, now will another birdie grow up there ? " I suppose he was thinking of his father's planting corn and more corn growing.

William Henry to his Sister.

My dear Little Sister, —

I 'm sorry your little birdie 's dead ! He was a nice singing birdie ! But I would n't cry. Maybe you 'll have another one some time, if you 're a good little girl. Maybe father 'll go to Boston and buy you one, or maybe Cousin Joe will send one home to you, in a vessel, or maybe I 'll catch one, or maybe a man will come along with birds to sell, or maybe Aunt Phebe's bird will lay

an egg and hatch one out. I would n't feel bad about it.
It is n't any use to feel bad about it. Maybe, if he
had n't been killed, he 'd 'a' died. Dorry says, "Tell her,
Don't you cry,' and I 'll give her something, catch her a
rabbit or a squirrel!" Says he 'll tease his sister for her
white mice. Says he 'll tease her with the tears in his
eyes, — or else her banties.

How do you like your teacher? Do you learn any
lessons at school? You must try to get up above all the
other ones. We 've got two new teachers this year.
One is clever, and we like that one, but the other one is n't
very. We call the good one Wedding Cake, and we call
the other one Brown Bread. Did grandmother tell you
about the Fortune Tellers? We went to-day and she
told mine true. She said my father was a very kind
man, and said I was quick to get mad, and said I had
just got something I 'd wanted a long time (watch, you
know), and said I should have something else that I'
wanted, but did n't say when. I wonder how she knew
I wanted a gun. I thought perhaps somebody told her,
and laid it to Old Wonder Boy, for we two had been
talking about guns. But he flared up just like a flash of
powder. "There. Now you need n't blame that on to
me!" says he. "You fellers always do blame everything
on to me!" Sometimes when somebody touches him he
hollers out, "Leave me loose! Leave me loose!"
Dorry says that's the way fellers talk down in Jersey. The Fortune Teller told W. B. that he came from
a long way off, and that he wanted to be a soldier, but
he 'd better give up that, for he would n't dare to go to war,
without he went behind to sell pies. All of us laughed to

hear that, for Old Wonder Boy is quick to get scared.
But he is always straightening himself up, and looking
big, and talking about his native land, and what he would
do for his native land, and how he would fight for his
native land, and how he would die for his native land.
He says that why she told him that kind of a fortune
was because he gave her pennies and not silver money.
His uncle that goes cap'n of a vessel has sent him a letter, and in the letter it said that he had a sailor aboard
his ship that used to come to this school.

I was going to tell you a funny story about W. B.'s
getting scared, but Dorry he keeps teasing me to go
somewhere. I made these joggly letters when he tickled

my ears with his paint-brush. Has your pullet begun to
lay yet? I hope my rooster won't be killed. Tell them
not to. Benjie says he had a grand great rooster. It
was white and had green and purple tail feathers, O, very
long tail feathers, and stood 'most as high as a barrel of
flour, with great yellow legs, and had a beautiful crow,
and could drive away every other one that showed his
head, and he set his eyes by that rooster, but when he
got home they had killed him for broth, and when he
asked 'em where his rooster was they brought out the

wish-bone and two tail feathers, and that was all there was left of him. I would n't have poor little kitty drowned way down in the deep water 'cause to drown a kitty could n't make a birdie alive again. Have your flowers bloomed out yet? You must be a good little girl, and try to please your grandmother all you can.

From your affectionate brother,

WILLIAM HENRY.

P. S. Now Dorry 's run to head off a loose horse, and I 'll tell you about Old Wonder Boy's getting scared. It was one night when — Now there comes Dorry back again! But next time I will.

W. H.

William Henry to his Sister, about Old Wonder Boy's Fright.

MY DEAR SISTER, —

I will put that little story I am going to tell you right at the beginning, before Dorry and Bubby Short get back. I mean about W. B.'s getting scared. But don't you be scared, for after all 't was — no, I mean after all 't was n't — but wait and you 'll know by and by, when I tell you. 'T was one night when Dorry and I and some more fellers were a sitting here together, and we all of us heard some thick boots coming a hurrying up the stairs, and the door came a banging open, and W. B. pitched in, just as pale as a sheet, and could n't but just breathe. And he tried to speak, but could n't, only one word at once, and catching his breath between, just so, — " Shut — the — door! — Do! — Do! — shut — the door! " Then we shut up the door, and Bubby Short stood his back up

against it because 't would n't quite latch, and now I will
tell you what it was that scared him.   Not at the first of
it, but I shall tell it just the same way we found it out.

Says he, " I was making a box, and when I got it done
't was dark, but I went to carry the carpenter's tools
back to him, because I promised to.   And going along,"
says he, " I thought I heard a funny noise behind me,
but I did n't think very much about it, but I heard it
again, and I looked over my shoulder, and I saw something white behind me, a chasing me.   I went faster, and
then that went faster.   Then I went slower, and then
that went slower.   And then I got scared and ran as fast
as I could, and looked over my shoulder and 't was keeping up.   But it did n't run with feet, nor with legs, for
then I should n't 'a' been scared.   But it came — O, I
don't know how it came, without anything to go on."

Dorry asked him, " How did it look ? "

" O, — white.   All over white," says W. B.

" How big was it ? " Bubby Short asked him.

" O, — I don't know," says W. B.   " First it looked
about as big as a pigeon, but every time I looked round
it seemed to grow bigger and bigger."

" Maybe 't was a pigeon," says Dorry.   " Did it have
any wings ? "

" Not a wing," says W. B.

" Maybe 't was a white cat," says Mr. Augustus,

" O, poh, cat ! " says W. B.

" Or a poodle dog," says Benjie.

" Nonsense, poodle dog ! " says W. B.

" Or a rabbit," says Bubby Short.

" O, go 'way with your rabbit ! " says W. B.   " Did n't
I tell you it had n't any feet or legs to go with ? "

"Then how could it go?" Mr. Augustus asked him.

"That's the very thing," said W. B.

"Snakes do," says Bubby Short.

"But a snake would n't look white," says Benjie.

"Without 't was scared," says Dorry.

I said I guessed I knew. Like enough 't was a ghost of something.

I said like enough of a robin or some kind of bird.

"Of what?" then they all asked me.

"That he'd stolen the eggs of," says Dorry.

"O yes!" says Old Wonder Boy. "It's easy enough to laugh, in the light here, but I guess you 'd 'a' been scared, seeing something chasing you in the dark, and going up and down, and going tick, tick, tick, every time it touched ground, and sometimes it touched my side too."

"For goodness gracious!" says Dorry. "Can't you tell what it seemed most like?"

"I tell you it did n't seem most like anything. It did n't run, nor walk, nor fly, nor creep, nor glide along. And when I got to the Great Elm-Tree, I cut round that tree, and ran this way, and that did too."

"Where is it now?" Dorry asked him.

"O, don't!" says W. B. "Don't open the door. 'T is out there."

"Come, fellers," Dorry said, "let 's go find it."

Benjie said, "Let 's take something to hit it with!" And he took an umbrella and I took the bootjack, and Bubby Short took the towel horse, and Mr. Augustus took a hair-brush, and Dorry took his boot with his arm run down in it, and first we opened the door a crack and did n't go out, but peeped out, but did n't see anything

6

there. Then we went out a little ways, and then we
did n't see anything. And pretty soon, going along towards the stairs, Bubby Short stepped on something.
"What's that?" says he. And he jumped, and we all
flung our things at it. "Hold the light!" Dorry cried
out.

Then W. B. brought out the light, and there was n't
anything there but a carpenter's reel, with a chalk line
wound up on it, and they picked it up and began to wind

up, and when they came to the end of it — where do you
s'pose the other end was? In W. B.'s pocket! and his
ball and some more things held it fast there, and that
chalk-line reel was what went bobbing up and down behind Old Wonder Boy every step he took, — bob, bob,
bobbing up and down, for there was a hitch in the line
and it could n't unwind any more, and the line under the
door was why 't would n't latch, and O, but you ought
to 've heard the fellers how they roared! and Bubby
Short rolled over on the floor, and Dorry he tumbled
heels over head on all the beds, and we all shouted and
hurrahed so the other fellers came running to see what
was up, and then the teachers came to see who was fling-

ing things round so up here, and to see what was the matter, but there could n't anybody tell what the matter was for laughing, and W. B. he looked so sheepish! O, if it was n't gay! How do you like this story? That part where it touched his side was when that reel caught on something and so jerked the string some. Now I must study my lesson.

Your affectionate brother,

WILLIAM HENRY.

P. S. When you send a box don't send very many clothes in it, but send goodies. I tell you things taste good when a feller's away from his folks. Dorry's father had a picture taken of Dorry's little dog and sent it to him, and it looks just as natural as some boys. Tell Aunt Phebe's little Tommy he may sail my boat once. 'T is put away up garret in that corner where I keep things, side of that great long-handled thing, grandmother's warming-pan. I mean that little sloop boat I had when I 's a little feller.

W. H.

Georgianna's Letter to William Henry.

MY DEAR BROTHER BILLY, —

Kitty is n't drowned. I've got ever so many new dolls. My grandmother went to town, not the same day my kitty did that, but the next day, and she brought me home a new doll, and that same day she went there my father went to Boston, and he brought me home a very big one, — no, not very, but quite big, — and Aunt Phebe went a visiting to somebody's house that very day, and she brought me home a doll, and while she was gone away Hannah Jane dressed over one of Matilda's old ones

new, and none of the folks knew that the others were
going to give me a doll, and then Uncle J. said that if it
was the family custom to give Georgianna a doll, he
would give Georgianna a doll, and he went to the field
and catched the colt, and tackled him up into the riding
wagon on purpose, and then he started off to town, and
when he rode up to our back door there was a great dolly,
the biggest one I had, and she was sitting down on the
seat, just like a live one. And she had a waterfall, and
she had things to take off and on. Then Uncle J. asked
me what I should do with my old dollies that were 'most
worn out. And I said I did n't know what I should.
And then Uncle J. said that he would take the lot, for
twenty-five cents a head, to put up in his garden, for
scarecrows, and he asked me if I would sell, and I said I
would. And he put the little ones on little poles and the
big ones on tall poles, with their arms stretched out, and
the one with a long veil looked the funniest, and so did
the one dressed up like a sailor boy, but one arm was
broke off of him, and a good many of their noses too.
The one that had on old woman's clothes Uncle J. put a
pipe in her mouth. And the one that had a pink gauze
dress, but 't is all faded out now, and a long train, but the
train was torn very much, that one has a great bunch of
flowers — paper — pinned on to her, and another in her
hand, and the puppy he barks at 'em like everything.
My pullet lays, little ones, you know. I hope she won't
do like Lucy Maria's Leghorn hen. That one flies into
the bedroom window every morning, and lays eggs on
the bedroom bed. For maybe 't would come in before I
got up. My class has begun to learn geography, and my

father has bought me a new geography. But I guess I sha' n't like to learn it very much if the backside is hard as the foreside is. Uncle J. says no need to worry your mind any about that old fowl, for he 's so tough he could n't be killed. I wish you would tell me how long he could live if it was n't killed, for Uncle J. says they grow tougher every year, and if you should let one live too long, then he can't die. But I guess he 's funning, do you? Our hens scratched and scratched up some of my flowers, and so did the rain wash some up that night it came down so hard, but one pretty one bloomed out this morning, but it has budded back again now. Aunt Phebe says she sends her love to you, tied up with this pretty piece of blue ribbon. She says, if you want to, you can take the ribbon and wear it for a neck bow. Grandmother says how do you know but that sailor that went to your school in Old Wonder Boy's uncle's vessel is that big boy, that bad one that ran away, you called Tom Cush?

Father laughs to hear about Old Wonder Boy, and he says a bragger ought to be laughed at, and bragging is a bad thing. But he don't want you to pick out all the bad things about a boy to send home in your letters; says next time you must send home a good thing about him, because he thinks every boy you see has some good things as well as some bad things.

A dear little baby has moved in the house next to our house. It lets me hold her, and its mother lets me drag her out. It 's got little bits of toes, and it 's got a little bit of a nose, and it says " Da da! da da! da da!" And when I was dragging her out, the wheel went over a poor little butterfly, but I guess it was dead before. O, its wings were just as soft! and 't was a yellow one. And I buried it up in the ground close to where I buried up my little birdie, side of the spring.

Your affectionate sister,

GEORGIANNA.

Among the other letters I find the following, from Tom Cush. As the people at Summer Sweeting place had been told the circumstances of his running away, it was not only proper, but just, that William Henry should send them this letter.

A Letter from Tom Cush to Dorry.

DEAR FRIEND, —

I have not seen you for a great while. I hope you are in good health. Does William Henry go to school there now? And does Benjie go, and little Bubby Short? I hope they are in good health. Do the Two Betseys keep shop there now? Is Gapper Skyblue alive now? I am in very good health. I go to sea now. That's where I went when I went away from school. I suppose all the boys hate me, don't they? But I don't blame them any for hating me. I should think they would all of them hate me. For I did n't act very well when I went to that school. Our captain knows about that school, for he is uncle to a boy that has begun to go. He's sent a letter to him. I wish that boy would write a letter to him, because he might tell about the ones I know.

I 've been making up my mind about telling you something. I 've been thinking about it, and thinking about it. I don't like to tell things very well. But I am going

to tell this to you.   It is n't anything to tell.   I mean it
is n't like news, or anything happening to anybody.   But
it is something about when I was sick.   For I had a fit
of sickness.   I don't mean afterwards, when I was so
very sick, but at the first beginning of it.

The captain he took some books out of his chest and
said I might have them to read if I wanted to.   And I
read about a man in one of them, and the king wanted
him to do something that the man thought was n't right
to do; but the man said he would not do what was wrong.
And for that he was sent to row in a very large boat
among all kinds of bad man, thieves and murderers and
the worst kind.   They had to row every minute, and
were chained to their oars, and above their waists they
had no clothes on.   They had overseers with long whips.
The officers stayed on deck over the rowers' heads, and
when they wanted the vessel to go faster, the overseers
made their long whip-lashes cut into the men's backs till
they were all raw and bleeding.   Nights the chains were
not taken off, and they slept all piled up on each other.
Sometimes when the officers were in a hurry, or when
there were soldiers aboard, going to fight the enemy's
vessels, then the men would n't have even a minute to
eat, and were almost starved to death, and got so weak
they would fall over, but then they were whipped again.
And when they got to the enemy's ships, they had to sit
and have cannons fired in among them.   Then the dead
ones were picked up and thrown into the water.   And
the king told the man that if he wanted to be free, and
have plenty to eat and a nice house, and good clothes to
wear, all he had to do was to promise to do that wrong

thing. But the man said no. For to be chained there would only hurt his body. But to do wrong would hurt his soul.

And I read about some people that lived many hundred years ago and the emperor of that country wanted these people to say that their religion was wrong and his religion was the right one. But they said, "No. We believe ours is true, and we cannot lie." Then the emperor took away all their property, and pierced them with red-hot irons, and threw some into a place where they kept wild beasts. But they still kept saying, "We cannot lie, we must speak what we believe." And one was a boy only fifteen years old. And the emperor thought he was so young they could scare him very easy. And he said to him, "Now say you believe the way I want you to, or I will have you shut up in a dark dungeon." But the boy said, "I will not say what is false." And he was shut up in a dark dungeon, underground. And one day the emperor said to him, "Say you believe the way I want you to, or I will have you stretched upon a rack." But the boy said, "I will not speak falsely." And he was stretched upon a rack till his bones were almost pulled apart. Then the emperor asked, "Now will you believe that my religion is right?" But the boy could not say so. And the emperor said, "Then you'll be burned alive!" The boy said, "I can suffer the burning, but I cannot lie." Then he was brought out and the wood was piled up round him, and set on fire, and the boy was burned up with the wood. And while he was burning up he thanked God for having strength enough to suffer and not lie.

Dorry, I want to tell you how much I've been thinking about that man and that boy ever since. And I want to ask you to do something. I've been thinking about how mean I was, and what I did there so as not to get punished. And I want you to go see my mother and tell her that I'm *ashamed.* Don't make any promises to my mother, but only just tell, " *Tom's ashamed.*" That's all. I don't want to make promises. But I know myself just what I mean to do. But I sha' n't talk about that any. Give my regards to all inquiring friends.

Your affectionate friend,

Tom.

P. S. Can't you tell things about me to William Henry and the others, for it is very hard to me to write a letter? Write soon.　　　　　　　　　　　　　　　　T.

Mr. Carver's visit to the Crooked Pond School alluded to in the following letter was quite an event for my Summer Sweeting friends, and caused an extra amount of cooking to be done in both families. Boys don't half appreciate the blessing of not being too old to have goodies sent them. Now goodies taste good to me, very good, but I have n't a friend in the world who would think of boiling up a kettleful of molasses into candy, or of making a waiterful of seed-cakes to send me. *Too old*, they say, — in actions, if not in words. How cruelly we are misjudged sometimes, and by those who ought to know us best! I shall never be too old to receive a box like that of William Henry's, never, never! — unless my whole constitution is altered and several *clauses* taken out of it.

I remember of seeing that waiter of " good seed-cakes " on grandmother's best room table, between the front windows, waiting to be packed in Mr. Carver's valise. Mr. Carver's black silk neck-handkerchief, tall hat, clean dickies, stockings,

I

two red and white silk pocket-handkerchiefs, and various other articles were distributed over the adjacent chairs, and his umbrella, in a brown cambric covering, stood near by. I have the impression that most of these things were ironed over, five or six times, as grandmother felt that apparel going away from home could not be too much ironed. Besides, it seemed to her impossible that such an event as Billy's father setting out on his travels should take place without extra exertions in some quarter.

Mr. Carver had other business which took him from home, but as " going to see Billy " was thought *enough to tell Mrs. Paulina*, why, it is enough for me to tell. " Mrs. Paulina " was an elderly woman, the wife of Mr. John Slade, one of the neighbors, and she was called " Mrs. Paulina," to distinguish her from several other Mrs. Slades.

Mrs. Paulina had her own opinion as to how money and time should be spent, — everybody's money and time. She was one of the prying sort, and had wonderful skill in ferreting out all the whys and wherefores of her neighbor's proceedings. It was a common thing at the Farm to say, when undertaking some new scheme, " Well, how much shall we tell Mrs. Paulina ? " It being a matter of course that she would inquire into it. The girls often amused themselves by giving her *blinding* answers just to see how she would contrive to carry her point. I remember their having great fun doing this, just after William Henry went away to school. Lucy Maria said 't was just like a conundrum to Mrs. Paulina, a great mammoth conundrum, and the poor thing must be told about " Old Uncle Wallace," or she would wear herself out, wondering " how Mr. Carver could possibly afford the money."

The " Old Uncle Wallace " thus brought to the rescue of Mrs. Paulina would probably not have came to her rescue, or to any woman's rescue, had he been free to choose, seeing that he lived and died a bachelor, and a stingy bachelor at that ! The old miser was a distant uncle, — either half-uncle, or grand-uncle, or half grand-uncle of the Mr. Carvers, and lived, that is before he died, in a town some twenty miles off. Billy's father was named for Uncle Wallace, and when a little boy, lived in the same neighborhood, and was quite a favorite with him.

The acquaintance with that distant branch of the family, however, had not been kept up, in fact I have no recollection of a single member of it ever coming to the Farm. They were people well to do in the world, and neither Mr. Carver nor Uncle Jacob were men to "honey round" rich relations. Certainly they never would have fawned upon the miserly old fellow, who had the reputation of being mean and tricky as well as miserly.

It seems, however, that "Uncle Wallace" did not wholly forget his namesake, for in his will he left him quite a valuable wood-lot near Corry's Pond, — some six or eight miles from the Farm, — and a few hundred dollars besides.

This occurred not a great while before my first ride out with Uncle Jacob. Mr. Carver had long felt that Billy was being spoiled at home, and the Crooked Pond School being recommended at that time as " really good," and " not too expensive," he resolved that while *feeling rich* he would place his son at that institution. And he was more especially inclined to do so for the reason that an old friend of his lived near there, and this friend's wife promised to see that the boy did not go about in actual rags. She is probably the person to whom William Henry refers in his first letters, as " the woman I go to have my buttons sewed on to."

The above circumstances were duly imparted to Mrs. Paulina, yet that perplexed woman got no relief. True, it was something to know where the money came from, but " How could a man," she asked, " spend so much money on eddication, when it might be drawing interest, or put into land? "

Mrs. Paulina could n't guess. She gave it up.

William Henry's Letter to his Grandmother.

MY DEAR GRANDMOTHER, —

I suppose my father has got home again by this time.
I like to have my father come to see me. The boys all
say my father is a tip-top one. I guess they like to have
a man treat them with so many peanuts and good seed-
cakes. I got back here to-day from Dorry's cousin's party. My father let me go. I wish my sister could have
seen that party. Tell her when I get there I will tell
her all about the little girls, and tell her how cunning the
little ones, as small as she, looked dancing, and about the
good things we had. O, I never saw such good things
before! I did n't know there were such kinds of good
things in the world.

Did my father tell you all about that letter that Tom
Cush wrote to Dorry? Ask him to. Dorry sent that
letter right to Tom Cush's mother. And when Dorry
and I were walking along together the next morning after
the party, she was sitting at her window, and as soon
as she saw us she said, " Won't you come in, boys?
Do come in!" And looked so glad! And laughed, and
about half cried, after we went in, and it was that same
room where we went before. But it did n't seem so
lonesome now, not half. It looked about as sunshiny as
our kitchen does, and they had flower-vases. I wish I
could get some of those pretty seeds for my sister, for
she has n't got any of that kind of flowers.

She seemed just as glad to see us! And shook hands
and looked so smiling, and so did Tom's father when he
came into the room. He had a belt in his hand that Tom

used to wear when he used to belong to that Base-ball Club. And when we saw that, Dorry said, " Why ! has Tom got back ? " Tom's mother said, " O no." But his father said, " O yes ! Tom 's got back. He has n't got back to our house, but he 's got back. He has n't got back to town, but he 's got back. He has n't got back to his own country, but he 's got back. For I call that getting back," says he, " when a boy gets back to the right way of feeling."

Then Tom's mother took that belt and hung it up where it used to be before, for it had been taken down and put away, because they did n't want to have it make them think of Tom so much.

She said when Tom got back in earnest, back to the house, that we two, Dorry and I, must come there and make a visit, and I hope we shall, for they 've got a pond at the bottom of their garden, and Tom's father owns a boat, and you must n't think I should tip over, for I sha'n't, and no matter if I should, I can swim to shore easy.

Your affectionate grandchild,

WILLIAM HENRY.

P. S. Bubby Short did n't mean to, but he sat down on my speckled straw hat, and we could n't get it out even again, and I did n't want him to, but he would go to buy me a new one, and I went with him, but the man did n't have any, for he said the man that made speckled straw hats was dead and his shop was burnt down, and we found a brown straw hat, but I would n't let Bubby Short pay any of his money, only eight cents, because I did n't have quite enough. Don't shopkeepers have the most money of all kinds of men ? Would n't you be a shopkeeper

when I grow up? It seems just as easy! If you was me would you swap off your white-handled jack-knife your father bought you for a four-blader? My sister said to send some of W. B.'s good things. He wrote a very good composition about heads, the teacher said, and I am going to send it, for that will be sending one of his good things. It's got in it about two dozen kinds of heads besides our own heads. W. B. is willing for me to copy it off. And Bubby Short wrote a very cunning little one, and if you want to, you may read it. The teacher told us a good deal about heads.

W. H.

W. B.'s Composition.

HEADS.

HEADS are of different shapes and different sizes. They are full of notions. Large heads do not always hold the most. Some persons can tell just what a man is by the shape of his head. High heads are the best kind.

Very knowing people are called long-headed. A fellow that won't stop for anything or anybody is called hot-headed. If he is n't quite so bright, they call him soft-headed ; if he won't be coaxed nor turned, they call him pig-headed. Animals have very small heads. The heads of fools slant back. When your head is cut off you are beheaded. Our heads are all covered with hair, except baldheads. There are other kinds of heads besides our heads.

First, there are Barrel-heads. Second, there are Pin-heads. Third, Heads of sermons, — sometimes a minister used to have fifteen heads to one sermon. Fourth, Headwind. Fifth, Head of cattle, — when a farmer reckons up his cows and oxen he calls them so many head of cattle. Sixth, Drumheads, — drumheads are made of sheepskin. Seventh, Heads or tails, — when you toss up pennies. Eighth, Doubleheaders, — when you let off rockets. Ninth, Come to a head — like a boil or a rebellion. Tenth, Cabbageheads, — dunces are called cabbageheads, and good enough for them. Eleventh, At Loggerheads, — when you don't agree. Twelfth, Heads of chapters. Thirteenth, Head him off, — when you want to stop a horse, or a boy. Fourteenth, Head of the family. Fifteenth, A Blunderhead. Sixteenth, The Masthead, — where they send sailors to punish them. Seventeenth, get up to the head, — when you spell the word right. Eighteenth, The Head of a stream, — where it begins. Nineteenth, Down by the head, — when a vessel is deep loaded at the bows. Twentieth, a Figurehead carved on a vessel. Twenty-first, The Cathead, and that 's the end of a stick of timber that a ship's anchor hangs by. Twenty-second, A Headland, or cape. Twenty-third, A Head of tobacco. Twenty-fourth, A Bulkhead, which is a partition in a ship. Twenty-fifth, Go ahead, — but first be sure you are right.

Bubby Short's Composition.

ON MORNING.

IT is very pleasant to get up in the morning and walk in the green fields, and hear the birds sing. The morning is the earliest part of the day. The sun rises in the morning. It is very good for our health to get up early. It is very pleasant to see the sun rise in the morning. In the morning the flowers bloom out and smell very good. If it thunders in the morning, or there 's a rainbow, 't will be rainy weather. Fish bite best in the morning, when you go a fishing. I like to sleep in the morning.

Here is a letter which, judging from the improvement shown in handwriting, and from its rather more dashing style, seems to have been written during William Henry's second school year.

William Henry's Letter about the "Charade."

MY DEAR GRANDMOTHER, —

I never did in all my life have such a real tiptop time as we fellers had last night. We acted charades, and I never did any before, and the word was — no, I must n't tell you, because it has to be guessed by actions, and when you get the paper that I 'm going to send you, soon as I buy a two-cent stamp, then you 'll see it all printed out in that paper. The teacher the fellers call

Wedding Cake, because he's such a good one, asked all the ones that board here to come to his house last night, and we acted charades, and his sister told us what to be, and what things to put on, and everything. You'll see it printed there, but you must please to send it back, for I promised to return.

There were n't females enough, and so Dorry he was the Fat Woman, and we all liked to ha' died a laughing, getting ready, but when we were — there, I 'most told!

O if you could ha' seen Bubby Short, a fiddling away, with old ragged clothes and old shoes and his cap turned wrong side out, then he passed round that cap — just as sober — much as we could do to keep in! I was a clerk and had a real handsome mustache done under my nose with a piece of burnt cork-stopple burned over the light. And she told me to act big, like a clerk, and I did.

Mr. Augustus was the dandy, and if he did n't strut, but he struts other times too, but more then, and made all of us laugh.

Old Wonder Boy was the boy that sold candy, and he spoke up smart and quick, just as she told him to, and the teacher was the country feller and acted just as funny, and so did his sister; his sister was the shopping woman. Both of them like to play with boys, and they 're grown up, too. Should you think they would? And they like candy same as we do. And when it came to the end, just as the curtain was dropping down, we all took hold of the rounds of our chairs, and jerked ourselves all of a sudden up in a heap together, and groaned, and so forth.

I wish you all and Aunt Phebe's folks had been there. We had a treat, and O, if 't was n't a treat, why, I 'll agree to treat myself. Three kinds of ice-creams shaped up into pyramids and rabbits, and scalloped cakes and candy, and *such* a great floating island in a platter! — Dorry said 't was a floating continent! — and had red jelly round the platter's edge, and some of that red jelly was dipped out every dip. O, if he is n't a tiptop teacher! Dorry says we ought to be ashamed of ourselves if we have missing lessons, or cut up any for much as a week, and more too, I say.

And so I can't tell any more now, for I mean to study hard if I possibly can.

Your affectionate grandson,

WILLIAM HENRY.

Please lend it to Aunt Phebe's folks.

CHARADE. (*Carpet.*)

FIRST SYLLABLE.

Chairs placed in two rows, to represent seats of cars. Passengers enter and take their seats. Placard stuck up, "Beware of Pickpockets," in capitals.

First. Enter two school-girls, M. and A., with books strapped about, lunch-box, &c. They are laughing and chatting. M. gives A. a letter to read. A. smiles while reading it, M. watching her face, then both look over it together. Afterwards, study their lessons. All this must be going on while the other passengers are entering.

Second. Business man and two clerks, one at a time. One takes out little account-book, another reads paper, another sits quietly, after putting ticket in his hat-band.

Third. Fat woman, with old-fashioned carpet-bag, umbrella, and bundles tied up in handkerchiefs; seats herself with difficulty.

Fourth. A clergyman, all in black, very solemn, with white neckcloth and spectacles.

Fifth. Yankee fellow from the country, staring at all new-comers.

Sixth. Dandy, with yellow gloves, slender cane, stunning necktie, watch-chain, and eyeglass comes in with a flourish, lolls back in his seat, using his eyeglass frequently.

Seventh. Lady with infant (very large rag-baby, in cloak and sunbonnet) and nurse girl. Baby, being fussy, has to be amused, trotted, changed from one to the other. Lady takes things from her pocket to please it, dancing them up and down before its face.

Eighth. Plainly dressed, industrious woman, who knits.

Ninth. Fashionable young lady, dressed in the extreme of fashion. She minces up the aisle, looks at the others, seats herself apart from them, first brushing the seat. Shakes the dust from her garments, fans herself, takes out smelling-bottle, &c. (Shout is heard.) " All aboard ! "

Tenth. In a hurry, Lady that's been a-shopping, leading or pulling along her little boy or girl. She carries a waterproof on her arm, and has a shopping-bag and all sorts of paper parcels, besides a portfolio, a roller cart, a wooden horse on wheels, a drum, a toy-whip (and various other things). Doll's heads stick out of a paper. Lady drops a package. Dandy picks it up with polite bow. Drops another. Yankee picks it up, imitating Dandy's polite bow. Gets seated at last, arranges her

bonnet-strings, takes off the child's hat, smooths its hair,
&c.

Steam-whistle heard. Every passenger now begins
the jerking, up-and-down motion peculiar to the cars.
This motion must be kept up by all, whatever they are
doing, and by every one who enters.

Enter Conductor with an immense *badge* on his hat, or
coat. Calls out " Have your tickets ready ! " Then
passes along the aisle, and calls out again, " Tickets ! "
The tickets must be large and absurd. Passengers take
them from pocket-books, gloves, &c. Fat old woman
fumbles long for hers in different bundles, finds it at last
in a huge leather pocket-book. Conductor, after *nipping*
the tickets, passes out.

Enter boy with papers, " Mornin' papers ! Herald,
Journal, Traveller ! " (Business man buys one.)
"Mornin' papers ! Herald, Journal, Traveller ! " (Clerk
buys one.) Paper boy passes out. Conductor appears,
calls out, " Warburton ! Warburton ! Passengers for
Bantam change cars ! " (Noise heard of brakes, jerking
motion ceases, school-girls leave, with those little hopping
motions peculiar to school-girls. Yankee moves nearer
fashionable miss. Two laborers enter. Steam-whistle
heard, jerking motion resumed.) Candy boy enters.
" Jessup's candy ! All flavors ! Five cents a stick ! "
(Lady buys one for baby.) " Jessup's candy ! All flavors ! Lemon, vanilla, pineapple, strorbry ! " (Yankee buys one, offers half to fashionable miss. She de-
clines. Crunches it himself.) Boy passes out.

Enter boy with picture-papers, which he distributes.
Some examine them, others let them lie. (Dandy buys

one.) Boy collects them and passes out. Enter a very little ragged boy, with fiddle, or accordion. After playing awhile, passes round his hat. Most of the passengers drop something in it. Exit boy.

Enter Conductor. "Tickets!" Collects tickets. (Steam-whistle heard.) Passengers pick up their things. Curtain drops just as the last one goes out. (This scene might be ended by the passengers, at a given signal, pulling their seats together, pitching over, and having the curtain fall on a smash-up.)

SECOND SYLLABLE.

LADY *in morning-dress and jaunty breakfast-cap, sadly leaning her head on her hand. On table near is toast, chocolate, &c. Enter* MAGGIE *with tray.*

Maggie. Ate a bit, mum, ate a bit. 'T will cheer ye up like !

Lady (looking up). No, no, I cannot eat. O, the precious darling ! It is now seventeen hours since I saw him last. Ah, he 's lost !

Maggie. And did ye slape at arl, mum ?

Lady. Scarcely, Maggie. And in dreams I saw my darling, chased by rude boys, or at the bottom of deep waters, in filthy mud, eaten by fishes, or else mauled by dreadful cats. Take away the untasted meal. I cannot, cannot eat.

Exit MAGGIE *with breakfast things. Enter* MIKE *with newspapers.*

Mike. Mornin' paper, mum.

Lady (catching it, and looking eagerly up and down its columns). Let me see if he is found. O, here ! "Found !

A diamond pin on —" Pshaw, diamond pin! Here it
is. "Dog found! Black and tan —" Faugh, black
and tan! My beauty was pure white. But, Mike
where's the notice of our darling's being lost?

Mike. Shure, an' it's to the side o' the house I put it,
mum, arl writ in illegant sizey litters, mum.

Lady (in alarm). And did n't you go to the printers
at all?

Mike. Shure an' be n't it better out in the brard daylight, mum, laning aginst th' 'ouse convanient like, an'
aisy to see, mum?

Lady. O Mike, you've undone me! Quick! Pen,
ink, and paper. Quick! I say.

Exit MIKE.

Lady (solus). It was but yesterday I held him in these
arms! He licked my face, and took from my hand the
bits of chicken, and sipped of my chocolate. His little
black eyes looked up, O so brightly! to mine. His little
tail, it wagged so happy! O, dear, lovely one, where are
you now?

Enter MIKE, *with placard on long stick, with these words in very large
letters.*

☞ Dog Lost! V Dollus! ReeWarD! InnQuire
Withinn! Live oR DeD!!!☜

Reads it aloud, very slowly, pointing with finger.

Mike. An' it's meeself larned the fine writin', mum,
in th' ould counthry.

Lady (excited). Pray take that dreadful thing away,
and bring me pen and paper!

Exit MIKE, *muttering. Knock heard at door.*

Lady. Come !

Enter MARKET-MAN, *in blue frock.*

Market-man. Good day, ma'am. Heard you 'd lost a
dog.

Lady (eagerly, with hand extended). Yes, yes ! Where
is he ?

Market-man. Was he a curly, shaggy dog?

Lady. Yes ! O yes ! Where did you find him ?

Market-man. Was your dog bright and playful?

Lady (in an excited manner). O, very ! very !

Market-man. Answered to the name of Carlo ?

Lady. Yes ! He did ! he did ! O, if I had him in
these arms !

Market-man (in surprise). Arms, ma'am ? Arms?
'T is a Newfoundland dog ! He could carry you in his
arms !

Lady (dejected). O cruel, cruel disappointment !

Market-man. What kind of a dog was yours ?

Lady. O, a dear little lapdog. His curls were white
and soft as silk !

Market-man (going). Good day, ma'am. If I see him,
I 'll fetch him.

Exit MARKET-MAN. MIKE *enters with writing materials, and goes out
again.* LADY *begins to write, repeating the words she writes aloud.*

Lady. Lost, strayed, or stolen. A curly — (*Tap at
door.*) Come !

Enter stupid-looking BOY, *in scanty jacket and trousers, and too large
hat.*

Lady. Did you wish to see me ?

Boy (drawling). Yes, ma'am.

Lady. About a dog?

Boy. Yes, ma'am.

Lady. Have you found one?

Boy. Yes, ma'am.

Lady. Is it a very small dog?

Boy. Yes, ma'am.

Lady. Sweet and playful?

Boy. Yes, ma'am?

Lady. Did you bring him with you?

Boy. Yes, ma'am (*pointing*). Out there.

Lady (*excited*). O, bring him to me. Quick! O, if it should be he! If it should! (BOY *brings in small dog, yellow or black or spotted.*)

Lady (*in disgust*). O, not that horrid creature! Take him away! Take him away!

Boy. Is n't that your dog?

Lady. No! no! O, can't you take the horrid animal away?

Boy (*going*). Yes, ma'am.

Exit BOY with dog. LADY prepares to write.

Lady. Stupid thing! Now I 'll write. (*Repeats.*) LOST, STRAYED, OR STOLEN. A CURLY, WHITE — (*Tap at the door.*) Come! (*Lays down pen.*)

Enter ragged BOY, with covered basket.

Lady. Have *you* found a dog?

Boy. No, I hain't found no dog.

Lady. Then what do you want?

Boy. Father sells puppies. Father said if you'd lost your dog, you'd want to buy one of 'em. Said you could take your pick out o' these 'ere five. (*Opens basket for her to look in.*)

Lady (*shuddering*).   Little wretches!   Away with them!

Boy. They 'll grow, father said, high 's the table.

Lady. Carry them off, can't you?

Boy. Father wants to know what you 'll take for your dog, running.   Father said he 'd give a dollar, an' risk the ketchin' on him.

Lady. Dollar? No. Not if he were dead! Not if I knew he were drowned, and the fishes had eaten him, would I sell my darling pet for a paltry dollar!

Boy (*going*). Good mornin'. Guess I 'll be goin'. If I find your dog, I won't (*aside*) let you know.

Exit BOY, *with bow and scrape.*

Lady (*writes again, and repeats*). LOST, STRAYED, OR STOLEN.   A CUR — (*Knock at the door.*)   Come! (*Lays down pen.*)

Enter MRS. MULLIGAN.

Mrs. Mulligan. An' is it yourself lost a dog, thin?

Lady (*eagerly*). Yes.   A small, white, curly, silky dog.   Have you seen him?

Mrs. Mulligan. Och, no.   But 't was barkin' all night he was, behint th' 'ouse.   An' the b'ys, — that 's me Pat an' Tim, they *drooned* him, mum, bad luck to 'em, in the mornin' arly.

Lady. And did you see him?

Mrs. Mulligan. No, shure.

Lady. And where is he now?

Mrs. Mulligan. O, it 's safe he is, Pat tould me, to the bottom o' No Bottom Pond, mum.

Lady. And how do you know 't is my dog?

Mrs. Mulligan. Faith, an' whose dog should it be, thin?

7

Lady. Send your boys, and I 'll speak with them.

Mrs. Mulligan (going). I 'll send them, mum. Mornin' mum.

Exit MRS. MULLIGAN. *Another tap at the door.*

Lady. O, this is not to be borne ! Come !

Enter COUNTRYWOMAN *with band-box, — not an old woman.*

Lady (earnestly). If it 's about a dog, tell me all you know at once ! Is he living ?

Countrywoman. Yes 'm, but he 's quite poorly. I think dogs shows their sickness, same as human creturs do. Course they have their feelin's.

Lady. Do tell quick.

Countrywoman. Just what I want, for I 'm in a hurry myself. So I 'll jump right inter the thick on 't. You see last night when my old man was ridin' out o' town in his cart, with some o' his cabbages left over, for garden sarse had n't been very brisk all day, and he was late a comin' out on account o' the off ox bein' some lame, and my old man ain't apt to hurry his critters, for a marciful man is marciful to his beasts, you —

Lady. But about the dog !

Countrywoman. Wal, the old man was a ridin' along, slow, you know, — I alwers tell him he 'll never set the great pond afire, — and a countin' over his cabbage-heads and settlin' the keg o' molasses amongst 'em, and a little jug of — (*nods and winks and smiles*), — jest for a medicine, you know. For we *never do*, — I nor the old man, — never, 'xcept in case o' sickness.

Lady (impatiently). But what about the dog ?

Countrywoman. Wal, he was a ridin' along, and jest

got to the outskirts o' the town, when he happened to see
two boys a squabblin' which should have a dog, — a little
teenty white curly mite of a cretur —

Lady. Yes! Go on! Go on!

Countrywoman. And he asked 'em would they take
fifty cents apiece and give it up. For he knew 't would
be rewarded in the newspapers. And they took the fifty.

Lady (eagerly). And what did he do with him?
Where is he now?

Countrywoman. Why, I was goin' to ride in with the
old man this mornin' to have my bunnet new done over,
and I took the dog along. And we happened to see that
'ere notice, and he and I together, we spelt it out!
(*Opening bandbox.*) Now look in here! Snug as a bug,
right in the crown o' my bunnet. Seems poorly, but
he 'll pick up. (*Takes out a white lapdog.*)*

Lady (snatches him, and hugs and kisses him.) 'T is
my Carlo. O my precious, precious pet! Ah, he is
too weak to move. I must feed him and put him to
sleep. (*Rises to go out.*)

Countrywoman. But the five dollars, marm!

Lady. O, you must call again. I can't think of any
paltry five dollars, now. (*Exit.*)

Countrywoman (calling out). I 'll wait, marm!

Enter MIKE.

Mike. An' what bisness are ye doin' here?

Countrywoman. Waiting for my pay.

Mike. Pay, is it? Och, she 'll niver pay the day.
She 's owin' me wages, an' owin' the cook, and Mrs.

---

* A white lapdog may be easily made of wool and wire.

Flarty that scoors, and the millinery lady, an' 't is " Carl
agin," she sez. " Carl agin. Can't ye carl agin ?"

Countrywoman. Then I 'll get mine now. (*Takes off
shawl, and sits down. Takes out long blue stocking, and
goes to knitting, first pinning on her knitting-sheath.* I
don't budge, without the pay.

MIKE looks on admiringly. Curtain drops.

WHOLE WORD.

CLERK *standing behind counter, with shawls and various dry goods to
sell. Also rolls or pieces of carpet, oil and other kinds. Various
placards on the walls, — " No credit." " Goods marked down !"
&c. Enter* OLD WOMAN.

Old Woman (speaking in rather high key). Do you
keep stockings ?

Clerk (handing box of stockings). O yes. Here are
some, very good quality.

Old Woman (examining them). Mighty thin, these
be.

Clerk. I assure you, they are warranted to wear.

Old Woman. To wear out, I guess.

Enter YOUNG MARRIED COUPLE.

Clerk. Good morning. Can we sell you anything to-
day?

Wife (modestly). We wish to look at a few of your
carpets.

Clerk. This way, ma'am.

Husband. Hem ! (*Clearing his throat.*) We will
look at something for parlors.

Clerk. Here is a style very much admired. (*Unrolls
carpet.*) Elegant pattern. We import all our goods,

ma'am. That's a firm piece of goods. You could n't do better. We warrant it to wear. All fast colors.

Old Woman (*coming near*). A good rag carpet 'll wear out two o' that.

Wife (*to Husband*). I think it is a lovely pattern. Don't you like it, Charley?

Husband. Hem — well, I have seen prettier. But then, 't is just as you say, dear.

Wife. O no, Charley. 'T is just as you say. I want to please you, dear.

Old Woman (*to Clerk*). Have you got any crash towelling?

Husband. What's the price of this carpet?

Clerk. Three dollars a yard. Here's another style (*unrolls another*) just brought in. (*Attends to Old Woman.*)

Husband (*speaking to Wife*). Perhaps we'd better look at the other articles you wanted. (*They go to another part of the store, examining articles.*)

Enter a spare, thin WOMAN, *in plain dress and green veil.*

Clerk. Can we sell you anything to-day?

Woman. I was thinking of buying a carpet.

Clerk. Step this way, ma'am. (*Shows them.*) We have all styles, ma'am.

Woman. I want one that will last. (*Examining it.*)

Clerk (*taking hold of it*). Firm as iron, ma'am. We've sold five hundred pieces of that goods. If it don't wear, we 'll agree to pay back the money.

Woman. I want one that won't show dirt.

Clerk. Warranted not to show dirt, ma'am. We warrant all our goods.

Woman. Can it be turned?

Clerk. Perfectly well, ma'am. 'T will turn as long as there's a bit of it left.

Woman. What do you ask?

Clerk. Well, we have been selling that piece of goods for three fifty, but you may have it for three dollars.

Woman. Could n't you take less?

Clerk. Could n't take a cent less. Cost more by wholesale.

Woman. I think I'll look further. (*Going.*)

Clerk. Well, now seeing it's the last piece, you may have it for two fifty.

Woman. I was n't expecting to give over two dollars a yard. (*Going.*)

Clerk. Now I'll tell you what I'll do. Say two and a quarter, and take it.

Woman. I have decided not to go over two dollars. (*Going.*)

Clerk (*crossly*). Well. You can have it for that. But we lose on it. In fact, we are selling now to keep the trade, nothing else. Twenty-five yards? I'll measure it directly.

Old Woman. Have you got any cotton flannel?

Enter FASHIONABLE LADY.

Clerk (*all attention, bowing*). Good morning, madam. Can we sell you anything to-day?

Fashionable Lady. I am looking at carpets this morning. Have you anything new?

Clerk. This way, madam. We have several new lots, just imported. (*Shows one.*)

Fashionable Lady. It must light up well, or it will never suit me.

Clerk. Lights up beautifully, madam.

Fashionable Lady. Is this real tapestry?

Clerk. O, certainly, madam. We should n't thin of showing you any other.

Fashionable Lady. What's the price?

Clerk. Well, this is a Persian pattern, and we can't offer it for less than six dollars. Mrs. Topothetree bought one off the same piece.

Fashionable Lady. 'T is a lovely thing, and when a carpet suits me, the price is no objection.

Old Woman (coming forward). Have you got any remnants? I wanted to get a strip to lay down afore the fire. (*Speaking to Lady.*) Goin' to give six dollars a yard for that? Guess you better larn how to make a rag carpet. Fust, take your old coats and trousers, and strip 'em up inter narrer strips, and jine the strips together, and wind all that up in great balls. That's your warp. Then take coarse yarn and color it all colors. That's your fillin'. Then hire your carpet wove, and that carpet 'll last.

Enter POLICEMAN *and a* GENTLEMAN.

Gentleman (pointing to Fashionable Lady). That is the person.

Policeman (placing his hand on her shoulder). This gentleman, madam, thinks you have — *borrowed* a quantity of his lace goods.

Fashionable Lady (with air of astonishment). I? Impossible! Impossible, sir!

Gentleman. I am sure of it.

Policeman. Will you have the goodness, madam, to come with us?

Curtain drops, while all are gazing at each other in amazement.

I procured a copy of the above charade for little Silas. There was a sociable, one evening, at his school, got up for the purpose of raising money to buy a melodeon, or a seraphine, I don't know which. I never do know which is a melodeon and which is a seraphine. I have an idea the first sounds more melodious.

They wanted a charade to act, and I sent them this of William Henry's. Silas took the character of the fellow from the country. They liked the charade very much. The brakeman had the forward wheels of a baby carriage for his brakes. Of course only one of the wheels was seen, and he made a great ado turning it.

At the end the cars ran off the track, and the curtain fell upon a general smash-up.

William Henry to his Grandmother.

DEAR GRANDMOTHER, —

The puddles bear in the morning and next thing the pond will, and I want to have my skates here all ready. 'Most all the boys have got all theirs already, waiting for it to freeze. They hang up on that beam in the sink-room chamber. Look under my trainer trousers that I had to play trainer in when I's a little chap, on that great wooden peg, and you'll find 'em hanging up under the trousers. And my sled too, for Dorry and I are going to have double-runner together soon as snow comes. It's down cellar. We went to be weighed, and the man said I was built of solid timber. Dorry he hid some great iron dumb-bells in his pockets for fun, and the man first he looked at Dorry and then at the figures, and then at his weights; he did n't know what to make of it. For I 've grown so much faster that we 're almost of a size.

First of it Dorry kept a sober face, but pretty soon he began to laugh, and took the dumb-bells out, and then weighed over, and guess what we weighed?   >

The fellers call us "Dorry & Co.," because we keep together so much. When he goes anywhere he says "Come, Sweet William!" and when I go anywhere I say "Come, Old Dorrymas!" ' There 's a flower named Sweet William. There is n't any fish named Dorrymas, but there 's one named Gurrymas. We keep our goodies in the same box, and so we do our pencils and the rest of our traps. His bed is 'most close to mine, and the one that wakes up first pulls the other one's hair. One boy that comes here is a funny-looking chap, and wears cinnamon-colored clothes, all faded out. He is n't a very big feller. He has his clothes given to him. He comes days and goes home nights, for he lives in this town. He 's got great eyes and a great mouth, and always looks as if he was just a-going to laugh. Sometimes when the boys go by him they make a noise, sniff, sniff, sniff, with their noses, making believe they smelt something spicy, like cinnamon. I hope you 'll find my skates, and send 'em right off, for fear the pond might freeze over. They hang on that great wooden peg in the sink-room chamber, that sticks in where two beams come together, under my trainer trousers; you 'll see the red stripes.

7 *

Some of us have paid a quarter apiece to get a football, and should n't you think 't was real mean for anybody to back out, and then come to kick? One feller did. And he was one of the first ones to get it up too. "Let's get up a good one while we're about it," says he, "that won't kick right out." Dorry went to pick it out, and took his own money, and all the rest paid in their quarters, and what was over the price we. took in peanuts. O, you ought to 've seen that bag of peanuts! Held about half a bushel. When he found the boys were talking about him he told somebody that when anybody said, "Let's get up something," it was n't just the same as to say he 'd pay part. But we say 't is. And we talked about it down to the Two Betseys' shop, and Lame Betsey said 't was mean doings enough, and The Other Betsey said, "Anybody that won't pay their part, I don't care *who* they be." And I 've seen him eating taffy three times and more, too, since then, and figs. And he comes and kicks sometimes, and when they offered some of the peanuts to him, to see if he 'd take any, he took some.

Now Spicey won't do that. We said he might kick, but he don't want to, not till he gets his quarter. He 's going to earn it. If my skates don't hang up on that wooden peg, like enough Aunt Phebe's little Tommy 's been fooling with 'em. Once he did, and they fell through that hole where a piece of the floor is broke out. You 'd better look down that hole. I 'm going to send home my Report next time. I could n't get perfect every time. Dorry says if a feller did that, he 'd know too much to come to school. But there 's some that do. Not very

many. Spicey did four days running. I could 'a got
more perfects, only one time I did n't know how far to
get, and another time I did n't hear what the question
was he put out to me, and another time I did n't stop to
think and answered wrong when I knew just as well as
could be. And another time I missed in the rules. You
better believe they are hard things to get. Bubby Short
says he wishes they 'd take out the rules and let us do
our sums in peace, and so I say. And then one more
time some people came to visit the school, and they
looked right in my face, when the question came to me,
and put me out. I should n't think visitors would look a
feller right in the face, when he 's trying to tell something. Dorry says that I blushed up as red as fire-coals.
I guess a red-header blushes up redder than any other
kind; don't you? I had some taken off my Deport-
ment, because I laughed out loud. I did n't mean to,
but I 'm easy to laugh. But Dorry he can keep a sober
face just when he wants to, and so can Bubby Short. I
was laughing at Bubby Short. He was snapping apple-
seeds at Old Wonder Boy's cheeks, and he could n't tell
who snapped 'em, for Bubby Short would be studying
away, just as sober. At last one hit hard, and W. B.
jumped and shook his fist at the wrong feller, and I felt
a laugh coming, and puckered my mouth up, and twisted
round, but first thing I knew, out it came, just as sudden,
and that took off some.

I shall keep the Report till next time, because this
time I 'm going to send mine and Dorry's photographs
taken together. We both paid half. We got it taken
in a saloon that travels about on wheels. 'T is stopping

here now.   Course we did n't expect to look very handsome.   But the man says 't is wonderful what handsome
pictures homely folks expect to make.   Says he tells
'em he has to take what 's before him.   Dorry says he 's
sure we look very well for the first time taking.   Says
it needs practice to make a handsome picture.   Please
ᵴsend it back soon because he wants to let his folks see it.
Send it when you send the skates.   Send the skates soon
as you can, for fear the pond might freeze over.   Aunt
Phebe's little Tommy can have my old sharp-shooter for
his own, if he wants it.   Remember me to my sister.

Your affectionate Grandson,

WILLIAM HENRY.

As the photograph above mentioned had altogether too
serious an expression, a younger one was used in drawing the
picture for the frontispiece.   Neither of the three do him jus-
tice, as neither of the three can give his merry laugh.

Grandmother to William Henry.

MY DEAR BOY, —

Your father and all of us were very glad to see that
photograph, for it seemed next thing to seeing you, you
dear child.   We could n't bear to send it away so soon.
I kept it on the mantel-piece, with my spectacles close
by, so that when I went past it I could take a look.
We sent word in to your aunt Phebe and in a few minutes little Tommy came running across and said his
"muzzer said he must bwing Billy's Pokerdaff in, wight
off."   But I told him to tell his muzzer that Billy's Pokerdaff must be sent back very soon, and was n't going

out of my sight a minute while it stayed, and they must come in. And they did. We all think 't is a very natural picture, only too sober. You ought to try to look smiling at such times. I wish you 'd had somebody to pull down your jacket, and see to your collar's being even. But Aunt Phebe says 't is a wonder you look as well as you do, with no woman to fix you. I should know Dorry's picture anywhere. Uncle Jacob wants to know what you were both so cross about? Says you look as if you 'd go to fighting the minute you got up.

Little Tommy is tickled enough with that sled, and keeps looking up in the sky to see when snow is coming down, and drags it about on the bare ground, if we don't watch him.

I had almost a good mind to keep the skates at home. Boys are so venturesome. They always think there 's no danger. I said to your father, "Now if anything should happen to Billy I should wish we 'd never sent them." But he 's always afraid I shall make a Miss Nancy of you. Now I don't want to do that. But there 's reason in all things. And a boy need n't drown himself to keep from being a Miss Nancy. He thinks you 've got sense enough not to skate on thin ice, and says the teachers won't allow you to skate if the pond is n't safe. But I don't have faith in any-pond being safe. My dear boy, there 's danger even if the thermometer is below zero. There may be spring-holes. Never was a boy got drowned yet skating, but what thought there was no danger. Do be careful. I know you would if you only knew how I keep awake nights worrying about you.

Anybody would think that your uncle Jacob had more money than he knew how to spend. He went to the city last week, and brought Georgiana home a pair of light blue French kid boots. He won't tell the price. They are high-heeled, very narrow-soled, and come up high. He saw them in the window of one of the grand stores, and thought he 'd just step in and buy them for Georgie. Never thought of their coming so high. I 'm speaking of the price. Now Georgie does n't go to parties, and where the child can wear them, going through thick and thin, is a puzzler. She might to meeting, if she could be lifted out of the wagon and set down in the broad aisle, but Lucy Maria says that won't do, because her meeting dress is cherry-color. Next summer I shall get her a light blue barege dress to match 'em, for the sake of pleasing her uncle Jacob. When he heard us talking about her not going anywhere to wear such fancy boots, he said then she should wear them over to his house. So twice he has sent a billet in the morning, inviting her to come and take tea, and at the bottom he writes, ☞ " Company expected to appear in blue boots." ☜ So I dress her up in her red dress, and the boots, and draw my plush moccasins over them, and pack her off. Uncle Jacob takes her things, and waits upon her to the table, and they have great fun out of it.

My dear Billy, I have been thinking about that boy that wears cinnamon-colored clothes. I do really hope you won't be so cruel as to laugh at a boy on account of his clothes. What a boy is, don't depend upon what he wears on his back, but upon what he has inside of his head and his heart. When I was a little girl and went to school in the old school-house, the Committee used to come, sometimes, to visit the school. One of the Committee was the minister. He was a very fine old gentleman, and a great deal thought of by the whole town. He used to wear a ruffled shirt, and a watch with a bunch of seals, and carry a gold-headed cane. He had white hair, and a mild blue eye, and a pleasant smile, that I have n't forgotten yet, though 't was a great many years ago. After we 'd read and spelt, and the writing-books and ciphering-books had been passed round, the teacher always asked him to address the school. And there was one thing he used to say, almost every time. And he said it in such a smiling, pleasant way, that I 've remembered it ever since. He used to begin in this way.

"I love little children. I love to come where they are. I love to hear them laugh, and shout. I love to watch them while they are at play. And because I love them so well, I don't want there should be anything bad about them. Just as when I watch a rosebud blooming; — I should be very sorry not to have it bloom out into a beautiful, perfect rose. And now, children, there are three words I want you all to remember. Only three. You can remember three words, can't you?"

"Yes, sir," we would say.

"Well, now, how long can you remember them?" he would ask, — "a week?"

"Yes, sir."

"Two weeks?"

"Yes, sir."

"A month?"

" Yes, sir."

" A year ? "

" Guess so."

" All your lives ? "

Then some would say, " Yes, sir," and some would say they guessed not, and some did n't believe they could, and some knew they could n't.

" Well, children," he would say at last, " now I will tell you what the three words are : Treat — everybody — well. Now what I want you to be surest to remember is ' everybody.' Everybody is a word that takes in a great many people, and a great many kinds of people, — takes in the washer-women and the old man that saws wood, and the colored folks that come round selling baskets, and the people that wear second-hand clothes, and the help in the kitchen, — takes in those we don't like and even the ones that have done us harm. ' Treat — everybody — well.' For you can afford to. A pleasant word don't cost anything to give, and is a very pleasant thing to take."

The old gentleman used to look so smiling while he talked. And he followed out his own rule. For he was just as polite to the poor woman that came to clean their paint as he was to any fine lady. He wanted to make us feel ashamed of being impolite to people who could n't wear good clothes. Children and grown people too, he said, were apt to treat the ones best that wore the best clothes. He 'd seen children, and grown folks too, who would be all smiles and politeness to the company, and then be ugly and snappish to poor people they 'd hired to work for them. A real lady or gentleman, — he used to end off with this, — "A real lady, and a real gentleman will — treat — everybody — well." And I will end off with this too. And don't you ever forget it. For that you may be, my dear boy, a true gentleman is the wish of

Your loving Grandmother.

P. S. Do be careful when you go a skating. If the ice is ever so thick, there may be spring-holes. Your father wants you to have a copy of that picture taken for us to keep, and sends this money to pay for it. I forgot to say that of course it is mean for a boy not to pay his part. And for a boy not to pay his debts is mean, and next kin to stealing. And the smaller the debts are the meaner it is. We are all waiting for your Report.

I did not think it at all strange that Uncle Jacob should buy the blue boots. It is just what I would like to do myself. I never go past one of those wonderful shoe-store windows, and look at the bright array of blue, yellow, and red, without wishing I had six little girls, with six little pairs of feet. For then I should have half a dozen excuses to go in and buy, and now I have n't one.

Georgie's boots looked pretty, with the nice white stockings her grandmother knit. And I could n't see any harm in her wearing a red dress with them. The red, white, and blue are the best colors in the world for me, and I 'll never turn against them !

"Three cheers for the Red, White, and Blue !"

William Henry to his Grandmother.

MY DEAR GRANDMOTHER, —

Excuse me for not writing before. Here is my Report. I have n't sniffed my nose up any at Spicey. I 'll

tell you why. Because I remember when I first came, and
had a red head, and how bad 't was to be plagued all the
time. But I tell you if he is n't a queer-looking chap!
Don't talk any, hardly, but he's great for laughing.
Bubby Short says his mouth laughs itself. But not out
loud. Dorry says 't is a very wide smile. It comes easy
to him, any way. He comes in laughing and goes out
laughing. When you meet him he laughs, and when you
speak to him he laughs. When he don't know the answer he laughs, and when he says right he laughs, and
when you give him anything he laughs, and when he
gives you anything he laughs. Though he don't have
very much to give. But he can't say no. All the boys
tried one day to see if they could make him say no. He
had an apple, and they went up to him, one at once, and
said, " Give me a taste." " Give me a taste," till 't was
every bit tasted away. Then they tried him on slate-
pencils, — his had bully points to them, — and he gave
every one away, all but one old stump. But afterwards
Mr. Augustus said 't was a shame, and the boys carried
him back the pencils and said they'd done with 'em.
Dorry says he's going to ask him for his nose some day,
and then see what he'll do. I know. Laugh. You
better believe he's a clever chap. And he won't kick.
Dorry likes him for that. Not till he's paid his quarter.
Mr. Augustus offered him the quarter, but he said, No,
I thank you. "Why not?" Mr. Augustus asked him.
He said he guessed he'd rather earn it. We expect the
teacher heard about it, and guess he heard about that feller that would n't pay his part, and about his borrowing
and not paying back, for one day he addressed the school

about money, and he said no boy of spirit, or man either,
would ever take money as a gift, long as he was able to
earn.   Course he did n't mean what your fathers give .
you, and Happy New Year's Day, and all that.   And to
borrow and not pay was mean as dirt, besides being
wicked.   He 'd heard of people borrowing little at a time
and making believe forget to pay, because they knew
't would n't be asked for.   The feller I told you about —
the one that kicks and don't pay — he owes Gapper Sky
Blue for four seed-cakes.   Mr. Augustus says that what
makes it mean is, that he knows Gapper won't ask for
two cents !   Gapper let him have 'em for two cents, because he 'd had 'em a good while and the edges of 'em were
some crumbly.   And he borrowed six cents from Dorry
and knows Dorry won't say anything ever, and so he 's
trying to keep from paying.   I guess his left ear burns
sometimes !

. Gapper can't go round now, selling cakes, because
he 's lame, and has to go with two canes.   But he keeps
a pig, and he and little Rosy make tiptop molasses candy
to sell in sticks, one-centers and two-centers, and sell 'em
to the boys when they go up there to coast.   I tell you
if 't is n't bully coasting on that hill back of his house!
We begin way up to the tip-top and go way down and
then across a pond that is n't there only winters and then
into a lane, a sort of downish lane, that goes ever so far.
Bubby Short 'most got run over by a sleigh.   He was
going " knee-hacket " and did n't see where he was going
to, and went like lightning right between the horses'
legs, and did n't hurt him a bit.

Last night when the moon shone the teachers let us

go out, and they went too, and some of their wives and some girls. O, if we did n't have the fun! We had a great horse-sled, and we 'd drag it way up to the top, and then pile in. Teachers and boys and women and girls, all together, and away we 'd go. Once it 'most tipped over. O, I never did see anything scream so loud as girls can when they 're scared? I wish 't would be winter longer than it is. We have a Debating Society. And the question we had last was, "Which is the best, Summer or Winter?" And we got so fast for talking, and kept interrupting so, the teacher told the Summers to go on one side and the Winters on the other, and then take turns firing at each other, one shot at a time. And Dorry was chosen Reporter to take notes, but I don't know as you can read them, he was in such a hurry.

"In summer you can fly kites.

"In winter you can skate.

"In summer you have longer time to play.

"In winter you have best fun coasting evenings.

"In summer you can drive hoop and sail boats.

"In winter you can snow-ball it and have darings.

"In summer you can go in swimming, and play ball.

"In winter you can coast and make snow-forts.

"In summer you can go a fishing.

"So you can in winter, with pickerel traps to catch pickerel and perch on the ponds, and on rivers. When the fish come up you can make a hole in the ice and set a light to draw 'em, and then take a jobber and job 'em as fast as you 're a mind to.

"In summer you can go take a sail.

"In winter you can go take a sleigh-ride.

"In summer you don't freeze to death.

"In winter you don't get sunstruck.

"In summer you see green trees and flowers and hear the birds sing.

"In winter the snow falling looks pretty as green leaves, and so do the icicles on the branches, when the sun shines, and we can hear the sleigh-bells jingle.

"In summer you have green peas and fruit, and huckleberries and other berries.

"In winter you have molasses candy and pop-corn and mince-pies and preserves and a good many more roast turkeys, (another boy interrupting) and all kinds of everything put up air-tight!

(Teacher.) Order, order, gentlemen. One shot at a time.

"In summer you have Independent Day, and that's the best day there is. For if it had n't been for that, we should have to mind Queen Victoria.

"In winter you have Thanksgiving Day and Fore-father's Day and Christmas and Happy New-Year Day and the Twenty-second of February, and that's Washington's Birthday. And if it had n't been for that we should have to mind Queen Victoria."

When the time was up the teacher told all that had changed their minds to change their sides, and some of the Summers came over to ours, but the Winters all stayed. Then the teacher made some remarks, and said how glad we ought to be that there were different kinds of fun and beautiful things all the year round. Bubby Short says he's sure he's glad, for if a feller could n't have fun what would he do? After we got out doors the summer ones that did n't go over hollered out to the other ones that did, "Ho! ho! Winter killed! Winter killed! 'Fore I 'd be Winter killed! Frost bit! Frost bit! 'Fore I 'd be Frost bit!"

I should like to see my sister's blue boots. I am very careful when I go a skating. There is n't any spring-hole in our pond. I don't know where my handker-chiefs go to.

Your affectionate Grandson,
WILLIAM HENRY.

P. S. Don't keep awake. I 'll look out. Bubby Short's folks write just so to him. And Dorry's. I wonder what makes everybody think boys want to be drowned?

The boys must have been much interested in that "Debating Society." When William Henry was at home he frequently started a question, and called upon all to take sides.

Georgiana to William Henry.

MY DEAR BROTHER, —

Yesterday I went to Aunt Phebe's to eat supper, and had on my light blue boots Uncle Jacob brought me when he went away. He dragged me over because 't was snowing, for he said the party could n't be put off because they had got all ready. But the party was n't anybody but me, but he 's all the time funning. Aunt Phebe's little Tommy he had some new rubber boots, but they did n't get there till after supper, and then 't was 'most his bedtime. But he got into the boots and walked all round with them after his nightgown was on, and the nightgown hung down all over the rubber boots. And when they wanted to put him in his crib he did n't want to take them off, so Uncle Jacob said better let the boots stay on till he got asleep, and then pull 'em off softly as she could. Then they put him in the crib and let the boots stick out one side, without any bed-clothes being put over them. But we guessed he dreamed about his boots, because soon as they pulled 'em a little bit, he reached down to the boots and held on. But when he got sound asleep then she pulled 'em off softly and stood 'em up in the corner. I carried my work with me, and 't was the handkerchief that is going to be put in this letter. Aunt Phebe thinks some of the stitches are quite nice. She says you must excuse that one in the corner, not where your name is, but next one to it. The snow-storm was so bad I stayed all night, and they made some corn-balls, and Uncle Jacob passed them round to me first, because I was the party, in the best waiter.

And we had a good time seeing some little pigs that the old pig stepped on, — six little pigs, about as big as puppies, that had little tails, and she would n't take a mite of care of them. She won't let them get close up to her to keep warm, and keeps a stepping on 'em all the time, and broke one's leg. She 's a horrid old pig, and Uncle Jacob was afraid they might freeze to death in the night, and Aunt Phebe found a basket, a quite large basket, and put some cotton-wool in it. Then put in the pigs. When 't was bedtime some bricks were put on the stove, and then he put the basket with the little pigs in it on top of the bricks, but put ashes on the fire first, so they could keep warm all night. And in the night they kept him awake, making little squealy noises, and he thought the fire would get hot and roast them, and once one climbed up over and tumbled down on to the floor and 'most killed himself so he died afterwards. And he says he feels very sleepy to-day, watching with the little pigs all night. For soon as 't was daylight, and before too, Tommy jumped out and cried to have his rubber boots took into bed with him, and then the roosters crowed so loud in the hen-house close to his bedroom window that he could n't take a nap. He told me to send to you in my letter a question to talk about where you did about summer and winter. Why do roosters crow in the morning?

Two of the little pigs were dead in the morning, beside that one that killed itself dropping down, and now two more are dead. She is keeping this last one in a warm place, for they don't dare to let it go into the pig-sty, for fear she would step on it or eat it up, for he says she 's worse than a cannibal. But I don't know what that is. He says they kill men and eat them alive, but I guess he 's funning. She dips a sponge in milk and lets that last little pig suck that sponge.

Grandmother wants to know if little Rosy has got any good warm mittens. Wants to know if Mr. Sky Blue has. And you must count your handkerchiefs every week, she says. Little Tommy went out with his rubber boots, and waded way into such a deep snow-bank he could n't get himself out, and when they lifted him up they lifted him right out of his rubber boots. Then he cried. Tommy's cut off a piece of his own hair.

Your affectionate sister,
GEORGIANA.

William Henry to his Sister.

My dear Sister, —

You can tell Grandmother that Lame Betsey knit a pair for Gapper Sky Blue, blue ones with white spots, and little Rosy has got an old pair. You are a very good little girl to hem handkerchiefs. I think you hemmed that one very well. It came last night, and we looked for that long stitch to excuse it, and Dorry said it ought to be, for he guessed that was the stitch that saved nine. When the letter came, Dorry and Bubby Short and Old Wonder Boy and I were sitting together, studying. When I read about the pigs I, tell you if they did n't laugh! And when that little piggy dropped out of the basket Bubby Short dropped down on the floor and laughed so loud we had to stop him. Dorry said, "Let's play have a Debating Society, and take Uncle Jacob's question." And we did. First Old Wonder Boy stood up. And he said they crowed in the morning to tell people 't was time to get up and to let everybody know they themselves were up and stirring about. Said he 'd lain awake mornings, down in Jersey, and listened and heard 'em say just as plain as day. "I 'm up and you ought to, too! And you ought to, too!"

Then Bubby Short stood up and said he thought they were telling the other ones to keep in their own yards, and not be flying over where they did n't belong. Said he 'd lain awake in the morning and heard 'em say, just as plain as day, "If you do, I 'll give it to you! I 'll give it to you oo oo oo!"

But a little chap that had come to hear what was going

8

on said 't was more likely they were daring each other to come on and fight. For he 'd lain awake in the morning and listened and heard 'em say, " Come on if you dare, for I can whip you oo oo!"

Then 't was my turn, and I stood up and said I guessed the best crower kept a crowing school, and was showing all the young ones how to scale up and down, same as the singing-master did. For I 'd lain awake in the morning and heard first the old one crow, and then the little ones try to. And heard the old one say, just as plain as day, "Open your mouth wide and do as I do! Do as I do!" and then the young ones say, " Can't quite do so! Can't quite do so!"

Dorry said he never was wide awake enough in the morning to hear what anybody said, but he 'd always understood they were talking about the weather, and giving the hens their orders for the day, telling which to lay and which to set, and where the good places were to steal nests, and where there 'd been anything planted they could scratch up again, and how to bring up their chickens, and to look out and not hatch ducks' eggs.

The teacher opened the door then to see if we were all studying our lessons, so the Debating Society stopped.

Should you like to hear about our going to take a great big sleigh-ride? The whole school went together in great big sleighs with four horses. We had flags flying, and I tell you if 't was n't a bully go! We went ten miles. We went by a good many schoolhouses, where the boys were out, and they 'd up and hurrah, and then we 'd hurrah back again. And one lot of fellers, if they did n't let the snowballs fly at us! And we wanted our

driver to stop, and let us give it to 'em good. But he
would n't do it.   One little chap hung his sled on behind

and could n't get it unhitched again, for some of our fellers kept hold, and we carried him off more than a mile.
Then he began to cry.   Then the teacher heard him, and
had the sleigh stopped, and took him in and he went all
the way with us.   He lost his mittens trying to unhitch
it, and his hands ached, but he made believe laugh, and
we put him down in the bottom to warm 'em in the
hay.   We 'most ran over an old beggar-woman, in one
place between two drifts, where there was n't very much
room to turn out.   I guess she was deaf.   We all stood
up and shouted and bawled at her and the driver held 'em
in tight.   And just as their noses almost touched her she
looked round, and then she was so scared she did n't know
what to do, but just stood still to let herself be run over.
But the driver hollered and made signs for her to stand
close up to the drift, and then there 'd be room enough.

When I got home I found my bundle and the tin box
rolled up in that new jacket, with all that good jelly in
it.   Old Wonder Boy peeped in and says he, " O, there 's
quite some jelly in there, is n't there ? "   He says down

in Jersey they make nice quince-jelly out of apple-parings, and said 't was true, for he 'd eaten some.   Dorry
said he knew that was common in Ireland, but never
knew 't was done in this country.   Dorry says you must
keep us posted about the last of the piggies.   Keep
your pretty blue boots nice for Brother Billy to see,
won't you?   Thank you for hemming that pretty handkerchief.   I 've counted my handkerchiefs a good many
times, but counting 'em don't make any difference.

From your affectionate Brother,
WILLIAM HENRY.

The course of true love it seems did not always run smooth
with Dorry and William Henry.

William Henry to his Grandmother.

MY DEAR GRANDMOTHER, —

This is only a short letter that I am going to write to
you, because I don't feel like writing any.   But when I
don't write then you think I have the measles, else
drowned in the pond, and I 'll write a little, but I feel so
sober I don't feel like writing very much.   I suppose
you will say, — what are you feeling so sober about?
Well, seems if I did n't have any fun now, for Dorry and
I we 've got mad at each other.   And he don't hardly
speak to me, and I don't to him either; and if he don't
want to he need n't, for I don't mean to be fooling round
im, and trying to get him to, if he don't want to.

Last night we all went out to coast, and the teachers
and a good many ladies and girls, and we were going to
see which was the champion sled.   But something else

happened first. The top of the hill was all bare, and
before they all got there some of the fellers were scuf-
fling together for fun, and Dorry and I we tried to take
each other down. First of it 't was all in fun, but then
it got more in earnest, and he hit me in the face so hard
it made me mad, and I hit him and he got mad too.

Then we began to coast, for the people had all got
there. Dorry's and mine were the two swiftest ones,
and we kept near each other, but his slewed round some,
and he said I hit it with my foot he guessed, and then
we had some words, and I don't know what we did both
say; but now we keep away from each other, and it
seems so funny I don't know what to do. The teacher
asked me to go over to the stable to-day, for he lost a
bunch of compositions and thought they might have
dropped out of his pocket, when we went to take that
sleigh-ride. And I was just going to say, " Come on,
Old Dorrymas ! " before I thought.

But 't is the funniest in the morning. This morning
I waked up early, and he was fast asleep, and I thought,
Now you 'll catch it, old fellow, and was just a going to
pull his hair ; but in a minute I remembered. Then I
dressed myself and thought I would take a walk out. I
went just as softly by his bed and stood still there a
minute and set out to give a little pull, for I don't feel

half so mad as I did the first of it, but was afraid he did. So I went out-doors and looked round. Went as far as the Two Betseys' Shop and was going by, but The Other Betsey stood at the door shaking a mat, and called to me, " Billy, where are you going to ? "

" Only looking round," I said. She told me to come in and warm me, and I thought I would go in just a minute or two. Lame Betsey was frying flapjacks in a spider, a little mite of a spider, for breakfast. She spread butter on one and made me take it to eat in a saucer, and I never tasted of a better flapjack. There was a cinnamon colored jacket hanging on the chair-back, and I said, " Why, that's Spicey's jacket ! " " Who ? " they cried out both together. Then I called him by his right name, Jim Mills. He's some relation to them, and his mother is n't well enough to mend all his clothes, so Lame Betsey does it for nothing. He earns money to pay for his schooling, and he wants to go to college, and they don't doubt he will. They said he was the best boy that ever was. His mother does n't have anybody but him to do things for her, only his little sister about the size of my little sister. He makes the fires and cuts wood and splits kindling, and looks into the buttery to see when the things are empty, and never waits to be told. When they talked about him they both talked together, and Lame Betsey let one spiderful burn forgetting to turn 'em over time enough.

When I was coming away they said, " Where's Dorry ? I thought you two always kept together." For we did always go to buy things together. Then I told her a little, but not all about it.

"O, make up! make up!" they said. "Make up and be friends again!" I'm willing to make up if he is. But I don't mean to be the first one to make up.

From your affectionate Grandson,

WILLIAM HENRY.

William Henry to his Grandmother.

MY DEAR GRANDMOTHER,—

I guess you'll think 't is funny, getting another letter again from me so soon, but I'm in a hurry to have my father send me some money to have my skates mended; ask him if he won't please to send me thirty-three cents, and we two have made up again and I thought you would like to know. It had been 'most three days, and we had n't been anywhere together, or spoken hardly, and I had n't looked him in the eye, or he me. Old Wonder Boy he wanted to keep round me all the time, and have double-runner together. He knew we two had n't been such chums as we used to be, so he came up to me and said, " Billy, I think that Dorry's a mean sort of a chap, don't you?"

" No, I don't," I said. " He don't know what 't is to be mean!" For I was n't going to have him coming any Jersey over me!

" O, you need n't be so spunky about it!" says he.

" I ain't spunky!" says I.

Then I went into the school-room, to study over my Latin Grammar before school began, and sat down amongst the boys that were all crowding round the stove And I was studying away, and did n't mind 'em fooling round me, for I'd lost one mark day before, and did n't mean to lose any more, for you know what my father promised me, if my next Report improved much. And while I was sitting there, studying away, and drying my feet, for we'd been having darings, and W. B. he stumped me to jump on a place where 't was cracking, and I went in over tops of boots and wet my feet sopping wet. And I did n't notice at first, for I was n't looking round much, but looking straight down on my Latin Grammar, and did n't notice that 'most all the boys had gone out. Only about half a dozen left, and one of 'em was Dorry, and he sat to the right of me, about a yard off, studying his lesson. Then another boy went out, and then another, and by and by every one of them was gone, and left us two sitting there. O, we sat just as still! I kept my head down, and we made believe think of nothing but just the lesson. First thing I knew he moved, and I looked up, and there was Dorry looking me right in the eye! And held out his hand — "How are you, Sweet William?" says he, and laughed some. Then I clapped my hand on his shoulder, "Old Dorrymas, how are you?" says I. And so you see we got over it then, right away.

Dorry says he was n't asleep that morning, when I stood there, only making believe. Said he wished I'd pull, then he was going to pull too, and would n't that been a funny way to make up, pulling hair? He's had a letter from Tom Cush and he's got home, but is going away again, for he means to be a regular sailor and get to be captain of a great ship. He's coming here next week. I hope you won't forget that thirty-three. I'd just as lives have fifty, and that would come better in the letter, don't you believe it would?   That photograph saloon has just gone by, and the boys are running down to the road to chase it.   When Dorry and I sat there by the stove, it made me remember what Uncle Jacob said about our picture.

Your affectionate Grandson,
WILLIAM HENRY.

William Henry to his Grandmother.

MY DEAR GRANDMOTHER, —

The reason that I've kept so long without writing is because I've had to do so many things.   We've been speaking dialogues and coasting and daring and snowballing, and then we've had to review and review and review, because 't is the last of the term, and he says he believes in reviews more than the first time we get it.   I tell you, the ones that did n't get them the first time are bad off now.   I wish now I'd begun at the first of it and got every one of mine perfect, then I should have easier times.   The coast is wearing off some, and we carry water up and pour on it, and let it freeze, and throw snow on.   Now 't is moonshiny nights, the teacher lets all the "perfects" go out to coast an hour.   Sometimes I get out.   And guess where Bubby Short and Dorry and I are going to-night!   Now you can't guess, I know you can't.   To a party!   Now where do you suppose the party is to be?   You can't guess that either.   In this town.   And not very far from this school-house. Somebody you've heard of.   Two somebodies you've heard of.   Now don't you know?   The Two Betseys! Suppose you'll think 't is funny for them to have a

8 *

L

party. But they're not a going to have it themselves. Now I'll tell you, and not make you guess any more.

You know I told you Tom Cush was coming. He came to-day. He's grown just as tall and as fat and as black and has some small whiskers. I did n't know 't was Tom Cush when I first looked at him. Bubby Short asked me what man that was talking with Dorry, and I said I did n't know, but afterwards we found out. He did n't know me either. Says I'm a staving great fellow. He gave Dorry a ruler made of twelve different kinds of wood, some light, some dark, brought from famous places. And gave Bubby Short and me a four-blader, white handled. He's got a fur cap and fur gloves, and is 'most as tall as Uncle Jacob. He told Dorry that he thought if he did n't come back here and see everybody, he should feel like a sneak all the rest of his life.

We three went down to The Two Betseys' Shop with him, and when he saw it, he said, " Why, is that the same old shop? It don't look much bigger than a hen-house ! " Says he could put about a thousand like it into one big church he saw away. Said he should n't dare to climb up into the apple-tree for fear he should break it down. Said he'd seen trees high as a liberty-pole. And when he saw where he used to creep through the rails he could n't believe he ever did go through such a little place, and tried to, but could n't do it. So he took a run and jumped over, and we after him, all but Bubby Short. We took down the top one for him.

The Two Betseys did n't know him at first, not till we told them. Dorry said, " Here's a little boy wants to buy

a stick of candy." Then Tom said he guessed he 'd take
the whole bottle full. And he took out a silver half a

dollar, and threw it down, but would n't take any change
back, and then treated us all, and a lot of little chaps that
stood there staring. Lame Betsey said, "Wal, I never!"
and The Other Betsey said, "Now did you ever? Now
who 'd believe 't was the same boy!" And Tom said he
hoped 't was n't exactly, for he did n't think much of that
Tom Cush that used to be round here. Coming back he
told us he was going to stay till in the evening, and have
a supper at the Two Betseys', us four together, but not
let them know till we got there. He 's going to carry
the things. We went to see Gapper Sky Blue, and Tom
bought every bit of his molasses candy, and about all the
seed-cakes. When I write another letter, then you 'll
know about the party.

Your affectionate Grandson,

WILLIAM HENRY.

P. S. Do you think my father would let me go to sea?

William Henry to his Grandmother.

MY DEAR GRANDMOTHER, —

We had it and they did n't know anything about it till we got there, and then they did n't know what we came for. Guess who was there besides us four! Gapper Sky Blue and little Rosy. Tom invited them. We left the bundles inside and walked in. Not to the shop, but to the room back, where they stay. They told us, " Do sit up to the fire, for 't is a proper cold day." They 'd got their tea a warming in a little round tea-pot, a black one, and their dishes on a little round table, pulled up close to Lame Betsey; seemed just like my sister, when she has company, playing supper. The Other Betsey, she was holding a skein of yarn for Lame Betsey to wind, and said their yarn-winders were come apart. Dorry said, " Billy, let 's you and I make some yarn-winders! " Now what do you think we made them out of? Out of ourselves! We stood back to back, with our elbows touching our sides, and our arms sticking out, and our thumbs sticking up. Then Dorry told her to put on her yarn, and we turned ourselves round, like yarn-winders.

Pretty soon Gapper Sky Blue and Rosy came. Then we brought in the bundles and let 'em know what was up, and they did n't know what to say. All they could say was, " Wal, I never! " and " Now did you ever? "

The Other Betsey said if they were having a party they must smart themselves up some. So she got out their other caps, with white ruffles, and put on her handkerchief with a bunch of flowers in the back corner, but put a black silk cape on Lame Betsey that had a muslin ruffle round it, or lace, or I don't know what, and a clean collar, that she worked herself, when she was a young lady, and a bow of ribbon, that she used to wear to parties, wide ribbon, striped, green and yellow, or pink, I can't tell, and both of 'em clean aprons, figured aprons, — calico, I think like enough, — with the creases all in 'em, and strings tied in front. I tell you if the Two Betseys did n't look tiptop! Then they unset that little round table, and we dragged out the great big one, that had n't been used for seventeen years. The Other Betsey's grandfather had it, when he was first married. When 't is n't a table, 't is tipped up to make into a chair, and had more legs than a spider. Little Rosy helped set the table. She never went to a party before.

O, but you ought to 've seen the plates! You know your pie-plates? Well, these were just like them. All white, with scalloped edges, blue scalloped edges. Only no bigger round than the top of your tin dipper. The knives and forks — two-prongers — had green handles. And the sugar-bowl and cream-pitcher were dark blue. Tom brought a good deal of sugar, all in white lumps, and a can of milk. He bought pies and jumbles and turnovers and ginger-snaps and egg-crackers and cake and bread at the bake-house, and butter and cheese and Bologna sausage — I can't bear Bologna sausage — and some oranges, that he brought home from sea. And the sweetest jelly you ever saw! Don't know what 't is made of, but they call it guava jelly, and comes in little boxes. I believe I could eat twenty boxes of that kind of jelly, if I could get it. Dorry says he don't doubt they make it out of apple-parings down in Jersey.

The Other Betsey stood up in a chair and took down her best china cups and saucers, that used to be her grandmother's, and had n't been took down for a good many years, and wiped the dust off. Little mites of things, with pictures on them. We boys did n't drink tea, only Tom Cush; we had milk in mugs. Mine was a tall, slim one, not much bigger round than an inkstand, and had pine-trees on it, blue pine-trees. Dorry had a china one that was about as clear as glass, that Lame Betsey's brother brought home when he went captain, and Bubby Short's had " A gift of affection " on it. That was one her little niece used to drink out of that died afterwards, when she was very little.

I tell you if that supper-table did n't look like a sup- per-table when 't was all ready! They set Lame Betsey at the head of the table, because she could n't get up, and Dorry said the one at the head must never get up, for it was n't polite. We took her right up in her chair to set her there. Then there was some fun quarrelling which should sit at her right hand, because that is a seat of honor. Tom said Gapper ought to, for he was the oldest. But he said it ought to be Tom, because he was the most like company. But at last she said 't would n't make any difference, because she was left-handed. The Other Betsey brought some twisted doughnuts out.

Now I 'll tell you how we sat.

Lame Betsey at the head, and the Other Betsey at the other end; Gapper Sky Blue and Rosy and Bubby Short on the right side, and Tom and Dorry and I on the left. And if we did n't have a bully time! The Two Betseys and Gapper used to know each other, and to go to school together, and they told such funny stories, made us die a laughing, and when I get home you 'll hear some.   Then Gapper told Tom Cush that now he was a sailor he ought to spin us a yarn. When I come home I 'll tell you the yarn Tom spun.   'T was all about an alligator he saw, and about going near it in a boat, and what the Arabs did, and what he did, and what the alligator did.   Wait till I come, then you 'll hear about it.   Both Betseys kept putting down their knife and fork, and looking up at him, just as scared, and kept saying, " Wal, I never ! " " Now did you ever ! "

Tom acted it all out.   First he cleared a place for a river.   Then he took a twisted doughnut for the alligator and a ginger-snap for a boat. I 'll tell you about it sometime.   Guess 't was n't all true, for you can put anything you 've a mind to in a yarn.   He told us about the beautiful birds, and when I told him about one my sister used to have, he said he 'd bring her home a Java sparrow.

Then he told us about drinking " Hopshe ! "   I 'll tell how, and I want all of you to try it.

Now suppose Hannah Jane was the one to try it.

First, she takes a tumbler of water in her hand, then you all say together, Hannah Jane and all, quite fast, —

> " A blackbird sat on a swinging limb.
> He looked at me and I at him.
> Once so merrily, — Hopshe !
> Twice so merrily, — Hopshe !
> Thrice so merrily, — Hopshe ! "

Now I shall tell where the fun comes in.

While all the rest say, " Once so merrily," Hannah Jane must drink one swallow quick enough to say the

"Hopshe!" with them. Then another swallow while they say, "Twice so merrily," and another while they say, "Thrice so merrily," and be ready to say the "Hopshe" with them, every time. We tried it, and I tell you if the "Hopshe's" did n't come in all sorts of funny ways! The Two Betseys told about some funny tricks they used to try, to see who was going to be their beau.

From your affectionate Grandson,

WILLIAM HENRY.

P. S. I saw a dollar bill in Gapper Sky Blue's hand after Tom Cush bade him good by. Dorry says how do I know but 't was more than a dollar bill, and I don't.

W. H.

There was a good deal left for the Two Betseys to eat afterwards. I had a letter from Mr. Fry.

William Henry to Aunt Phebe.

DEAR AUNT, —

There is going to be a dancing-school, and Dorry's mother wants him to go, and he says he guesses he shall, so he may know what to do when he goes to parties, and his cousin Arthur, that does n't go to this school, says 't is bully when you 've learned how. Please ask my grandmother if I may go if I want to. Dorry wants me to if he does, he says, and Bubby Short says he means to too, if we two do, if his mother 'll let him. Dorry's mother says we shall get very good manners there, and learn how to walk into a room. I know how now to walk into a room, I told him, walk right in. But he says his mother means to *enter* a room, and there 's more to it than walking right in. He don't mean an empty room, but company and all that. I guess I should be scared to go, the first of it; I guess I should be bashful, but Dorry's cousin says you get over that when you 're used to it. Good many fellers are going. Mr. Augustus, and Old Wonder Boy, and Mr. O'Shirk. Now I suppose you can't think who that is! Don't you know that one I wrote about, that kicked and did n't pay, and that would n't help water the course? The great boys picked out that name for him, Mr. O'Shirk. The O stands for owe, and Shirk stands for itself. I send home a map to my grandmother, I 've just been making, and I tried hard as I could to do it right, and I hope she will excuse mistakes, for I never made one before. 'T is the United States. Old Wonder Boy says he should thought I 'd stretched out " Yankee Land " a little bigger. He calls the New England States "Yankee Land." And he says they make a mighty poor show on the map. But Mr. Augustus told him the brains of the whole country were kept in a little place up top, same as in folks. So W. B. kept still till next time. Dorry said he 'd heard of folks going out of the world into Jersey. If I go to dancing-school, I should like to have a bosom shirt, and quite a stylish bow. I think I 'm big enough, don't you, for bosom shirts? I had perfect this forenoon in all. I 've lost that pair of spotted mittens, and I don't know where, I 'm sure. I know I put them in my pocket. My hands get just as numb now with cold! Seems as if things in my pockets got alive and jumped out. I was clapping 'em and blowing 'em this morning, and that good, tiptop Wedding Cake teacher told me to

come in his house, and his wife found some old gloves of
his.   I never saw a better lady than she is.   When she
meets us she smiles and says, " How do you do, William
Henry ?" or Dorry, or whatever boy it is.   And when
W. B. was sick one day she took care of him.   And
she asks us to call and see her, and says she likes boys !
Dorry says he's willing to wipe his feet till he wears a
hole in the mat, before he goes in her house.   For she
don't keep eying your boots.   Says he has seen women
brush up a feller's mud right before his face and eyes.
My hair grows darker colored now.   And my freckles
have 'most faded out the color of my face.   I'm glad
of it.

From your affectionate Nephew,
WILLIAM HENRY.

Aunt Phebe to William Henry.

MY DEAR BILLY, —

We are very much pleased indeed with your map.
Dear me, how the United States have altered since they
were young, same as the rest of us !   That western part
used to be all Territory.   You could n't have done anything to please your grandmother better.   She's hung it
up in the front room, between Napoleon and the Mourn-
ing Piece, and thinks everything of it.   Everybody that
comes in she says, " Should you like to see the map my
little grandson made, — my little Billy ?"   You 'll always
be her little Billy.   She don't seem to think you are
growing up so fast.   Then she throws a shawl over her
head, and trots across the entry and opens the shutters,
and then she 'll say, " Pretty good for a little boy."   And

tells which is Maine, and which is New York, and points out the little arrow and the printed capital letters. Folks admire fast as they can, for that room is cold as a barn, winters. The last one she took in was the minister. Your grandmother sets a sight o' store by you. She's proud of you, Billy, and you must always act so as to give her reason to be, and never bring her pride to shame.

We are willing you should go. At first she was rather against it, though she says she always meant you should learn to take the steps when you got old enough, but she was afraid it might' tend to making you light-headed, and to unsteady your mind. This was the other night when we were talking it over in your kitchen, sitting round the fire. Somehow we get in there about every evening. Does seem so good to see the blaze. Your father said if a boy had common sense he'd keep his balance anywhere, and if dancing-school could spoil a fellow, he wasn't worth spoiling, worth keeping, I mean. I said I thought it might tend to keep you from toeing in, and being clumsy in your motions Your Uncle J. said he didn't think 't was worth while worrying about our Billy getting spoiled going to dancing-school, or anybody's Billy, without 't was some dandyfied coot. "Make the head right and the heart right," says he, "and let the feet go, — if they want to." So you see, Billy, we expect your head's right and your heart's right. Are they?

The girls and I have turned to and cut and made you a couple of bosom shirts and three bows, for of course you will have to dress rather different, and think a little more about your looks. But not too much, Billy! Not too much! And don't for gracious sake ever get the notion that you're good-looking! Don't stick a breast-pin in that shirt-bosom and go about with a strut! I don't know what I had n't as soon see as see a vain young man. I do believe if I were to look out, and you should be coming up my front yard gravel path with a strut, or any sort of dandyfied airs, I should shut the door in your face. Much as I set by you, I really believe I should. Lor! what are good looks? What are you laying out to make of yourself? That's the question. Freckles are not so bad as vanity. Any-body'd think I was a minister's wife, the way I talk. But, Billy, you have n't got any mother, and I do think so much of you! 'T would break my heart to see you grow up into one of those spick-and-span fellers, that are all made up of a bow and a scrape and a genteel smile! Though I don't think there's much danger, for common sense runs in the family. No need to go with muddy boots, though, or linty, or have your bow upside down. You 've always been more inclined that way. Fact is, I want you should be just right. I have n't a minute's more time to write. Your Uncle J. has promised to finish this.

DEAR COUSIN BILLY, —

This is Lucy Maria writing. The blacksmith sent word he was waiting to sharpen the colt, and father had to go. He's glad of it, because he never likes to write letters. I 'm glad you are going to dancing-school. Learn all the new steps you can, so as to show us how they 're done. Hannah Jane's beau has just been here. He lives six miles off, close by where we went once to a clam-bake, when Dorry was here. Georgiana's great doll, Seraphine, is engaged to a young officer across the road. He was in the war, and draws a pension of a cent a week. The engagement is n't out yet, but the family have known it several days, and he has been invited to tea. He wore his best uniform. Seraphine is invited over there, and Georgie is making her a spangled dress to wear. The wedding is to come off next month. I do wish I could think of more news. Father is the best hand to write news, if you can only get him at it. Once when I was away, he wrote me a letter and told me what they had for dinner, and what everybody was doing, and how many kittens the cat had, and how much the calf weighed, and what Tommy said, and seemed 'most as if I 'd been home and seen them. Be sure and write how you get along at dancing-school, and what the girls wear.

Your affectionate Cousin,

LUCY MARIA.

William Henry to Aunt Phebe.

MY DEAR AUNT, —

Thank you for the bosom shirts and the ones that helped make them. They 've come. I like them very much and the bows too. They 're made right. I lent Bubby Short one bow. His box had n't come. He kept running to the expressman's about every minute. We began to go last night. If we miss any questions to-day, we shall have to stay away next night. That 's going to be the rule. O, you ought to 've seen Dorry and me at

it with the soap and towels, getting ready! We scrubbed
our faces real bright and shining, and he said he felt like
a walking jack-o'-lantern. I bought some slippers and
had to put some cotton-wool in both the toes of 'em to
jam my heels out where they belonged to. I don't like
to wear slippers. My bosom shirt sets bully, and I bought
a linen-finish paper collar. I have n't got any breastpin.
I don't think I'm good looking. Dorry does n't either.
I know he don't. That's girls' business. We had to
buy some gloves, because his cousin said the girls wore
white ones, and nice things, and 't would n't do if we
did n't. Yellowish-brownish ones we got, so as to keep
clean longer. But trying on they split in good many
places, our fingers were so damp, washing 'em so long.
Lame Betsey is going to sew the holes up. When we
got there we did n't dare to go in, first of it, but stood
peeking in the door, and by and by Old Wonder Boy
gave me a shove and made me tumble in. I jumped up
quick, but there was a great long row of girls, and they
all went, " Tee hee hee! tee hee hee!" Then Mr. Tornero stamped and put us in the gentlemen's row. Then
both rows had to stand up and take positions, and put one
heel in the hollow of t' other foot, and then t' other heel in
that one's hollow, and make bows and twist different ways.
And right in front was a whole row of girls, all looking.
But they made mistakes theirselves sometimes.

First thing we learned the graces, and that is to bend
way over sideways, with one hand up in the air, and
the other 'most way down to the floor, then shift about on
t' other tack, then come down on one knee, with one hand
way behind, and the other one reached out ahead as if

't was picking up something a good ways off. We have
to do these graces to make us limberer, so to dance easier.
I tell you 't is mighty tittlish, keeping on one knee and
the other toe, and reaching both ways, and looking up in
the air. I did something funny. I 'll tell you, but don't
tell Grandmother. Of course 't was bad, I know 't was,
made 'em all laugh, but I did n't think of their all pitching over. You see I was at one end of the row and W. B.
was next, and we were fixed all as I said, kneeling down in
that tittlish way, reaching out both ways, before and behind, and looking up, and I remembered how he shoved
me into the room, and just gave him a little bit of a
shove, and he pitched on to the next one, and he on to
the next, and that one on to the next, and so that whole
row went down, just like a row of bricks! Course
everybody laughed, and Mr. Tornero did too, but he soon
stamped us still again. And then just as they all got
still again, I kept seeing how they all went down, and I
shut up my mouth, but all of a sudden that laugh shut
up inside made a funny sort of squelching sound, and he
looked at me cross and stamped his foot again. Now I
suppose he 'll think I 'm a bad one, just for that tumbling
in and shoving that row down and then laughing when I
was trying to keep in! He wants we should practise the
graces between times, to limber us up. Dorry and I do
them up in our room. Guess you'd laugh if you could see,
when we do that first part, bending over sideways, one
hand up and one down. I tried to draw us, but 't is a
good deal harder drawing crooked boys than 't is straight
ones, so 't is n't a very good picture. The boys that go
keep practising in the entries and everywhere, and the

other ones do it to make fun of us, so you keep seeing
twisted boys everywhere. Bubby Short was kneeling
down out doors across the yard, on one knee, and I
thought he was taking aim at something, but he said he
was doing the graces. I must study now. Bubby Short
got punished a real funny way at school to-day. I'll tell
you next time. I'm in a hurry to study now.

Your affectionate Nephew,

WILLIAM HENRY.

P. S. Dorry's just come in. He and Bubby Short
and I bought "Seraphine" some wedding presents and
he's done 'em up in cotton-wool, and they'll come
to her in a pink envelope. Dorry sent that red-stoned
ring and I sent the blue-stoned. We thought they'd do
for a doll's bracelets. Bubby Short sends the artificial
rosebud. He likes flowers, — he keeps a geranium.
We bought the presents at the Two Betseys' Shop.
They said they'd do for bracelets. Dorry says, "Don't
mention the price, for 't is n't likely everybody can make
such dear presents, and might hurt their feelings." We
tried to make some poetry, but could n't think of but two
lines.

> When you 're a gallant soldier's wife,
> May you be happy all your life!

Dorry says that's enough, for she could n't be any more
than happy all her life. "Can too!" W. B. said. "Can
be good!" "O, poh!" Bubby Short said; "she can't
be happy without she's good, can she?" But I want to
study my lesson now.   W. H.

Those bosom shirts are the best things I ever had.

W. H.

Although it would have been a vast sacrifice, I think I would have almost given my best pair of shoes for a chance of seeing Billy when dressed to go to the dancing-school. A boy in his first bosom shirt is such an amusing sight. You can easily pick one out in a crowd by his satisfied air, and stiff gait ; by the setting back of the shoulders, and the throwing out of the chest, — as if that smooth, white, starched expanse did not set out enough of itself ! Some have a way of looking up at gentlemen, as much as to say, *We* wear bosom shirts ! But of course those of us boys and men who have passed through this experience remember all about it.

Lucy Maria to William Henry.

DEAR COUSIN, —

That famous wedding came off yesterday afternoon. There were fifteen invited. I do wish I had time to tell you all about it. Mother made a real wedding-cake. Georgie has hardly slept a wink for a week, I do believe, thinking about it. The young soldier wore his epaulets, having been made General the day before. The bride was dressed in pure white, of course, with a long veil, of course, too, and orange blossoms, real orange blossoms that I made myself. The presents were spread out on the baby-house table. Perhaps you don't know that Georgie has a baby-house. It is made of a sugar-box, set up on end papered with housepaper inside, and brown outside. It has a down below, an up stairs, and garret. I do wish I had time to tell you all about the wedding, but Matilda 's a churning, and I promised to part the butter and work it over, if she would fetch it. I do wish you could hear her singing away, —

"Come, butter, come! come, butter, come!
Peter stands at the gate, waiting for his buttered cake.
Come, butter, come!"

Besides the baby-house table, the presents were laid on
the roof of the baby-house. There were sontags, shoes,
hats and feathers, and all sorts of clothes, the rosebud,
your jewelry, and more besides, also spoons, dishes, grid-
irons, vases and everything they could possibly want, to
keep house with, even to flatirons and a cooking-stove.
The hands of the happy couple were fastened together,
and they stood up (there was a pile of books behind
them). Then the trouble was, who should be the minister? At last we saw that funny Dicky Willis, your
old crony, peeping in the window, and made him come
in and be the minister. He was just the right one for
it. He charged the bridegroom to give his wife everything she asked for, and keep her in dry kindlings, and
let her have her own way, and always wipe his feet, and
not smoke in the house, and never find fault; and
charged her to sew on his buttons, and have plum-pud-
ding often, and let him smoke in the house, and never
want any new clothes, and always mind her husband,
and let him bring in mud on his feet, and always have
a smiling face, even if the baby-house was a burning
down over their heads, and then pronounced them man
and wife. I could fill up half a dozen sheets of paper,
if I had time, but I'm afraid of that butter. Everybody shook hands with them, and kissed them, and the
wedding-cake was passed round, and then the children
played

"Little Sally Waters, sitting in the sun,
Crying and weeping for her lost one."

In the midst of everything Tommy came in with Georgiana's atlas, and said he 'd found " two kick-cases." He meant those two black hemispheres, that are pictured out in the beginning. Mother put a raisin in his mouth, and hushed him up. The happy couple have gone on a wedding tour to Susie Snow's grandmother's *country seat*. It is expected that they will live half the time with Georgie, and half at the General's head-quarters. But their plans may be altered ; this is a changing world, and a young couple can't always tell what 's before them. I do wish you 'd write how you get on at dancing-school, and what the great girls wear, about my age. O dear what an age it is ! 'T is dreadful to think of ! 'Most eighteen ! Did you ever hear of anybody being so old ? Now truly I 'm 'most ashamed to own how old I am. Eighteen next month ! Hush, don't tell ! Keep it private ! I do wish I could grow backwards, and grow back into a baby-house if 't were nothing but a sugar-box. I do long to cut my hair off and go in a long-sleeved tier, and I 've a good mind to. We don't think you made a very good beginning. Guess your Mr. — I can't think of his name — thought there was need enough of your learning to enter a room. Mother 's going to put a note in this letter. I 've made her promise not to scold you, but she 's got something particular to say. Father will too. I told him 't would be just what you would like, one of his letters. Matilda says the butter has sent word it 's coming. Write soon.

From your affectionate Cousin,

LUCY MARIA.

I was very sorry not to be able to attend the wedding. My

present was half a dozen holders. The woman with whom I board said I could n't give a bride anything more useful. Her little daughter made them for me, at the rate of two cents apiece. They were an inch wide, and all had loops at the corners.

A Note from Uncle Jacob.

How are you, young man? .

I am very glad you go to dancing-school. Boys, as a general thing, are too fond of study, and 't is a good plan to have some contrivance to take their minds off their books. I suppose you'd like to know what is going on here at home. Your grandmother sits by the fire knitting some mittens for you to lose, so be sure you do it. [She says, tell him to be sure when he goes to dancing-school to wear his overcoat.] Your aunt Phebe is making jelly tarts. Says I can't have any till meal-time. [Tell him to be sure and get cooled off some before he comes away.] Your grandmother can't help worrying about that dancing-school. Matilda is picking over raisins for the pies. She won't sit very close to me. Now Tommy has come in, crying with cold hands. Lucy Maria is soaking them in cold water. I don't doubt he'll get a tart. Yes, he has. First he cries, and then he takes a bite. [Tell him not to go and come in his slippers.] Aunt Phebe says, "Now there's William Henry growing up, you ought to give him some advice." But I tell her that a boy almost in his teens knows himself what's right and what's wrong. Now Georgiana has come in crying. Says she stepped her foot through a puddle of ice. Grandmother has set her up

to dry her foot. Now she'll get a tart, I suppose! Yes
she has. [Tell him to look right at the teacher's feet.]
That's good advice if you expect to learn how. Now
your aunt says I'm such a good boy to write letters
she's going to give me this one that's burnt on the
edge. [Tell him to brush his clothes and not go linty.]
More good advice. I guess now I've got the tart I
won't write any more. Of course we expect you to do
just about right. If you neglect your studies and so
waste your father's money, you'll be an ungrateful
scamp. If you get into any contemptible mean ways,
we shall be ashamed to own you. Do you mean to do
anything or be anything now or ever? If you do, 't is
time you were thinking about it.

UNCLE JACOB.

All between the brackets are messages from your
grandmother.

J. U.

A Note from Aunt Phebe.

DEAR BILLY, —

When you get as far as choosing partners, there's a
word I want to say to you, though, as you're a pretty
good dispositioned boy, maybe there's no need; still you
may not always think, so 't will do no harm to say it.
There are always some girls that don't dance quite so
well, or don't look quite so well, or don't dress quite so
well, or are not liked quite so well, or are not quite
so much acquainted. Now I don't want you to all the
time, but sometimes, say once in an evening, I want
you to pick out one of these for your partner. I

know 't is n't the way boys do. But you can. Suppose you don't have a good time that one dance. You were n't sent into the world to have a good time every minute of your life ! How would you like to sit still all the evening ? I 've been spectator at such times, and I 've seen how things go on ! Why, if boys would be more thoughtful, every girl might have a good time, besides doing the boys good to think of something besides their own comfort. If I were you I would n't try to make fun, but try to learn, for though your father was willing you should go, and wants to do everything he can for you, he has to work hard for his money. Lucy Maria is waiting to hear how you get on.

Your affectionate

AUNT PHEBE.

William Henry to Lucy Maria.

DEAR COUSIN, —

I was going to write to you before, how I was getting along, but have had to study very hard. We 've been five times. The girls wear slippers and brown boots and other colors, and white dresses and blue and all kinds, and long ribbons, and a good many pretty girls go. If girls did n't go, I should like to go better. I mean till we know how, for I 'd rather make mistakes when only boys were looking. And I make a good many, because he says I don't have time and tune. He says my feet come down sometimes right square athwart the time. So I watched the rest, and when they put their feet down, I did mine. But that was a stroke too late, he said. Said "time and tune waits for no man." I like to promenade, because a feller can go it some then. We learn all kinds of waltzes and redowas and polkas. I can polka with one that knows how. Whirling round makes me light-headed just as Grandmother said. But I get over it some. We are going to do the German at the last of it._ The worst of it is cutting across the room to get your partners. He calls out when we 're all standing up in two rows, " First gentleman take the first lady ! " Now, supposing I 'm first gentleman, I have to go way across to first lady with all of 'em looking, and fix my feet right way, one heel in the other hollow, and then make my bow, and then she has to make that kind of kneeling-down bow that girls do, and then we wait till all of 'em get across one by one. Then we take the step a little while, and then launch off round the hall, polking, or else get into quadrilles. And if we do we make graces to the partners and the corners. I like quadrilles best, because you can hop round some and have a good time, if you have a good partner. You can dance good deal better with a good partner. Last time I had that one the fellers call " real estate," because you can't move her she don't ever get ready to start, and when 't is time to turn stands still as a post.

Dorry and I practise going across after partners, up in our room. You ought to 've seen us yesterday ! Dorry was the lady. If he did n't look funny ! He fixed the table-cloth off the entry table, to make it look like his mother's opera-cape, and fastened a great sponge on for a waterfall, and fizzled out his hair, and had a little tidy on top his head, and that red bow you sent me right in front of it. Then he stood out by the

window, and kept looking at his opera-cape, and smooth-
ing it down, and poking his hair, and holding his handkerchief, the way girls do, and kept whispering, or making believe, to Bubby Short, the way girls do. Then I
went across and made my bow, and he made that kneeling-down bow, and then we tried to polka redowa, but
our boots tripped us up, and we could n't stand up, and
laughed so we tumbled down, and did n't hear anybody
coming till he knocked, and 't was the teacher, come to
see what the matter was. Not Wedding Cake, but Old
Brown Bread, and he said dancing must n't be brought
into our studies, and scolded more, but I saw his eyes
laughing, looking at Dorry. One of the boys tumbled
down stairs, doing the graces in the entry, too near the edge,
and it 's forbidden now. Some of the first-class fellers
put up a notice one night in the entry, great printed
letters.

That owl stands for Minerva. I could n't make a very
good one because I 'm in such a hurry to do my examples. The goddess of wisdom used to be named Minerva. She was painted with an owl. I 've been reading
it in the Classical Dictionary. Dorry and Bubby Short
and I have just been to the Two Betseys to get our
gloves sewed up, and the Other Betsey said she used to
dance like a top. Then she held her dress up with her

thumbs and fingers, and took four different kinds of balances. Made us die a laughing, she hopped up and down so.

Your affectionate Cousin,

WILLIAM HENRY.

P. S. That TO is n't left out in the notice, it's my own mistake.

The remaining letters were probably written during his last term at the school.

Matilda's Letter to William Henry.

DEAR COUSIN, —

Lucy Maria keeps telling me that I promised to write you a letter, but I wish I had n't promised to write you one, because I don't like to write letters very well, for I can't think of anything to write. But Lucy Maria she likes to, and that would do just as well as for me to. But mother says I ought to often, so as to get me in the habit of it. I don't have very much time to write very long letters, for the girls are getting up a Fair, and I am helping do the old woman in her shoe, and gentlemen's pincushions, and presents for the arrow table, where the arrow swings round and points to your present, and so I don't get very much time between schools. For we have to write compositions every week now, and all the girls think the teacher is just as mean as he can be to make us. We want he should take off some of the compositions and put more on to our other lessons; but no. He thinks 't is the best thing we can do. He don't care about anything else, I believe. Susie Snow says she

9 *

believes he's all made up of composition. Our next subject is "Economy" and we've got to put in time wasted, and health wasted, and money wasted. Susie Snow is going to put in hers that girls should never waste their time writing compositions.

I wish I could think of some news to tell. Lucy Maria could get news in a sandy desert, I believe. But she don't have to go to school. Hannah Jane has n't got home from Aunt Matilda's yet. The minister and his wife and all his children have been here to spend the day. They are very fond of jelly. Mother gave them that tall gilt tumbler full, that Cousin Joe brought home from sea, with gilt flowers on it. 'T is very pleasant weather. I wish you'd come back and hoe my flower-garden, the weeds are thick as spatters, and I don't have much time. The dog stepped on my sensitive plant. Some of my seeds have n't come up. Father says I better go down after them. That Root of Bliss I set out, good for the headache, that Cousin Joe brought home from the island of Sumatra, that's in the Mediterranean Sea, or else in the Indian Ocean, the hens scratched up four times, and I've brought it in the house and stuck it in a cigar-box. Father told me to shake pepper over it because 't was used to pepper at home, but I can't tell what he means and what he don't, he funs so. Our new cow hooks down rails and goes where she wants to.

O Billy! now I can tell you some news. But 't is quite bad news. It happened two weeks ago. We all felt very sorry about it, and some of us cried. I could n't help it. You know our cow that was named Reddie, the one we raised up from a bossy-calf with milk-porridge till 't was big enough to eat grass? Well, she got in the bog. We were just eating supper. Georgiana was eating supper at our house that night. Tommy had n't got home from school, and we were all wondering where he was. Father said he did n't doubt he 'd gone to find his turtle. He had a turtle that got loose and ran away. Mother was just saying he 'd have to have cold dip toast for his supper, for she makes it a rule not to keep things about for him when he don't come straight home to his meals. He 'd rather play than eat. 'T is only a little school he goes to. Not very far off. Five scholars, that 's all. Little bits of ones. But I must tell about our cow.

We began to hear a great screaming, and could n't think what the matter was. 'T was Tommy. And next thing he came running through the yard, crying and hollering both together, " Father ! Father ! Cow ! Reddie ! " Much as he could do to speak. Father knew in a minute what 't was, for he knew she was pastured close to the bog, and he ran and we all ran, and Mr. Snow and some other men that found it out came with us. O poor cow ! She was in more than half way up, and making dreadful moaning noises, and shook her head and tried to stir, but every stir made her go deeper in. Men and boys waded in, but they could n't do anything.

" Rails ! rails ! " they all called out, and we pulled them out of the fences and they tried to prise her up with them, but the bog was so soft she sank in so they could n't do anything with her. Much as they could do to keep up themselves. Mr. Snow was prising with a rotten rail, and it broke, and he went down in the wet. Old Mr. Slade, that goes with two canes, came there bareheaded and sat down on the bank. He told them to go get some boards. There were n't any, any nearer than Mr. John Slade's new house, and that was too far off, and father said 't was too late, for she was in, then, up to the top of her back. 'Most all the women and girls came away then, for we could n't bear to stay any longer to see her suffer. She kept her nose pointed up high as she could, and her eyes looked very mournful.

In the morning father told me I should never see Reddie again. They got her up, but not soon enough. She 's buried now, under the poplar-tree, in that field we bought of Mr. Snow. She was a good, gentle cow, and seemed to know us. Mother says she seemed like one of the family. Georgiana about spoiled her new boots in the bog. Our new cow is n't the best breed, but she 's part best. The cream is considerable yellow, but not very. She gives about eight or nine quarts. Milk has risen a cent. Mother declares she will not measure her milk in that new kind of quart, that don't hold much over a pint. Lucy Maria and all of us are trying to have mother go get her picture taken. But she says she can't screw her courage up, and can't take the time. Your father says he wants to see her good clever face in a picture. Too bad blue eyes take light. But she might be taken looking down, Lucy Maria says, mending Tommy's trousers, that would be natural. He 's always making barn-doors in his trousers, he 's such a climbing fellow.

L. M. and I have most earned money enough, and

father's going to make up the rest, and we are going to
hire a cheap piano, that Mr. Fry told us about, and I'm
going to be a music teacher, I guess. I'm going to begin
next month. I shall take of Miss Ashley. I shall have
to walk a mile. O goody! goody! dum, dum, dum!
Sha' n't I be glad! But Susie Snow says I shall sing
another tune after I've taken a little while. Father says
if I begin to take I must go through. Says I must
promise to practise two hours a day. I'd just as soon
promise that as not. 'T is just what I like. Only think,
I shall have a piano in this very house. Seems if I
could n't believe it! I can play for you to dance.
Wish I knew how to dance. Susie Snow has come
after me to go take a walk. Now, William Henry, you
must answer this letter just as immediately as possible.

From your affectionate Cousin,
MATILDA.

P. S. Cousin Joe has sent me a smelling-bottle, a little
gilt one he brought home, that's got ninety-four different
smells in it. Mother is writing you a note. She says
you can't dance on her carpet. Father says he's sorry
he did n't learn the graces, and means to when you come
again. We can dance in the barn. Tommy has just
come in. He says he knows his B A C's. He's a
funny boy. He means A B C's. But he always gets
the horse before the cart. One day we tried to make
conundrums, and Georgiana made this, — see if you can
answer it: Which is best, to have plum-cake for supper
and only have a little mite of a piece, or cookies, and
have as many as you want?

Georgiana's kitty has just jumped over the fence. She's after my morning-glories again. Just as fast as I fasten 'em up, she goes to playing with the strings and claws 'em down again. Lucy Maria drew a picture of her doing it.

M.

A Note from Dorry.

DEAR WILLIAM HENRY'S GRANDMOTHER, —

William Henry wants I should tell you not to be scared when you see another boy's handwriting on the back of this letter, and not to think he's got cold, or got anything else, like measles, or anything of that kind, and not to feel worried about his not writing for so long, for he is all right except the first joint of his forefinger. He crooked that joint, or else uncrooked it, playing base ball. 'T was a heavy ball and he took it whole on that joint, and 't is so stiff he can't handle a penholder. He thinks you will all wonder why he does n't write, and worry about his getting sick or something, but he never felt better. Appetite very good. He has received his cousin Matilda's letter, and will answer it when he can. He wants to know what she'd think if she had to write poetry for composition. Our teacher told us we must each write one verse about June: I put three of them in for you to see, but don't put our names.

"O I love the verdant June,
  When the birds are all in tune,
  When the rowers go out to row,
  When the mowers go out to mow,
    O, sweetly smells the fragrant hay,
    As we ride on the load and stow it away."

" In June we can sail
In the gentle gale,
 On the waters blue,
And catch cod-fish
That make a good dish,
And mackerel too."

" In June the summer skies are clear,
And soon green apples do appear.
And though they 're hard and sour, we know
That every day they 'll better grow.
This teaches us that boys, also,
Every day should better grow."

P. S. He wants I should tell you 't is tied up in a rag all right and don't hinder his studying. Says he wishes his cousin Lucy Maria would write him one of her kind of letters, that she knows how to write, and tell what they are all doing and what they talk about, and when his finger is well he will answer all the letters they will write to him.

Very respectfully,
BILLY's FRIEND, DORRY.

Aunt Phebe's Note.

MY DEAR BILLY, —

Grandmother worries about that finger. Do ask Dorry to write again, or else take the penholder in your middle one, though we mistrust that 's damaged, or you 'd have written before this. I 've had my picture taken and send you one to keep. Look at it often, and if you 've done anything wrong, think it shakes its head at you! Little wrong things, or big ones, all the same. For little wrongs are more dangerous, because we think they 're of no account. But they show what's in a person, same as a little pattern of goods tells what the whole piece is. Show me half an inch of cotton and I'll tell you what color the whole spool is.

I'd no idea of having my picture taken. I was right in the heart of baking, when your Uncle J. drove up and said he'd harnessed up on purpose. 'T was all a contrived plan between him and the girls. I saw them smiling together when Mattie brought out my black alpaca. I thought the girls seemed mighty ready to take hold and finish up the baking. But he got caught in his own trap, for Lucy Maria went with us, to make sure my collar and things looked fit to be taken, and she set her foot down we shouldn't leave the saloon till he'd had his, for she was going to have a locket with us both inside, and I had to be done over small. What an operation it is to have your picture taken! If we could only take ether and be carried through! He put my head in a clamp, and crossed my hands, and pinned up a black rag for me to look at, and told me to look easy and natural, and smile a very little! I'm sure I tried to, but your Uncle J. says 't is a very melancholy face, and Lucy Maria says the cheek-bones cast a shadow! Your father says the worst of it is, it does look like me! I think it's too bad to make fun of it, after all I passed through! Your Uncle J. took things easy and joked with the man, and was laughing when the cover was taken off and did n't dare to unlaugh, he says, so he came out all right, with a laughing face, as he always is. The girls want we should be taken large and hang up, side by side, in two oval frames, over the mantel-piece. But their father says he sha' n't be hung up alive, if he can help himself.

It is n't likely I shall write to you again very soon. Cousin Joe and his accordion are coming, and he 'll bring his sisters, and the young folks about here know them, and I expect there 'll be nothing but frolicking.   Then there 'll be some of your Uncle J.'s folks after that, so you see we 'll be all in a hubbub and I shall have to be the very hub of the hubbub, I suppose.   Lucy Maria says, " Tell William Henry to send us a charade, or something to amuse the company with."   Write when you can.

With a great deal of love, your affectionate

AUNT PHEBE.

P. S.   Take good care of your finger.   A finger-joint would be a great loss.   I think cold water is as good as anything.   Grandmother wishes you had some of her carrot salve.   Let us hear from you in some way. Grandmother wants to know if the Two Betseys don't make carrot salve.

I must add here that Lucy Maria was not the girl to give up those pictures in " two oval frames."   For by perseverance, and partly with my assistance, the thing was secretly managed, and managed so well that Uncle Jacob actually carried them out home himself, in a bundle to Lucy Maria, without knowing it !   And they now hang in triumph over the fireplace in the " girls' chamber."

Lucy Maria to William Henry.

DEAR BILLY, —

'T is a pity about that forefinger.   Pray get it well enough to handle a pen, 't is so long since you 've written.

So you want home matters reported. Eatable matters of course will be most interesting. Milk and butter, plenty. Gingerbread (plain), ditto. Gingerbread (fancy), scarce. Cookies, quiet. Plum-cake, in demand. Snaps, lively. Brown-bread, firm. White-bread (sliced), dull. Biscuits (hot), brisk. Custard, unsteady. Preserves not in the market.

What do we do, and what do we talk about? Why, we talk about our cousin William Henry, and what we do can't be told within the bounds of one letter. Think of seven cows' milk to churn into butter, besides a cheese now and then, and besides working for the extra hands we hire this time o' year! I should have written to you before, when we first heard of your accident, if I could have got the time. Hannah Jane is away, and we've let Mattie go with Susie Snow to Grandma Snow's again for a few days. Grandma Snow likes to have Mattie come with Susie, for 't is rather a still, dull place. So you must think we are quite lonesome here now, and we are, especially mother. Father tells her she'd better advertise for a companion. I've a good mind to advertise to be a companion. What do companions do? The old lady might be cross, or the old gentleman, but that would n't hurt me, so long as I kept clever myself. Don't doubt I'd get fun out of it some way. There's fun in about everything I think.

I've been trying to get father and mother to go to Aunt Lucy's and stay all night. But father thinks there would n't be anybody to shut the barn-door, and mother thinks there would n't be anybody to do anything, though I've promised to scald the pans, and do up the starched things, and keep Tommy out of the sugar-bowl. He takes a lump every chance he can get. Takes after his father. Father puts sugar on sweetened puddings, if mother is n't looking! We've made some verses to plague Tommy, and when Mattie gets her piano, they're going to be set to music.

SONG.

A Sweet Tommy.

As turns the needle to the pole,
So Tommy to the sugar-bowl.
> Tra la la, tra la la !
>> Sweet, sweet Tommy !

Tommy always takes a toll
Going by the sugar-bowl.
> Tra la la, tra la la !
>> Sweet, sweet Tommy !

Were Tommy blind as any mole,
He'd always find the sugar-bowl.
> Tra la la, Tra la la !
>> Sweet, sweet Tommy !

He's a funny talking fellow. We took him into town last night, to see the illumination. This morning we heard him and Frankie Snow telling Benny Joyce about it. Father and I were listening behind the blinds. Made father's eyes twinkle. Don't you know how they twinkle when he's tickled ?

"You did n't see the *rumination* and we did!" we heard Tommy say.

"Rumination? What's a rumination?" asked Benny.

"O hoo! hoo!" cried Tommy. "Denno what a rumination is ! "

"Why," said Frankie, "don't you know the *publicans?* Wal, that 's it."

"O poh!" said Benny. "Publicans and sinners! I knew they 's coming!"

"And soldiers!" said Frankie. "O my! All a marching together!"

"O poh!" said Benny. "I see 'em go by. Paint-pots on their heads, and brushes *in* 'em! I was n't goin' to chase!"

"Guess nobody would n't let ye?" said Frankie.

"Did n't either!" cried Tommy, "did n't have paint-pots!"

"Did!" said Benny. "Guess my great brother knows!"

"Guess we know," said Frankie, "when we went!"

"And the town was all *celebrated,*" said Tommy. And the houses all *gloomed* up! And horses! O my!

"O poh!" said Benny. "When I grow up, I 'm goin' to have a span!"

If mother does go, she 'll take Tommy, for she would n't sleep a wink away from him over night. Father pretends he 'd go if he had a handsome span. Says he has n't got a horse in the barn good enough to take mother out riding. When Mammy Sarah was here washing, she told him how he could get a good span. You know he 's always joking about taking summer boarders. Says Mammy Sarah, "Now 't is a wonder to me you don't do it, for summer boarders is as good as a gold-mine. Money runs right out of their pockets, and all you have to do is to catch it." She says we could make enough out of a couple of them, in a month's time, to buy a handsome span, and she is n't sure but the harness.

I think we begin to be a little in earnest about summer
boarders.   For we have rooms enough, in both houses
together, and milk and vegetables, and mother's a splendid cook.   Mammy Sarah says, "They ain't diffikilt,
and after they've been in the country couple of weeks,
they don't eat so very much more than other folks."

Father says he wants to take them more for the entertainment than the money.   He wants rich ones, but ·
not the sensible kind, that know money is n't the only
thing worth having.   Says what he wants is that silly,
stuck-up kind, that put on airs, and make fools of themselves, they 'd be so amusing!   Thinks the best sort for
our use would be specimens that went up quite sudden
from poor to rich, like balloons, all filled with gas.   I
believe there 'd be lots of fun to be made out of them.
I 've seen one or two.   Gracious!   You 'd think they
were n't born on the same planet with poor folks.   Mother 'd rather have the really well-informed, sensible kind,
that we may learn something from them.   A couple of
each would be just the thing.   How do you like mother's
picture?   We don't feel at all satisfied with it.   If she
could only be taken at home!   Then she 'd look natural.
Father says the world is going ahead so fast, he believes
the time will come when every family will have its own
picture-machine, much as it has its own frying-pan.
Then when folks have on their best expressions, why, clap
it right before them.   Then they 'll look homish.   Says
what he wants is to have mother's face when she 's just
made a batch of uncommon light biscuits, or when Tommy 's said something smart.   Won't there be funny pictures when we can hold up a machine before anybody any

minute, like a frying-pan, and catch faces glad, or mad,
or sad, or any way? I made believe take Tommy's and
then showed them to him on a piece of paper. Guess
I'll put them in the letter. They'll do to amuse you.
I draw an hour or so every day. First, I have to
make my hour. Sometimes I have to make more. For
I will read a little, if the world stops because of it. But
about the faces. First one is when he was crying be-

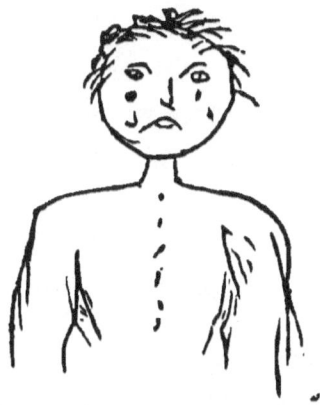

cause he couldn't have sugar on his potatoes. Next one
is when he was spunky at Frankie Snow for bursting
his little red balloon. The pleased-looking face is when
father brought him home a little ship all rigged, and the
laughing one is when the cow put her head in the window. We tell him we'll have them framed and hung
up so he can see just how he looks. Mother says 't is
all very well to laugh at Tommy, but she guesses some
older ones' pictures would n't always look smiling and
pleasant, take them the year through!

As soon as your finger is itself again do write, for we
miss your letters. We expect to have gay times here
this summer. Company coming, but we sha' n't make

company of them. Except to have splendid times. What
shall we do evenings? If you go anywhere where there
is anything going on, do write us about it, so we can go on
the same way. When are you coming? Write me a
good long letter when you can.

Your affectionate Cousin,

LUCY MARIA.

Your father is going to write you a letter. Quite
wonderful for him. O William Henry, you don't know
how much I think of your father, and what a good man
he is! I guess you 'd better write to your grandmother
before you do me; she 's so pleased to have you write to
her.

Father wants to know when that ball hit you if you
bawled.

Lucy Maria's "picture-taker" made a great deal of fun for
them, and possibly did some good. She constructed a queer
long-handled affair, and, at the most unexpected moments,
this would be thrust before the faces of different members of
the family, more especially Tommy, Matilda, or Georgiana,
and their "pictures" would be sure to appear to them soon
after, "glad, or mad, or sad, or any way."

And the plan of "summer boarders" also furnished entertainment. The talk on this subject was quite amusing, particularly when it touched the subject of "advertising." Lucy
Maria suggested this ending: —

"None but the silly, or the really well-informed need apply."
But Mr. Carver thought such a notice would fail of bringing
a single boarder. For silly people did not know they were
silly, and the really well-informed were the very last ones to
think themselves so.

William Henry to Aunt Phebe.

DEAR AUNT PHEBE, —

I thank you for taking your time to write to me, when you have so much work to do. My forefinger has about recovered the use of itself. The middle one did go lame a spell, but now 't is very well, I thank you. Mrs. Wedding Cake did them up for me. I think she 's a very kind woman. Dorry says he 'd put a girdle round the earth in forty minutes, or lay down his life, if she wanted him to, or anything else, for the only woman he knows that will smile on boys' mud and on boys' noise.

Ten of us went on an excursion with the teacher, half-price, to Boston, and had a long ride in the cars, over forty miles. We went everywhere, and saw lots of things. Went into the Natural History building. You can go in for nothing. You stand on the floor, at the bottom and look way up to the top. All round inside are galleries running round, with alcoves letting out of them, where they keep all sorts of unknown beasts and birds and bugs and snakes. Some of those great birds are regular smashers! 'Most dazzles your eyes to look at their feathers, they 're such bright red! I 'd just give a guess how tall they were, but don't believe I 'd come within a foot or two. Also butterflies of every kind, besides skeletons of monkeys and children and minerals and all kinds of grasses and seeds, and nuts there such as you never cracked or thought of! They are there because they are seeds, not because they are nuts. And there 's a cast of a great ugly monster, big as several elephants, that used to walk round the earth before any men lived in it. If he was n't a ripper! Could leave his hind feet on the ground and put his fore paws up in the trees and eat the tops off! They call him a Megotharium! I hope he's spelt right, though he ought not to expect it, and I don't know as it makes much difference, seeing he lived thousands of years before the flood, and lucky he did, Dorry says, for the old ark could n't have floated with many of that sort aboard. He was n't named till long after he was dead and buried. Patient waiter is no loser, Dorry says, for he's got more name than the ones that live now, and is taken more notice of. We saw a cannon-ball on the side of Brattle Street Church, where 't was fired in the Revolution, and we went to the top of the State House. Made our knees ache going up so many steps, but it pays. For you can look all over the harbor, and all round the country, and see the white towns, and steeples, for miles and miles. Boston was built on three hills and the State House is on one of them. I can't write any more, now.

W. B. has left school, because his father got a place for him in New York. His father thought he was old enough to begin. He's a good deal older than I am.

From your affectionate Nephew,

WILLIAM HENRY.

10

How do you like this picture of that great Mego — I won't try to spell him again — eating off the tree-tops? The leaves on the trees then were different from the ones we have, now. Dorry made the leaves, and I made the creature.

A Letter to William Henry from his Father.

MY DEAR SON, —

Perhaps you have thought that because I am rather a silent man, and do not very often write you a letter, that I have not very much feeling and do not take interest in you. But no one knows how closely I am watching my boy as Time is bringing him up from boyhood to manhood.

Sometimes your grandmother worries about your being where there may be bad boys; but I tell her that among so many there must be both good and bad, and if you choose the bad you show very poor judgment. I think if a boy picks out bad companions it shows there is something bad in himself.

She says I ought to keep giving you good advice, now you are just starting in life, and charge you to be honest and truthful and so forth. I tell her that would be something as it would be if you were just starting on a pleasant journey, and I should say, " Now, William Henry, don't put out your own eyes at the beginning, or cut the cords of your legs!" Do you see what I mean? A boy that is *not* honest and truthful puts out his own eyes and cripples himself at the very beginning.

There is a good deal said about arriving at honor and distinction. I don't want you to think about *arriving* at honor. I want you to take honor to start with. And as for distinction, a man, in the long run, is never distinguished for anything but what he really is. So make up your mind just what you want to pass for, and be it. For you will pass for what you are, not what you try to appear. Go into the woods and see how easily you can tell one tree from another. You see oak leaves on one, and you know that is oak all the way through. You see pine needles on another, and you know that is pine all the way through. A pine-tree may want to look like an oak, and try to look like an oak, and think it does look like an oak, as it can't see itself. But nobody is cheated. So a rascally fellow may want to appear fair and honest, and try to appear fair and honest, and think he does appear fair and honest, as he can't see himself. But, in the long run, nobody is cheated. For you can read a man's character about as easy as you can the leaves on the trees. Sometimes I sit down in a grocery store and hear the neighbors talked about, and 't is curious to find how well everybody is known. It seems as if every man walked round, labelled, as you may say, same as preserve jars are labelled, currant, quince, &c. Only he don't know what his label is. Just as likely as not a man may think his label is Quince Marmelade, when 't is only Pickled String Beans!

Just so with boys. Grown folks notice boys a great deal, though when I was a boy, I never knew they did. The little affairs of play-time and school-time, and their home-ways are all talked over, and by the time a boy is twelve years old, it is pretty well known what sort of a man he will make.

Now don't mistake my meaning. I don't want you to

be true because people will know it if you are not, but
because it is right and noble to be so. I want you to be
able to respect yourself. Never do anything that you
like yourself any the less for doing.

A boy of your age is old enough to be looking ahead
some, to see what he is aiming at. I don't suppose you
want to drift, like the sea-weed, that lodges wherever the
waves toss it up! Set up your mark, and a good high
one. And be sure and remember that, as a general thing,
there is no such thing as luck. If a man seems to be a
lucky merchant, or lawyer, or anything else, 't is because
he has the talent, the industry, the determined will, that
make him so. People see the luck, but they don't always
see the "taking pains" that's behind it. I remember you
wrote us a letter once, and spoke of a nice house, with
nice things inside, that you meant to have by "trying
hard enough." There's a good deal in that. We've
got to try hard, and try long, and try often, and try again,
and keep trying. That house never 'll come down to you.
You've got to climb up to it, step by step. I don't know
as I have anything to say about the folly of riches. On
the contrary, I think 't is a very good plan to have money
enough to buy books and other things worth having. I
don't see why a man can't be getting knowledge and
growing better, at the same time he is growing richer.
Some poor folks have a prejudice against rich folks. I
have n't any. Rich people have follies, but poor people
copy them if they can. That is to say, we often see poor
people making as big fools of themselves as they can,
with the means they have. Money won't hurt you, Billy,
so long as you keep common sense and a true heart.

We are all watching you and thinking of you, here at home. If you *should* go wrong 't would be a sad blow for both families. Perhaps I ought to tell you how I feel towards you, and how, ever since your mother's death, my heart has been bound up in you and Georgie. You would then know what a crushing thing it would be to me if you were found wanting in principle. But I am not very good, either at talking or writing, so do remember, dear boy, that even when I don't say a word, I'm thinking about you and loving you always. God bless you !

From your affectionate

FATHER.

W. B., it seems, from his own account, set sail on the great sea of commerce with flying colors, and favorable winds, — probably the Trade-winds.

Old Wonder Boy to William Henry.

DEAR FRIEND, —

I like my place, and think it is a very excellent one. It is " Veazey & Summ's." When you get a place it is my advice that you should procure one in New York, as New York is greatly superior to Boston. Boston is a one-horse place. I would n't be seen riding in that slow coach. Washington Street could be put whole into Broadway, and not know it was there hardly, for you could travel both sides and all round it. Our store is a very excellent store. Some consider it greatly superior to Stewart's. All our clerks dress in very superior style and go in very good society, and so I learn to use very good language. We keep boys to do the errands, and porters. All the stylish people do their trading here. The young ladies like to trade with me very much. The New York ladies are greatly superior to any other ladies. The firm think a great deal of me, so I expect to be promoted quite fast. I am learning to smoke. I have got a very handsome pipe. The head clerk thinks it has got a very superior finish to it. We two are quite thick. How are all the fellers? Write soon. Remember me to all inquiring friends, and excuse handwriting.

Your friend,
WALTER BRIESDEN.

William Henry to Matilda.

DEAR COUSIN, —

Now I'm going to answer your letter, and then I sha' n't have to think about it any longer. I was sorry to hear about poor Reddie. But if it had been Tommy, then it would have been a great deal worse. Think of that. Dorry and I have been wishing 'most a week about something, and now I'll tell you what 't is about. About a party. 'T is going to be at Colonel Grey's. He lives in a large light-colored brick house, with a piazza round it, and a fountain, and bronze dogs, and everything lovely. It is Maud Grey's birthday party. Sixteen years old. Old and young are going to be invited, because her little sister's birthday comes next day to hers. Now sometimes when there's a party some of the biggest of our fellows get invited, because there are not very many young gentlemen in town, and they are glad to take some from the school. But we two never have yet. But Dorry thinks we stand a better chance now, for we've been to dancing-

school, and will do to fill up sets with. Maud Grey
did n't go as a scholar, but she went spectator sometimes,
and took my partner's place once, when her string of
beads broke. Dorry was in the same set. I never
polkaed better in my life, for she took me round and made
me keep time whether I wanted to or not, but I told
Dorry I felt just like a little boy that had been lifted over
a puddle. He's afraid she won't remember us, but I
guess I'm afraid she will, and then won't invite such a
bad dancer. We two thought we'd walk by the house,
just for fun, and make ourselves look tall. So we held up
our chins, and swung two little canes we'd cut, going
along, for small chaps are plenty enough, but young gentlemen go off to college, or stores, soon 's they're of any
size. The blinds were all shut up, but Dorry said there
was hope if the slats were turned the right way. Blind
slats here move all ways. Yesterday, in school-time, I
saw a colored man coming towards the school-house, and
thought 't was Cicero, the one that works for Colonel Grey,
coming with the invitations, and made a loud "hem!"
for Dorry to look up, and a hiss, to mean Cicero, and
pointed out doors. 'T was n't very loud, but that one we
call Brown Bread, that has eyes in the back of his head,
and ears all over him, and smells rat where there is n't
any, and wears slippers, so you can't hear him, even if
't is still enough to drop a pin, — I thought he was over
the other side of the room, tending to his own affairs, but
all of a sudden he was standing just back of me, and I
had to lose a recess just for that. And 't was n't Cicero
after all, but the one that comes after the leavings. —
(Somebody knocks.)

Afternoon. — Hurrah! We're going! The one that knocked at the door was Spicey, with our invitations. When I come home I'll bring them home to show. They came through the post-office. We expect they all came to the professor, with orders to pick out the ten tallest ones, for they are directed in his writing. I never went to such a party, and should n't know how to behave, if 't was n't for Dorry. First thing you do is to go up and speak to the lady of the house and the lady of the party. I mean after you've been up stairs, and looked in the looking-glass and smoothed down your hair. Mine always comes up again. I've tried water and I've tried oil, and I've tried beef-marrow, but 't is bound to come up. Dorry says I ought to put it in a net. Don't you remember that time I had my head shaved off close, and how it looked like an orange? I'm glad 't is n't so red as it was. 'T is considerable dark now. When you come down you walk up to the lady of the house and say " How do you do?" and shake hands, and when you go home you have to bid her good-night, and say you've had a very pleasant time, and shake hands again. Not shove out your fist, as if you were shoving a croquet-ball, but slow, with the fingers about straight, and not speak it out blunt, as if you were singing out " good-night!" to the fellers, but quite softly and smiling. Dorry's been showing me beforehand. Bubby Short stood up in the floor, and had the bed-spread tied round him with a cod-line, for a trail, and shavings for curls. He was the lady of the house and we walked up to him, and said, " How do you do, Mrs. Grey?" and so forth. Dorry drew this picture of

us. He draws better than I do. I will write about the party.

From your Cousin,
WILLIAM HENRY.

William Henry to his Grandmother.

MY DEAR GRANDMOTHER, —

Now if you will be a good little grandmother, and promise never to worry any more, then I 'll tell you about that party. We had to wear white gloves. I 'll begin at the outside. The piazzas had colored lights hanging round them, and there were colored lights hung in the trees and the gateways. 'T was a foggy night, and those colored lights lighted up the fog all around, so when you came towards the place it looked just like a great bright spot in the midst of darkness. There was a tall lady, standing in the middle of the room, with a splendid dress on, dragging way behind her, and I went right up to her, and just got my foot the way Mr. Tornero told us, and the palm of my hand right, when Dorry

10 *   o

jerked me back by my jacket and said she was n't the
right one. You see we got belated, going back after our
clean pocket-handkerchiefs, and hurried so that Dorry
fell down and muddied his trousers' knees, but lucky
't was close to the Two Betseys' shop, for we went in
there and got sponged up, but we had to wait for 'em to
dry. Lame Betsey said she used to take care of Maud
Grey when she was a little scrap, and she wanted to make
her a birthday present. So they both hunted round, to
see if they had anything. In the desk they found a little
thin book, a funny-looking old blue-covered book, "Advice to a Young Lady," that was given to Lame Betsey
when she was young. The title was on the blue cover.
'T was a funny-looking thing and it smelt snuffy. She
asked me to give it to Maud, after she 'd written her
name in it. I tell you now Lame Betsey makes quite
good letters! I did n't want to take the book, but I did,
for both Betseys are clever women.

All this was the reason we got belated, and Mrs. Grey
had got mixed up with the other people, but we found
her and did the right thing by her. And Maud too.
I don't think any of you would believe that I could be-

have so well! so polite I mean. Course I did n't feel bashful any! O no!

They had four pieces, and they played as if they knew how. I did n't dance at the first of it. Did n't dare to. 'T was too light there. The carpets were covered with white. Then chandeliers, and lamps, and wax candles, and flowers everywhere they could be, set up in vases,—one lady called vases, varzes,—and hanging-baskets. I never was in such a beautiful place. The ladies sang at the piano, and the young gentlemen turned their leaves over. O you ought to 've heard 'em when the tunes went up, up, up! Enough to make you catch your breath! Seemed as if it could never get down again. I don't like that kind. But Dorry said 't was opera style and nobody was to blame but me, if I did n't like it. Now John Brown's Body, I like that, and when they all sang that, I joined right in, same as any of them. For I knew I knew that tune. But first one looked round at me, and then another looked round at me, as if something was the matter. I thought I saw 'em smiling. Then I kept still. But I did n't know I was singing wrong. O, I do wish I knew what this singing is! Seems easy enough. Now when the tune goes up loud, I go up loud, and when that goes down low, I go down low. But Dorry says it is n't singing. Says 't is discord. But I can't tell discord from any other cord, and he says the harder I try, the worse noise I make. I do wish I could roar out that Glory Hallelujah! for I feel the tune inside of me, but it never comes out right. Dorry laughs when I set out to sing. He says I chase the tune up and down all the way through, and never hit it ! Now, if 't is right inside, why can't it come out right ? I don't see !

We went into a large room to eat refreshments, and I wish Aunt Phebe could see the things we had. And taste of them too. I saved the frosting off my cake for Tommy. 'T is wrapped up in a paper in my trunk. 'T is different from your frosting, good deal harder. I had a sort of funny time in that room. Somebody had to hit my elbow when I was passing custard to a girl, and joggled over a mess of it on to her white dress and my trousers. I whipped out my pocket-handkerchief to sop it up, and whipped out that little blue book. Somebody picked it up, and one young man, that had been cutting up all the evening, Maud Grey's cousin, he got hold of it and read her name and called out to her to come get her present, and made a good deal of fun about it, and began to read it loud. She wanted to know who brought it, and somebody told her I was the one. I began to grow red as fire, but all of a sudden I thought, Now, Billy, what 's the use ? So I said very plain, " Miss Grey, Lame Betsey sent you that book." She did n't laugh very much, only smiled and asked me to tell Lame Betsey she was glad that she remembered her. Guess she thought I looked bashful, for afterwards she asked me if I would n't try a polka with her. I don't think she 's very proud, for when I was looking at a painted vase, she came and told me how it was done, for all I was n't much acquainted with her. She talked to me as easy and sociable as if she 'd been Lucy Maria.

A company of us got together in one of the rooms

and ate our ice-creams there, and while we were eating them, we beheaded words.   Lucy Maria must read this letter, for she 'll want to know how.   When you behead a word you take off the first letter.   It's fun, when you get beheading them fast.   The spelling must n't be changed.   Dorry made some of these.   I did n't.   I could n't think fast enough.

Behead an article of dress, and you leave a farming tool.   .

Shoe — hoe.

I 'll put the rest of the answers at the bottom, so as to give all of you a chance to guess what they are.

1. Behead what leads men to fight, and you leave the cause of much misery, sin, and death.

2. Behead what young ladies are said to be fond of, and you leave a young lady.

3. Behead what comes nearest the hand, and you leave what comes nearest the heart.

4. Behead something sweet, and it leaves an address to the sweet.

5. Behead part of a coach, and you leave part of yourself.   Behead that, and you leave a fish.

6. Behead a rogue, and you leave a musician.

7. Behead an old-fashioned occupation, and you leave what prevents many a parting.

8. Behead a part of ladies' apparel, and you leave what is higher than the king.

9. Behead what always comes hard, and you leave what makes things go easy.

10. Behead a weapon, and you leave a fruit.   Behead that, and you leave part of the body.

1. Drum, rum.	6. Sharper, harper.
2. Glass, lass.	7. Spin, pin.
3. Glove, love.	8. Lace, ace.
4. Molasses, O Lasses!	9. Toil, oil.
5. Wheel, heel, eel.	10. Spear, pear, ear.

Sometimes they make them in rhyme.

> Behead what is born in the fire,
>   And lives but a moment or so, —
>   For it can't live long you know, —
> And you leave what all admire.
>   Where grass so green doth grow,
>   And trees in many a row.
> Behead this last, and you leave in its place
> What once preserved the human race.

Spark, park, ark.

> Behead a musical term so sweet,
> And you leave what runs without any feet.
> Behead again, and, sad to tell,
> You leave what is sick and never gets well.
>   To what is left add the letter D,
>   And you have a lawyer of high degree.

Trill, rill, ill.   "LL. D."

I've got something a good deal funnier to tell, but
I'm going to write all about that in Lucy Maria's
letter.   I guess she'll be very glad when she gets that
letter, for 't will tell her how to do something very funny.
I will send her the story of it too, so she won't have to
make up anything herself.   Don't you think I had a
pretty good time?   I hope my sister is well, and hope
you all are.   Lucy Maria must read this letter.   She

could make those beheadings quicker'n lightning. I am well. Don't believe I shall ever be sick.

From your affectionate Grandson,

WILLIAM HENRY.

P. S. I've been to a lecture on good health. The man said there were two parts to the air, a good part and a poison part, and every time we breathe we keep in the good part, and breathe out the poison part. So if a room were sealed up, air-tight, a man living in it would soon die, for he would use up all the good part and leave the poison part. So we ought to always let fresh air in, that has n't been breathed. He says in a crowded room, if there is no fresh air coming in, we have to use over what other folks have breathed, whether they are sick or well.

W. H.

What with our young friend's frequent visits to the Two Betseys, his attendance at the dancing-school, and going to parties and to lectures, it would seem as though his time was not wholly taken up with his studies. Among William Henry's letters to Lucy Maria I find the following one about the Dwarf, and with it, in Lucy Maria's handwriting, I find a copy of the Narrative alluded to.

William Henry to Lucy Maria.

DEAR COUSIN, —

I guess you will want to know how this was done, that I'm going to write about, so I will tell you about it, then you will know how to make one out of Tommy, but I guess a bigger boy would be better. It does n't make much difference about the size, if he can keep a sober face while somebody tells a story about him, and do the things he's told to. I could n't guess how 't was done till Bubby Short told me. Bubby Short was the dwarf. He was invited on purpose, because he is up to all kinds of fun, and can act dialogues, be an old man, or old woman, or anything you want him to. I will tell you exactly how 't was done, so you will know. And I will send you the Narrative to copy. But you can't keep it very long. It was given to Bubby Short. The showman was Maud Grey's cousin. He was dressed in a turban, with long robes, and he had black rings made round his eyes, and his face was tatooed with a lead-pencil. Course he made up the story and made the pictures to it too. But he pretended he got them in the dwarf's country, that was named "Empskutia." I thought maybe you'd like to read it, then if you made one you could think of something to say. 'T was only meant for the little ones, he said, but we all liked to hear it. No matter if it was nonsense, we did n't care. Now, I 'll begin.

First, they had a table, with a long table-cloth on it that touched the floor. It must touch the floor, so as to hide the *real* feet of the one that 's going to be the dwarf. When Bubby Short was all ready he sat down to the table, same as if he 'd been doing his examples or eating his dinner, — sat facing the company and waited for the curtain to rise. Course you have to have a curtain. The table-cloth covered the lower part of him. His own hands and arms were turned into feet and legs for the dwarf. I 'll tell you how. The arms had little trousers on them, and the hands were put into nice little button-boots, so they looked like legs and feet. He was all stuffed out above his waist, and had on a stiff shirt bosom, and breastpin, and necktie, and false whiskers, and a wig made of black curled hair, and a tasselled cap, with a gilt band round it. He crooked his arms at the elbows and laid them flat on the table, with the button-boots towards the curtain, so when the curtain went up it looked like a little dwarf sitting down, facing the company. Now I must tell you where the dwarf's arms and hands came from. For you know that Bubby Short's arms and hands were made into legs and feet for the dwarf. Now to make arms, he had on a little coat, with the sleeves of it stuffed out to look like arms, and then a stuffed pair of white cotton gloves was sewed on to the sleeves, to look like hands, and these gloves were pinned together by the fingers in front of his waist so as to look like clasped hands.

The showman asked him to do different things. Asked him to try to stand up. Then Bubby Short began to get up, very slow, as if 't was tough work to do it, and let his arms straighten themselves down, and looked just as if there was a little short fellow standing on the table. I thought like enough you 'd like to know how, so as to make one some time, out of Tommy or some bigger boy that knows how to whistle. The showman made his dwarf whistle a funny tune, and told us 't was an air of his native country. Then made him step out the tune with his little button-boots, and it seemed just like a little dancing dwarf. The showman said that was the national dance of his country. I guess Uncle Jacob would like to see one. I guess his eyes would twinkle.

When the curtain went up you ought to 've heard the folks roar! Some of them thought 't was real. When the company asked him if he could move his arms, he shook his head, no. Then the showman said he could make him do it, by whispering a charm in his ear. So he went close up and whispered, and took out the pin that pinned the gloves, in a secret way, and then the arms dropped apart. All the way he could move his arms was by shaking his body, and then only a little. The showman said the fearful accident that stopped his growth lost him the use of his arms, though he could dance and whistle and make a bow [*here he made him make a bow*], and could scratch his ear with his boot [*here he scratched his ear with the button-boot-toe*], but his brain was strong as anybody's. Then afterwards he told how much he knew. But you can read about it in the Narrative. He made him crook his knees sideways. He could do this easy enough, for 't was only the elbows bending outwards. Then he made him sit down again. I don't believe any of you ever saw anything so funny. The showman kept a very sober face all the time, and 'most made us believe every word of his story was true, and at the end he spoke very loud and acted it out, like an orator.

Your affectionate Cousin,

WILLIAM HENRY.

P. S. Will you please send back the picture of that creature we sent you once? We want to do something with it. I put in the Narrative some of the things the audience did.

NARRATIVE.

My dear young Friends, —

Hyladdu Alizamrald, the unfortunate gentleman now before you, was born in the country of Empskutia, on the borders of the great unknown region of Phlezzogripotamia, which lies beyond the sources of the river Phlezzra. He was the only child of a nobleman, whose wealth was unbounded, and whose power was immense. The day of his birth was made a day of rejoicing throughout the city. Not only were fountains of wine set flowing, that none might go athirst (for the Empskutians are driest when they 're happiest), but living fountains of milk also, that every child might, on that happy day, drink its fill of the pure infantine fluid. It is perhaps needless to remark that these last were cows, driven in from the surrounding plains.

Hyladdu was an infant of great promise, and bade fair to become the pride of his native land, instead of being — of being — pardon my emotion. [*Showman puts handkerchief to his eyes. Hyladdu wipes away a tear with his boot-toe.*] Yes, gentlemen and ladies [*calmer*], at his birth there seemed to be no reason why Hyladdu's head should not rise as far towards the clouds as will yours, my smiling young friends before me. Briefly, he was not born a dwarf. Shall I relate how this sweet flower of promise was nipped in the bud? [*The audience cry, " Yes! yes!" Hyladdu takes his handkerchief in both boots and wipes his eyes.*]

Listen, then. When Hyladdu had reached the age of eighty-one days — eighty-one being the third multiple of three — his parents, according to the custom of the country, summoned to the cradle of the young child a Thulsk.

The Thulski are a tall, mysterious race of prophets, known only in Empskutia, who attain to an unknown age. Many of them cannot even remember their own boyhood. These prophets are reverenced by all the people. As year after year is added to their life, they grow thin, dark, and shrivelled, like mummies. The skin is dry and hangs loose about the bones. The hair is long and white, and every year adds to its length and its whiteness, while the eyes seem blacker and more piercing. They wear very high black caps, square, and carry in the hand a peculiar flower, a snow-white flower, having five petals, which grows in secret places, and which, even if found, no other person ever dare to pluck, lest its peculiar smell should work a charm upon them. None but the Thulski themselves know when and where the Thulski die. If they have graves they are unknown graves, though it is a common belief in the country that the mysterious white-petalled flower blooms only in their burial-places. During life they live apart from all others, seldom speaking, even when mingled in the busy crowd.

The order of the Thulski is kept up in this way. Their chief, clad in long dark robes, wanders silently the streets, and when, among the children at play, he discovers one who has some peculiar mark about him, — the nature of this mark is unknown, — he beckons, and the child follows him. Must follow him. For that silent beckoning joins him to their order. He is from that moment a Thulsk, and has no wish to escape.

Now, although to be a Thulsk is to be certain of long life, yet no mother desires this fate for her child, but, on the contrary, children aré warned against them, and have among themselves a secret sign, a rapid motion of the fingers, which means " scatter ! "   And if, when they are at play, the white-haired prophet is seen, though even at a great distance, this sign is rapidly made, and the little flock disappears so instantly, one would suppose the earth had swallowed them.   You will see, before my melancholy story is finished, what all this has to do with Hyladdu's misfortune.

As I was saying, when he had attained the age of eighty-one days, — eighty-one being the third multiple of three, — his parents, according to the custom of the Empskutians, summoned one of these prophets to the cradle of their child, that his fortunes might be foretold.

The weird, shrivelled old Thulsk, with his flowing white hair, wrapped his dark robes about him, and sat silently at the low cradle, gazing upon the sleeping child. At length he arose, with a look of sorrow, and would have departed without uttering a single word.

" Speak ! speak ! " cried the father.

" Ah, do not speak ! " murmured the mother ; for she perceived that the prophet foresaw evil.   " Yet speak, yes, speak ! " she cried.   " Let us know the worst, that we may prepare ourselves."

The prophet then made a reply, of which these five words are a translation : —

" Sorrow cometh sufficiently soon.   Wait ! "

But, on being very earnestly entreated, he disclosed that before the beautiful infant attained his sixth year —

six being the double of three — he would sustain injuries from a fall, by which either his mind or his body would be blighted. Which, it was not given him to say. He added that it grieved him to still further disclose that he himself would be in some way connected with the child's misfortune, though in what way even his prophetic vision could not foresee.

Now it may readily be supposed that the parents spared no pains to ward off from their child this unknown danger. The upper windows were immediately fastened down, fresh air being secured by means of hinges on each square of glass. As soon as he could walk sentinels were placed at every flight of stairs, and to keep him out of the cellar, a neighboring wine-merchant was invited to store his goods there, so that wine-butts took up every inch of room, from floor to ceiling. Ladders and movable steps he was not allowed the sight of, and as it seems as natural for boys to climb trees as to breathe the air around them, every tree in the grounds was protected by sharp iron teeth.

The longing which every boy has to climb is called the climbing instinct. In Hyladdu the climbing instinct was nipped in the bud, — smothered, crushed, kept under. He was forbidden to swing on gates, taught to avoid fence-posts, lamp-posts, and flag-staffs, and to look upon hills as summits of danger. Of shinning, he knew but the name. And that the very idea of climbing might be kept from his mind, all climbing plants were rooted out from the grounds; not even a morning-glory was allowed to run up a string! By these means the anxious parents hoped to prevent what the Thulsk had foretold, from coming to pass. "For," said they, "if he never goes up, he can never fall down." But mark now how all these precautions were the very means of making the prophecy prove true. For, had he only been taught to climb, and had been accustomed to high places, that sad accident might not have taken place and the blighted individual before you might now have been one of the flowers of his country! [*Emotion.*] Pardon me, friends. Tears come unbidden. [*Showman holds handkerchief to his eyes. Dwarf ditto, with boots.*]

Imagine now the dear child, grown a beautiful boy of five summers, — a boy of beaming blue eyes, and a rosy cheek! of flaxen curls and a graceful montion! The idol of his parents, the joy of his friends! Sweet in disposition, of tender feelings, quick to learn, truthful, affectionate, gentle in his manners, winning in his ways, no wonder that he was so well beloved!

It was only one short week before his sixth birthday, and his friends were trembling with joy, that the fatal time had so nearly passed, when the calamity which had so long hung over him like a cloud descended upon him like a thunderbolt! In other words, he lacked but a week of six, and all were rejoicing that the danger was nearly passed, when the event happened.

Hyladdu, being, like most boys, of a playful turn of mind, was sometimes permitted to join in the games of other children, in front of his father's mansion, ta-tended always by a faithful servant. On this particular day they were amusing themselves by playing with some silver-coated marbles, a box of which had been pre-sented to Hyladdu by his grandmother, who was one of the court ladies.

A very pretty group they were. The children of that country, like their fathers, were dressed in long white robes, with bright sashes. On their heads they wore caps of blue or scarlet, which turned up with points before, behind, and at each side. On each point a little silver bell was hung, that the servants might have less difficulty in following them about. Their shoes were pointed at the toes.

Among those silver marbles was an "alley" of great beauty, glistening with rubies, and inlaid with pearl. This alley never was played for in earnest. [*Here the dwarf beckons to the showman, and whispers in his ear.*] He informs me that the laws forbade playing in earnest. I will now finish as rapidly as possible.

In the course of the game, this precious "alley" rolled a long distance, until it came to a brick in the pavement, which was set slanting, or had become so by a sinking of the ground underneath. This brick gave the "alley" a turn sideways to the left, and it rolled at last through a crack in the garden fence, and hid itself in the grass. The servant, in great haste, darted through the gate in search of it.

Meanwhile, slowly down the street, though at a distance, a Thulsk was approaching. It was the same who had nearly six years before sat by Hyladdu's cradle. He walked silently on, his eyes cast down, his hands clasped, holding between them the five-petalled flower. One of the boys, perceiving him, made the sign of warning. Instantly they scattered, like a flock of pigeons, leaving their little silver-belled caps on the ground. Hyladdu, seeing the cellar open, would have hidden himself there, but no space was left between the wine-butts.

A much larger boy seized his hand and pulled him into a strange house, and then, in his fright, dragged him through long passage-ways, and up seven flights of stairs; for the Empskutians build their houses to an immense height. Here they sat down to breathe awhile, and Hyladdu begged the boy to go for the faithful servant, that he might lead him home.

Now no sooner was the boy gone than Hyladdu began to look about him, and presently he discovered a slender staircase going still higher. Having climbed seven flights with help, he felt no fear in attempting the eighth alone. This slender staircase conducted him to the roof of the building. [*Emotion and handkerchief.*] Excuse my emotion. But when I think what might have happened, if something else had not happened to prevent, when I think that he might have fallen from that immense height, to be dashed in pieces beneath, I — I — But I will let my story take its course.

And now let me tell you that the people of Empskutia were very fond of the beautiful. The streets were adorned with ornamental trees, and over the roofs of the houses were trained flowering vines, which ran to the highest peak of cupola or chimney, and, blooming sweetly there, filled the whole air with fragrance. It was the custom of the people to place stout iron hooks along the eaves of their dwellings, from which were suspended immense flower-pots of various beautiful designs. In these pots the flowering vines took root and from thence not only climbed the roof, but trailed gracefully down, thus giving the city a festive appearance, like a never-ending gala-day.

When Hyladdu looked out from the top of that last eighth flight, the long-smothered instinct of climbing burst out like a hidden fire. It would not be restrained. Ah, now will be seen the folly of crushing that instinct. Had he only have been accustomed to dizzy heights, made familiar with danger, how different might have been his fate! [*Emotion.*]

The instinct of climbing, as I said, was now strong upon him! No sooner did he perceive that there was still a height to gain than he resolved to gain that height. Nothing less would satisfy him than sitting astride the ridgepole, where a pair of bright-feathered birds had built their nest, and were then feeding their young. He ventured out, made his way cautiously up, holding on by the vines. Ah, could his parents have seen him then!

He arrived at the top, and there, seated on that lofty pinnacle, surrounded by beautiful flowers, he gazed on the scene below, and enjoyed a new happiness. For the first time in his life he looked down from a height! for the first time in his life he gazed abroad over a wide extended country!

Such pleasure he had never known, and the faithful servant, anxiously searching, might have found him there, still enjoying it, but for a pretty little bluebird, that flew suddenly down and startled him, while he was gazing at some object far away. This little bird came flying through the air, and alighted for an instant on the child's head, thinking perhaps to make its nest in the soft curls, or it might have thought his rosy lips were cherries. The suddenness with which it came startled

Hyladdu. He trembled, he lost his hold, slipped, then caught by a vine, it gave way, he slipped again, but, having no skill in climbing, slipped lower and lower, and would have fallen from the roof and been dashed in pieces, but for that custom which was mentioned just now, of suspending large flower-pots from the eaves. It happened that his course lay directly towards one of these iron hooks. He dropped, therefore, into the immense flower-pot beneath, where he lay as secure as a babe in its cradle!

From this frightful position he was at length rescued by one of the hook and ladder company of that city, and placed in his mother's arms. His own arms were nearly paralyzed by his frantic efforts to cling to some support, so that ever afterwards he could move them but very slightly, as you perceive. [*Dwarf moves his arms slightly, by shaking his body.*] And though the child's life was spared, yet the terrible fright had the effect of stopping his growth! Yes, my young friends, Hyladdu never grew more, except in wisdom! The innocent cause of all this, the poor sorrowing grandmother, died of remorse!

And now my story becomes a more pleasing one to tell. Although the child's body remained dwarfed in size, yet his heart grew in goodness, and his mind grew in knowledge, and he was beloved and respected by all. Debarred earthly mountains, he mounted the heights of learning. The climbing instinct, which his body could not satisfy, was developed in his mind. He craved books, he craved whole libraries. Teacher after teacher came, all exhausting upon him their treasures of knowledge.   Music and drawing, studied scientifically, were his amusements.   He mastered astronomy, mineralogy, algebra, conchology, trigonometry, physiology, engineering, metaphysics, technology, geology, phrenology, also foreign languages unnumbered, with all the literature belonging to each.   [*Sensation in the audience.*]   And when at last the storehouses of wisdom seemed exhausted, a report reached him of a great country beyond the seas, called the United States of America, in whose excellent schools there remains something yet to learn! [*Applause from the audience.*]

He studied the written language of that country, read its history, and resolved to seek its shores.   For he longed to behold the land of the Revolutionary War; to read the Declaration of Independence, and to stand upon the grave of Old John Brown!   [*Applause.*]

He had heard of Bunker's Hill.   Travellers said that upon whomsoever rested the shadow of its monument, that person possessed forever after the unflinching bravery of those who bled and perished there!   [*Cheers.*] He had heard of Plymouth Rock [*Cheers*], and been told that his foot once planted firmly upon it, he would feel springing up within him all the heroism, the self-sacrifice, and the everlasting perseverance of the glorious Pilgrim Fathers!   [*Prolonged cheering.*]

I have now, my young friends, told you, very briefly, the history of this remarkable character.   His age is thirty-four years.   He is of a cheerful disposition, having long ago resolved to look his misfortune steadily in the face and make the best of it.   In books, where are treasures stored up by the scholars of all past time, he

finds a never-ending pleasure.   Though dwarfed in stat-
ure, he is resolved to make a man of himself, and will
fight it out on that line if it takes all summer.   For he
early adopted for his motto, these beautiful lines of Dr.
Watts, —

> " Were I so tall as to reach the pole,
>   Or grasp the ocean in my span,
> I should be measured by my soul.
>   The mind 's the standard of the man."

(Curtain falls.)   [*Applause.*

I once heard the above narrative repeated by Joe in a
truly theatrical manner.   On the same occasion I also saw
the picture of the " creature " to which William Henry refers
in his postscript to the Dwarf Letter.

Uncle Jacob hailed me one day as I was coming from my
office, and after driving close to the curbstone, informed me
that Cousin Joe and his accordion had arrived, both in good
health and spirits.   Also, that Billy's school had met with a
very sudden vacation, caused either by flues, or furnaces, or
both, having something the matter with them, and the young
rascal would be at home that evening, and I must come
without fail.   " Of course you know," said he, " 't is a pretty
hard thing for Billy having to give up his studies, so he 's
coming home to his friends.   Nothing like being among
friends when you 're in trouble ? "

Now this was by no means a remarkable event.   Only a
boy coming home for a few days to see his folks.   Still, an
occasion which worked Grandmother up to the pitch of putting on her best cap should not be passed over in silence.

I went out to the Farm that evening, and on arriving found
Cousin Joe, and the accordion, and Aunt Phebe's family, with
a few relatives whom I had never met before, all assembled at
Grandmother's.   They had made up a fire in the " Franklin

fireplace." This "Franklin fireplace" was a sort of iron framework, projecting from the chimney into the room. The top was flat, with brass balls on the corners. It had iron sides, which "flared out," and a rounded iron hearth of its own, about an inch above the brick hearth, and shining brass andirons.

No one could wish for a brighter room, I thought, for there was the light from the fire, the light from the "lights," and the light from all those smiling faces! An inviting supper-table was set out, covered dishes were "keeping warm" on the hearth and "frame," and everything was ready and wait-ing for William Henry. Mr. Carver had gone to the sta-tion, and they were expected back every moment.

Georgiana was very busy over a skein of blue sewing-silk. She informed me that that was the first whole skein of sewing-silk she ever had in all her life, and that it came from a bun-dle of all colors, which Cousin Joe gave to Hannah Jane. It brought trouble with it, as it is said all earthly possessions do, and snarled at all her attempts to coax it on to a spool. Tommy, sober as a judge, was holding it for her to wind. He sat in a little chair, with his legs crossed. His mother said he was very particular to cross his legs, so as to seem more like a man.

Lucy Maria had just persuaded Grandmother to put on her best, double-stringed, white-ribboned cap, in honor of Wil-liam Henry. It was the very one he brought her so long ago, but was still as good as new, having very seldom seen the light of day, or of evening, since it first came home in the bandbox. She had also been coaxed into her second-best dress, and then into the rocking-chair. Lucy Maria tied her cap under the chin, with the narrow strings, and smoothed down the wide ones.

"You have no idea, Grandmother," said she. "You have n't the faintest idea how well you look!"

"'T is too dressy for me," said Grandmother. "It don't feel natural on my head."

"Now I should think," said Uncle Jacob, "that a cap would feel more natural on anybody's head than anywhere!"

"It looks natural," said Lucy Maria, "I'm sure it does. Looks as if it grew there!"

"And only think how 't will please Billy!" said Aunt Phebe.

The "*Map of the United States*" had been brought out of the front room, and placed over the mantel-piece. And Lucy Maria, for fun, she said, and to pay a delicate compli-

ment to the artist, had fastened a few sprays of upland cranberry around it. And, also, for fun, she pinned up near it a little picture, which I had quite a laugh over, and which, she said, was the renowned Megotharium, in the act of feeding, drawn by the famous artist, William Henry, assisted by his brother artist, Dorry. The picture, she added, was not an *original*, but merely a copy done by a female. A photograph of these two artists, sitting side by side, was exhibited, underneath the picture.

Cousin Joe said that *creature* beat all his going to sea. This young sailor, by the way, must have made a jolly shipmate. He was full of his jokes and his tricks. Tried to twirl Tommy round, by rubbing him between his two hands,

as one does a top, telling him that was the way the Hottentots did to take the mischief out of boys!

Aunt Phebe said she thought if the Hottentots knew any
way of taking the mischief out of boys, and were out of
work, they might find employment in this country.

Tommy begged to play "one tune," and was allowed to.
Cousin Joe declared that "that accordion was played every
wave of the way across the Atlantic," either by himself or by
one of the sailors, and that sometimes the mermaids sang to its
music! Asked Tommy if he would like to hear the tune the
mermaids sang? Tommy said he should rather wait till after
supper. This was the way in which, company being present,
the young chap let it be known that he was hungry.

Grandmother wondered, then, why they did n't come, and
went to look out of the window, putting up both hands, to
keep the light of the room from her eyes; then opened the
outside door, to listen for the whistle; then went to look at
the kitchen clock; then came back, saying it was a good deal
past the time, and what could be the matter?

She little knew who was behind, following her on tiptoe
into the room. William Henry himself! He was creeping
in at the sink-room door, just as she turned to come back from
looking at the clock, and followed softly behind. She did n't
notice how very smiling we all looked. Billy shook his finger
at us, to hush us.

"I hope there has n't anything happened to the cars," said
she.

"I hope so too!" shouted Billy. And, by a miraculous
jump, he planted himself, square foot, in front of his grandmother, who, of course, walked straight into his arms!

Then everybody shouted, and clapped, and shook hands,
and kissed. The cap got twisted about, and as if there were
not confusion enough, Cousin Joe began to caper about, and
to play on his accordion tunes that were never played before!

Such a splendid fellow as Billy was! Such a hearty, laughing, breezy fellow, with his thick head of hair, "not so red as it was," and his honest, good-natured face! I did n't wonder they were all so glad to see him.

"Welcome home, shipmate!" shouted Cousin Joe. "Welcome home! How long 'll you be in port? And worked away at Billy's hand as if he 'd been pumping out ship.

"'Most a week," said Billy. "Mind my forefinger."

"Don't take long to stay at home a week," said Cousin Joe, tossing up his accordion.

"That 's so," said Uncle Jacob. "Come, let 's be doing something!"

"That means, let 's be eating something," said Aunt Phebe. "Come, girls, put everything on the table! Billy, how tall and spruce you do look! Poor Grandmother, she 's losing her little Billy!"

"But what 's her loss is his gain!" said Uncle Jacob. "I speak to sit next the frosted cake. Where 's Tommy?"

Tommy came in, tugging Billy's carpet-bag, which he found in the kitchen, hoping, no doubt, there were goodies inside for him.

We had a delightful "supper-time," Grandmother, of course, piling Billy's plate with everything good.

"I see," said Mr. Carver, "that whatever boys eat at home grandmothers expect will agree with them!"

The happy "young rascal" meanwhile bore the separation from his studies with amazing fortitude! Told no end of funny stories about the boys, and about parties, and about the Two Betseys. And twice, during supper, he exclaimed, "I do hope nothing has happened to those cars. They were such good cars!"

My visits to the farm were always delightful, but during that supper-time, and during that evening, I grudged every moment as it flew away.

11 *

Uncle Jacob was in high glee, and insisted on being taught "the graces," and on having his wife taught "the graces." Then Lucy Maria "set her foot down" that every one should stand in the row, and Billy should be Mr. Tornero. And, being a girl of resolution, she coaxed every one into line, except Grandmother, who said her rheumatism should do her some service then, if never before.

"The graces" were then taught, and learned, amid shouts of laughter, Cousin Joe playing for us, and I'll venture to say that had Mr. Tornero been present, he would have been astonished at our steps, and also at the music!

Afterwards we had the dwarf shown off, Cousin Joe being the showman. He declared after looking over the "Narrative," that Empskutia was a place well known to him, and that he had often sailed up the "river Phlezzra," to trade with the natives. Lucy Maria dressed him in a large-figured red and green bedspread, pinned on to look like a loose robe, with flowing sleeves, and girded about the waist with cords and tassels taken from Aunt Phebe's parlor curtains. He wore an immense lace collar, and a turban made of a white muslin handkerchief (one that was Grandmother's mother's) and besprinkled with artificial flowers. His face was tattooed with a lead-pencil, and dark circles drawn around his eyes. He held in his hand a slender rod, or wand.

The dwarf was a young cousin of William Henry's (not Tommy), and he did his part well, whistling, bowing, dancing, sneezing, rising, sitting, with a perfectly sober face.

The showman then read the "Narrative," adding thereto such ridiculous incidents, and such comical remarks, that the audience were convulsed with laughter, and the face of the dwarf twitched alarmingly. These twitchings, he (the showman) said, were not unusual, and were the effects of the sad occurrence then being narrated. The closing portions of the story were declaimed in a powerful voice. He "acted out" the "pole" and the "span," and at the third line, "I must be measured by my *soul*," laid his hand upon his heart in the most impressive manner, and remained in that position till the curtain fell.

After this "John Brown" was sung, and William Henry was permitted to roar out that "Glory Hallelujah" as loudly as he pleased.

The following letter must have been written some time after William Henry met with the *affliction* which was so touchingly alluded to by Uncle Jacob, as above related, and which that wretched youth felt could only be endured in the bosom of his family! In the interval it appears that he had been removed from the Crooked Pond School, and that Dorry had left also, to finish preparing himself for college in some higher seminary of learning.

William Henry's Letter after leaving School.

DEAR DORRY, —

I did n't know I was going to come away from school so soon after you did, but there was a new High School begun in our town about a mile and a half off, and my father thought I could learn there, and learn to farm it some too. But I don't think much of farming it. Course 't is fun to see things grow, after you 've planted the seeds, and then watched 'em all the way up. My grandmother says my father likes his corn so well, that he pities it in a dry time, and when a gale blows it down he pities it as much as if he 'd been blown down himself. Weeds are enough to make a feller mad, coming up fast as you kill 'em and sucking all the goodness out of the ground that don't belong to them. Suppose they think 't is as much theirs as anybody's.

I suppose you are studying away for college. I don't know whether I wish I could go or not. I guess my head would n't hold all 't would have to be put into it before I went, and in all that four years too! Now I want to know if a feller can remember all that? I mean remember the beginning after all the other has been piled top of it? I don't know what I shall be yet. For there is something bad about everything, Grandmother says, and I believe it. Now I don't want to be a farmer, because 't is hard work and poor pay, — in these parts. I guess I should like to go to Kansas. But there are the Indians after your scalp, and fever and ague, and grasshoppers, and potato-bugs, and bean-bugs, and army-worms to eat up everything, and droughts to dry up everything, and floods to wash it away, and hurricanes to blow it down, and Uncle Jacob says if a man comes through all these alive, with a few grains of corn, the man that wants to buy 'em is a hundred miles off! But my father says, what is a man good for that don't dare to go to sail without 't is on a mill-pond! For smooth water can't make a sailor. And if a man is scared of lions, how will he get through the woods. So I don't know yet what I shall be. What should you, if you did n' go to college? Go into a store? I tell you, Dorry, that if I was a dry-goods clerk, fenced in behind a counter, I do believe I should ache to jump over and *put* for somewhere and go to doing something. But my father says you can't always tell a man by what his business is. For you 've got to allow for head work. And because he sells shoe-strings, 't is no sign he has n't got anything in his head but shoe-strings ; and because a

man drives nails, 't is no sign he has n't got anything but
nails in his head. " Now suppose," says he, " that a man
sells dry goods all day, can't he have some thoughts stowed
away in his brains that he got out of books, or got up
himself? And when he 's walking along home and back,
and evenings, can't he out with 'em and be thinking 'em
over? I s'pose 't is n't time for me to have thoughts yet,
s'pose they 'll be dropping along in a year or two, " or
three at the most," as Lord Lovell said. One thing I
mean to have, and that is a good house with all the fix-
ings, and money to spend, and money to give away if I
want to. So whatever I get started on, I mean to pitch
in and shove up my sleeves, and go at it. Father says
I must be thinking the matter over, and not make my
mind up right off. They say going to sea is a dog's life.
I should like to go long enough to see what Spain looks
like, and China, and other places. Maybe I shall learn
a trade. Now, for instance, a carpenter's. That don't
seem much of a trade. Mostly pounding. . But they
say if you keep on, and are smart at it, why, you get
to taking houses, and then you are not a carpenter any
longer, but a "builder," and money comes in.

I 'm going to let her rest a spell. Though I 'm so old
I can't help looking ahead some sometimes, to see where
I 'm coming out.

Did n't you feel homesick any when you were coming
away from school? I did, — " quite some," as W. B. used
to say. I went round to all the places, and paddled in
the pond, and lay down on the grass to take one more
drink out of the brook, and climbed up in the Elm, and
ran up and down our stairs much as half a dozen

times, without stopping, for I thought I never should again.

I whittled a great sliver off the base-ball field fence to fetch away; did n't we use to have good times there? Bubby Short gave me his pocket-book, and I gave him mine. They had about equal, inside. I went to bid Gapper good-by, day before I came off, and gave Rosy my little penknife.

Then I went to bid the two Betseys good-by, and they wiped their eyes, and seemed about as if they 'd been my grandmothers, and said I *must* come to eat supper with them that afternoon. So I went. Me all alone! Had a funny kind of a time. We sat at that round, three-legged stand, and I 'll tell you what we had. Bannock and butter, sausages, flapjacks, and scalloped cakes. All set on in saucers, for there was n't much room. They had about supper enough for forty. For they said they knew their appetites were nothing to judge a hungry boy by, and I must eat a good deal and not go by them, and kept handing things to me, and every once in a while they 'd say, " Now don't be scared of it, there 's more in the buttery?" George! Dorry, I wish you could have seen that punkin-pie they had! 'T was kept in a chair, a little ways off. I don't see what 't was baked in. The Other Betsey said that was just such a kind of a pie as her mother used to make. I out with my ruler, and asked if I might measure it. 'T was about two feet across, and about four inches thick. She said she thought 't was a good time to make one, when they were going to have company. When I took my piece I had to hold my plate in my hand, for there was n't room on the stand. They wished you'd been there, and so did I, and so would you, if you 'd seen that pie. They did n't take down their best dishes, that we had that other time, but called me one of the family and used the poor ones. I had to look out about lifting up the spoon-holder, because the bottom had been off, once, and mind which sugar-bowl handle I took hold of, for one side it was glued on. But everything held. I can't bear tea, but they said 't was very warming and resting, and I 'd better. I guess they put in about six spoonfuls of sugar! They wanted to know all about you, and said you were a smart fellow.

They wanted me to take some little thing out of the store, to remember them by. So I looked and looked to find something that did n't cost very much, and at last I pitched upon a pocket-comb. The Other Betsey put on her glasses and scratched a B. on it, and said it could stand for the two of 'em. But I told her she better make two B.'s, for that would seem more like the Two Betseys, and she did. Lame Betsey said one B. ought to go lame, and the Other Betsey said she guessed they both would, for she had poor eyesight, and her hand shook, and nothing but a darning-needle to scratch with. If I do break the comb I shall keep the handle, for I think the Two Betseys are tip-top. I wish they could come and see my grandmother. Would n't the three of 'em have a good time!

Send a feller a letter once in a while, can't ye? Say, now, you Dorry, don't get too knowing to write to a feller?

Your friend,

WILLIAM HENRY.

At this point the correspondence properly closes. As a faithful editor, I have endeavored to let it tell its own story, but must frankly acknowledge that at times, the pleasant memories recalled by these Letters have tempted me, too far, perhaps, beyond editorial bounds. This fault I freely confess, hoping to be as freely forgiven. Were it known how much I have left unsaid, while longing to say it, I should receive not only forgiveness but praise.

In closing, I cannot do better than to add to the collection an extract from a letter written to Mr. Carver by the Principal of the Crooked Pond School.

It seems that William Henry's new teacher proposed his taking up Latin, and that Mr. Carver being somewhat undecided about the matter, wrote to the Principal of the Crooked School, asking his opinion. The Principal's reply, in as far as it discusses the Latin question, would scarcely be in order here. But the closing portion will, I know, be read with pleasure by all who have taken an interest in William Henry. He speaks of him thus : —

". . . . Allow me, sir, in concluding, to congratulate you on the many good qualities of your son. He is one of the boys that I feel sure of. We regret exceedingly his leaving us, and I assure you that he carries with him the best wishes of all here, — teachers, pupils, and townspeople. I shall watch his course with deep interest. A boy of his manly bearing, kind disposition, and high moral principle will surely win his way to all hearts, as he has done to ours.

With regard to his studies, though not, perhaps, a remarkably brilliant scholar, he has, on the whole, done well. For the first few months, it is true, we rather despaired of awakening an interest. He was too fond of play, too unwilling to come under our pretty strict discipline. Observing how heartily he entered into all games, and that he excelled in them, it occurred to us, that if the same ambition and pluck shown on the playground could be aroused in the schoolroom, our object would be gained. This, by various means, we have tried to accomplish, and I am happy to add, with good success. Your son, sir, is a boy to be proud of.

Very truly yours,

It so happened that I called at the Farm the very day on which this reply was received, and just as Grandmother had finished reading it.

As I entered the room she looked up, and without speaking handed me the letter. Tears stood in her eyes, and I saw that something had touched her deeply.

" Any bad news ? " I asked.

"No," she answered, in a tremulous voice. "But to think of that schoolmaster's finding out what was in that child!''

THE END.

Cambridge: Printed by Welch, Bigelow, and Company.